MANU
and The Butterfly Farm

Marlene Dee Gray Potoura

Paperback ISBN: 978-1-7638456-6-4

First Published in 2025 by

First Nations Writers Festival International Limited T/as First Nations Publishers

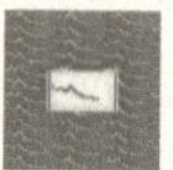

A Registered Charity (ABN 79 655 932 979)

2/53 Junction St, Nowra NSW 2540, Australia

Phone: +61 491 851 353

Email: firstnationswritersfestival@gmail.com
Web: www.firstnationswritersfestival.org
FB: www.facebook.com/firstnationswritersfestival.com

Cover Design: Busybird Publishing
Typeset: Busybird Publishing
Line Edited: Anna Borsi AM 2025
Printed and bound in Australia by IngramSpark

A catalogue record for this book is available from the National Library of Australia

Contents

Prologue

This story is set in the late 1990s and the early 2000s, a time when Lae Town[1] was on the brink of change from technology through the internet; yet the values of family and hard work remained steadfast. Whilst I've used real names of towns and places, the characters in this narrative are entirely fictional. This creative writing piece is crafted for both young and old, illustrating that family is everything in the Islands and that hard work is essential to our growth and happiness.

Although we may stumble and face setbacks, our work ethic should remain unwavering. Life often presents challenges that test our resolve, but it is through these trials that we discover our true strength. Success manifests in countless forms—it can be a small victory in the face of adversity or a significant achievement that changes our lives. It is not dictated by our backgrounds, where we live, who raises us, or what we eat. Instead, success hinges on our ability to identify our aspirations, set meaningful goals, and commit ourselves fully to the effort required to achieve them.

No man is an island; no one accomplishes anything entirely on their own. The culture of caring for one another within families and communities is universal. Each person, regardless of their corner of

---

1 Papua New Guinea

the world, originates from unique families and tribes, forming the rich traits of humanity.

At its core, survival is paramount. Yet, it is not just about enduring; it is about thriving. The bonds of friendship, support, and the profound need to love and be loved represent the essence of our humanity. These connections enrich our lives, providing a foundation upon which we can build our dreams. In recognising the importance of community and kinship, we cultivate an environment where everyone can flourish.

In the end, it's the love we share, the lessons we learn, and the lives we touch that define our journey. Together, we can navigate the complexities of life, drawing strength from each other as we strive for our own versions of success.

Acknowledgements

I would like to thank Professor Martin Wiemers for all the information on butterflies.

I also thank my friend Ken Estes for helping me with the Nevada part of the story.

Thank you to First Nations Writers Festival.

Words

Aibika leaves: Spinach-like edible leaves from the aibika plant, commonly used in cooking.

Bilum: The most significant string or wool; woven bag in Papua New Guinea (PNG).

Bos tumas: A respectful or affectionate way to address someone.

Bosman: Someone who has earned respect; a leader or a person on the path to becoming a well-recognised leader.

Bosmeri: Someone who is a leader, often earning respect and recognition through wealth and kindness.

Bubu: Grandparents male or female. It is also a respectful term for the elderly in PNG.

Kulau: Green coconut.

Kumu: Greens or green leafy vegetables commonly utilised in local cuisine.

Lewa: Love.

Masalai: A forest ghoul or spirit in local folklore.

Meri blaus: The most significant national blouse or dress in PNG.

Mumu: An important traditional earth oven used in PNG cooking.

Naiswan: A form of positive compliment

O, O: A form of casually addressing someone.

Patapata: A seat made from natural materials, primarily coconut trunk and bamboo.

"The universe is ever-watchful, bestowing its blessings upon those who labour diligently and make their intentions clear. When you pour your heart into your work, the cosmos conspires in your favour, transforming effort into opportunity."

(Marlene Dee)

1

Love, Hunger, Struggle

*B*umbu Settlement is a challenging place to live, marked by the unyielding realities of unemployment and the daily struggles faced by its residents. The air is thick with dust, and the streets are riddled with deep potholes that fill with stagnant water, remnants of the unrelenting rainy season. Food scarcity looms large for families who find themselves without work, with roadside markets offering only slim opportunities to earn enough to fill their empty stomachs—often relying on coins or the kindness of a neighbour or generous buyer. The scant resources available barely sustain families, forcing them into a daily struggle for survival.

Manu and his grandparents lived in a small hut; their weary faces etched with the lines of hardship and resilience. Unemployment weighs heavily on them, and each day unfolds as a relentless battle. They tend to a modest vegetable garden, nurturing what little they can grow, whilst also selling firewood at the Kamkumung roadside market. Here, they sell bundles of firewood for K2[2], and once the

____

2 Kina, the national currency. Similar to a dollar, however with different relational value.

firewood is sold, they use the money to buy food from the Tucker Stalls and fresh vegetables from the nearby market.

Despite the constant challenges, Bubu Naris, Manu's grandmother, always manages to stash away a portion of their earnings, saving for Manu's school fees each year. Her hope for his education shines through the hardships, reminding them both that even in difficult times, the promise of a better future is worth striving for. Each day, amidst the struggles, they hold onto moments of joy and connection, finding strength that they find in the love they have for each other.

Mondays and Wednesdays were their firewood collecting days, a vital routine in their lives. They ventured to the banks of the Bumbu River, where they searched for driftwood washed ashore by the currents. After gathering the wood, Bubu Pellie skillfully chopped it into manageable pieces with his old axe, while Bubu Naris expertly tied the wood into neat bundles.

The most challenging part of the process was carrying the firewood up the narrow cliff that loomed above them. They always took their time, carefully navigating the rocky terrain. However, one day, while climbing, Manu lost his footing and slid down the rocks. If it hadn't been for a sturdy root he managed to grab onto, he could have fallen into the jagged depths below.

"Bubu Pellie! Help!" Manu shouted, panic rising in his voice.

"Hold on, Manu! I'm coming!" he called out, his heart racing.

In a moment of quick thinking, Bubu Pellie tossed his load of firewood onto a flat stone and rushed to pull Manu back to safety.

Meanwhile, Bubu Naris, overwhelmed by the fear of losing her grandson, dropped her own load on the roadside and collapsed onto the narrow path, sobbing uncontrollably.

"Oh, Manu! My sweet boy!" she cried, her voice trembling.

"Bubu Naris, please!" Pellie urged, glancing back at her as he struggled to reach Manu. "He's okay! Just a little further!"

As Pellie grasped Manu's hand and pulled him up, he turned to Bubu Naris. "He's safe now. Look! He's back on solid ground."

Manu, panting and shaken, looked at his grandmother. "I'm alright, Bubu Naris. I was scared, but I held on tight."

Bubu Naris wiped her tears and managed a shaky smile. "You scared me half to death, Manu! Promise me you'll be more careful next time."

"I promise, Bubu," he replied earnestly, his eyes wide with sincerity. "I didn't mean to worry you."

"Let's get home," Bubu Pellie said, placing a reassuring hand on Naris's back. "We'll talk about it there."

That experience became a pivotal moment in their lives, strengthening their bond as they navigated the challenges of Bumbu Settlement. Together, they learned that even in the face of fear, their love and support for one another could conquer any obstacle.

After they managed to carry the firewood up the cliff, they carefully arranged the bundles behind their little hut. Once all the wood was stacked neatly, they would take ten bundles at a time on certain days and head to the Kamkumung roadside market to sell them.

This routine became their daily way of life, that provided a sense of purpose amid the challenges they faced. Each trip to the market was not just about selling firewood; it was a chance to connect with the community as well, share stories, and find small moments of joy amidst their hard work.

Manu always rushed home after school to help his grandparents, whether it was collecting driftwood or selling bundles of firewood at the Kamkumung roadside market. They whole heartedly committed themselves to their tasks, determined to survive the harsh conditions of Bumbu Settlement. In a town where jobs were scarce and appropriate income seemed out of reach, they worked tirelessly, relying on each other and their resourcefulness.

Manu's dedication to his grandparents not only strengthened their bond, but also instilled in him a deep sense of responsibility and resilience in the face of adversity. That is how life is.

On a cold, misty morning, Bubu Naris woke up with a swollen neck that made swallowing food nearly impossible; even drinking water was a struggle. Manu was heartbroken to see her moaning and crying in pain. It was truly devastating.

Bubu Naris had always been the strong, silent one, the one who instinctively knew how to care for others when they fell ill. Life seemed unusually cruel—one day she was vibrant and healthy, and the next, she was struck by illness. She had never been one to succumb to sickness or physical pain.

"Bubu Naris, please try to eat something," Manu urged, his voice filled with concern as he sat beside her on the bed. "I can make you some broth."

"I can't, Manu," she replied weakly, wincing as she attempted to swallow. "It hurts too much."

Bubu Pellie entered the room, sensing the heavy atmosphere. "What's going on?" he asked, his brow furrowed with worry. "Is she feeling worse?"

"Yes, she can't even drink water," Manu said, his eyes glistening with unshed tears. "It's not fair, Bubu Pellie. She's always been so strong."

Bubu Naris looked at them both, her heart aching at their concern. "Oh, my dear ones, I'm so sorry to worry you," she said, her voice a fragile whisper as she wiped the tears flowing from her eyes.

These tears were not just for herself; they were for her grandson; whose face bore lines of worry and sadness she had never seen before. In that moment, she realised that what she had long hidden was finally emerging.

When Bubu Pellie gently suggested taking her to Saint Mary's Health Centre, she declined sharply. "I feel dizzy and don't want to walk in this scorching sun!" she snapped, a reaction that was completely out of character for her. With a heavy sigh, she rolled out her mat on the grass beneath the coconut tree and lay down.

"The dry coconuts will fall on you, dear," Bubu Pellie called out softly, concern written on his face as he approached her. "Let's find a safer spot."

"I'll be fine, Pellie! I just need a moment," she replied, her voice tinged with frustration.

He knelt beside her, gently brushing a stray hair from her forehead. "You're not fine, Bubu Naris. You're not yourself today. Please, let me help you."

She met his gaze, her expression softening. "I know you worry, but I just need some peace. The sun will pass, and I'll be okay."

"Your well-being is what matters most to me," he said, his tone calm yet firm. "We can go together. I'll make it easy for you."

"I said no, Pellie. Go and cook breakfast for your grandson and stop pestering me!" she snapped. It was the first time Manu had ever heard her speak to her husband like that.

Manu sat quietly on the patapata next to their hut, his heart heavy with worry, as he watched, Bubu Naris raised her hand, dismissively waving her husband away. She gathered her mat and moved into the shade of the guava tree, where she slept deeply until late afternoon.

When Bubu Pellie gently woke her at 6:30 PM for dinner, she simply shook her head, picked up her mat, and returned to their hut to sleep, further deepening Manu's concern for her well-being.

Before daybreak, Bubu Pellie rose early and roasted three kaukaus over the fire, their earthy aroma mingling with the crisp morning air. He then boiled three packets of Maggi noodles, carefully serving them into their mugs. Each of them received a kaukau to accompany the meal. Bubu Naris attempted to sip the noodle soup, but struggled to swallow, her discomfort painfully evident.

As Manu watched her, tears welled in his eyes, realising just how serious the growth on Bubu Naris's throat had become. It was now unmistakable, a stark reminder of her suffering. *'Oh, why?'* he thought, the same rhetorical question echoing in his mind since yesterday, filled with helplessness.

Bubu Pellie gently touched Manu's shoulder, urging him to eat quickly. "You'll be late for school if you don't hurry," he said, his voice a mix of concern and encouragement. Despite his own worries, Manu tried to focus on the meal, knowing that each moment mattered.

When Manu returned home from school, he found the hut empty. A wave of worry washed over him as he sat outside, gazing down at the Bumbu River. Where were his grandparents? What had happened while he was away? Was Bubu Naris very sick?

He knew he had to silence the dark thoughts swirling in his mind. *'I must not think negatively,'* he told himself firmly. *'They will come back and tell me that everything is okay.'* He repeated these affirmations like a mantra, trying to shield himself from the anxiety creeping in.

With each breath, he focused on pushing away the fears, hoping for the best and holding onto the belief that his grandparents would return soon, safe and sound.

He stepped inside their hut and began to start a fire, the flickering flames bringing a sense of warmth to the chilly air. Carefully, he peeled four kaukaus and placed them in a pot, then ventured into the yard to pick a dry coconut. After husking it, he turned to scraping the flesh, filling the air with a rich, nutty aroma.

He squeezed the fresh coconut cream over the kaukaus and hung the pot over the fire, watching the flames dance beneath it. Next, he ran to their small vegetable garden and gathered a handful of aibika leaves, rinsing them in water before placing them in a coconut leaf woven basket.

As the kaukaus boiled, he opened the lid of the pot and added the aibika leaves on top, along with a sprinkle of salt and a packet of Maggie chicken cube. He replaced the lid, ensuring everything would cook perfectly. He blew gently on the fire to keep it steady, and felt a deep sadness gnawing at his heart as thoughts of Bubu Naris filled his mind.

Finally, when the food was ready, he carefully lifted the pot from the fire and opened the lid just a bit to let the steam escape, ensuring the aibika leaves wouldn't overcook. As he prepared the meal, he held onto the hope that they would all share it together soon, despite the sadness weighing heavily on him.

He locked the door of their hut, carefully hiding the key under the steps where only he and his grandparents knew its location. After that, he went behind the hut, gathered two bundles of firewood, and set off toward the firewood market.

On his way, he encountered Naisa and Kep, who usually sold candles at the Kamkumung market.

"Hey, bestie! Long time no see. Great to see you!" they greeted Manu with bright smiles.

"Hey! It's been a while. Nice to see both of you," Manu replied, shaking hands with them.

"Manu, you should really consider quitting the firewood. Candles sell faster. Look, you can sell two candle sticks for 50 toea![3] With all the PNG Power blackouts, people are buying more candles than ever," Kep urged, trying to persuade him.

"I'll stick to firewood, boys," Manu told them, waving goodbye as they reached the junction.

"Alright, boss! All the best!" Naisa and Kep called out, their voices trailing behind him.

Naisa was an orphan, and Manu had heard the tragic stories about his father. He had been a woodcutter, and when Naisa was just a few weeks old, he went into the forest to chop wood but never returned. The men of the settlement organised a search, and Bubu Pellie joined them as they scoured the forest. Their calls echoed in the trees until one of the men spotted a leg sticking out from beneath a fallen tree that Naisa's father had chopped.

"They say he must have disrespected something in the forest and met his fate," the whispers circulated throughout the settlement.

---

3 Similar to cents, different relational value

Not long after, Naisa's mother passed away, leaving him to navigate the world alone.

"Poor Neuva," Bubu Naris had sobbed as she prepared for the funeral at their little church down the road.

At around six years old, Naisa had learned to survive in the settlement, sleeping wherever he found hospitality. Alongside Kep, who was Manu's age, they teamed up to make a living selling candles, forging a bond in their shared struggles.

When he arrived at the roadside market, Manu set down the two bundles of firewood and sat beside them, waiting patiently. Before long, a tall, dark-skinned woman parked her fancy four-wheel-drive Toyota vehicle at the firewood market. As she stepped out, Manu noticed her effortless coolness; she conversed with everyone, walked barefoot, and bought a substantial amount of firewood.

Then, he realised she was walking directly toward him.

"Good afternoon, young man. How much are you selling your bundles for?" she asked, her smile warm and inviting.

"Good afternoon, bosmeri. It's K2 per bundle," Manu replied politely, his voice clear and steady.

"Bring them both to my vehicle, please," she instructed, her tone friendly yet authoritative.

Manu carried the two bundles of firewood over to her car, placing them in the back of the Toyota Land Cruiser alongside the other firewood she had purchased. As he turned back, the woman approached him and placed a K20 note in his palm.

"Bosmeri, wait here, and I'll go change this at the Tucker Stall to give you your K16 change," Manu said with a smile and was about to run off when she gently held his hand.

"No, take the K20. You keep the change, young man," she said, her smile brightening her already charming demeanor as she climbed into her vehicle.

"Thank you, bosmeri," Manu replied, unsure of what else to say, his heart swelling with gratitude.

She waved goodbye to Manu and the other firewood sellers before driving away.

"Bosmeri is always like that when she comes here. She never asks for her change. I wish all the firewood buyers were like her," Muino, who sold his uncle's firewood, remarked as he counted the money she had told him to keep.

"She got a bundle of firewood from me, gave me K10, and told me to keep the change," Muino added with a grin, chewing on a piece of plastic containing roasted peanuts.

When Manu returned home, he found Bubu Pellie outside their hut, diligently husking some dried coconuts, but Bubu Naris was nowhere in sight.

"Bubu Pellie!" Manu shouted, rushing into his welcoming arms.

"And where is Bubu Naris?" he asked, a wave of sudden tears welling in his eyes.

"Oh, Manu," Bubu Pellie replied, his voice heavy with sorrow. "Bubu Naris is very sick. She's been admitted to Angau Memorial Hospital."

Manu stood there, rooted to the spot as Bubu Pellie continued to husk the coconuts. The rhythmic sound of the husking echoed in the stillness of the evening, but Manu felt lost for words, his heart heavy with worry. The only thought echoing in his mind was a painful, relentless "why?"

Bubu Pellie paused, his weathered hands stilling for a moment. "Sometimes, the weight of the world feels unbearable, my boy. But we must keep moving forward."

Manu handed the K20 to Bubu Pellie, recounting the remarkable act of kindness from the woman who had bought the two bundles of firewood earlier that day.

Bubu nodded, a smile creeping onto his face. "You see, Manu, there are truly generous souls in this world who understand the beauty of giving. These individuals have often faced the harsh realities of life, knowing first-hand the struggles many endure just to put food on the table. After years of hard work, they've found their footing and now enjoy a comfortable life. Yet, they never forget the profound impact that a simple act of kindness can have on someone else's journey."

When they finished packing the dried coconuts into a sturdy sack, they walked on to the main road as the streetlights flickered to life, casting a warm glow on the dusty road. Manu looked up, watching cars pass by, their headlights cutting through the darkness.

"Let's get to Angau Hospital," Bubu Pellie said as he encouraged Manu to walk faster. "We need to sell these coconuts at the eatery before it gets too late."

Together, they set off into the night, the sack of coconuts on Bubu Pellie's shoulder, swinging gently as he walked. Shadows danced around them as they navigated the quiet streets, the sound of their footsteps mingling with the distant hum of engines.

As they approached the junction, they spotted Maoru waiting, her silhouette framed by the light of a nearby streetlamp.

"Maoru!" Manu called out, relief flooding his voice. "You won't believe what's happened. Bubu Naris has been admitted to Angau Hospital."

Maoru's face fell, concern drawn across her features. "Oh no, what happened? Is she okay?"

"We're not sure yet," Manu replied, his voice heavy. "But you can come around tomorrow and see your friend. Also, could you help us sell the firewood? We could use the extra money."

"Of course, I will," Maoru answered, her eyes glistening with sudden tears.

Manu and Bubu Pellie continued on to Angau Hospital, the weight of their worries mingling with the flickering streetlights. They arrived at the hospital just before 7:30PM and walked to the eatery at the back of the left wing of the hospital.

2

Goodbye Bubu Naris

The next morning was Saturday so Manu stayed on at the hospital, as Bubu Pellie went to their church for community work and to let their church members know that his wife was in hospital and everyone has to help her in their prayers.

Bubu Naris slept silently or staring at the ceiling and did not say much.

After lunch they had visitors from their church, especially the women that were close to Bubu Naris.

The moment Maoru stepped into the hospital room, the weight of her despair filled the air. She cried her heart out, her sobs echoing off the sterile walls expressing her love for Bubu Naris. The nurses, tending to other patients, had to gently ask her to keep her voice down, explaining how the cries of anguish could disturb those suffering from unspeakable ailments nearby.

"Please, Maoru," one nurse who goes to their church said softly, her expression a blend of sympathy and concern. "We know it's hard, but there are others who need quietness to heal."

Maoru nodded, wiping her tears with the back of her hand, but the sorrow in her heart was too profound to contain. She took a deep breath, trying to steady herself as she approached Bubu Naris's bed, her heart breaking at the sight before her. Bubu Naris sat up and hugged Maoru and they stayed like that for the next hour, until the good church women, had to drag Maoru away and leave the hospital, as the visiting hour was over and the nurses were getting the patients ready for the doctors to check them.

Bubu Naris lay there, gravely ill, her once-vibrant spirit now reduced to a frail figure, barely recognisable. The room, filled with the sterile scent of antiseptic, felt heavy with sorrow. As the doctor explained the swollen mass encircling her throat to Bubu Pellie, Manu hung on every word, each description striking him like a physical blow, reverberating through his chest.

The lump had grown alarmingly large, making the simple act of swallowing food and water a torturous endeavour. Bubu Naris's voice emerged as a raspy whisper, fragile and strained, each attempt to communicate met with a grimace of pain. Her eyes, usually bright and full of life, now reflected a haunting mix of frustration and fear, conveying emotions that words could no longer express.

Manu's heart ached as he watched her struggle. The woman who had once filled their home with warmth, laughter, and stories of resilience now lay diminished, her strength waning. Each laboured breath seemed to echo the weight of their shared memories, reminding him of the vibrant life she had led. It was unbearable to witness such a decline, and he felt a deep sense of helplessness wash over him.

In that moment, the reality of her condition settled like a dark cloud, suffocating and oppressive. Manu clenched his fists, determined to hold onto hope, even as despair threatened to take root. He silently vowed to be there for her, to fight alongside her in whatever way he could, even as the shadows of uncertainty loomed large.

"It hurts so much, my loves," she managed to say, her voice barely above a whisper. The words cut deep, and Manu felt his heart shatter with each syllable.

He could see the toll that illness had taken on her: the light that once danced in her eyes was dimmed, replaced by a haunting shadow of suffering. It broke Manu's heart to witness the decline of his once-vibrant and industrious Bubu Naris, a woman who had filled their lives with warmth and laughter. Memories flooded his mind—her hearty laughter, her stories that connected their family to lands afar, the way she would sing in the kitchen while cooking meals that filled their stomachs. The meals cooked by her were delicious and filling. Even now the food at the hospital eatery had no taste, though it looked like high quality.

"Why is this happening?" Manu thought, his heart aching at the sight of his Bubu Naris, fragile and in pain. The room felt suffocating, filled with the sterile scent of antiseptic and the quiet beeping of machines, each sound amplifying the despair that hung in the air.

On Sunday, Maoru came to the hospital at 5 AM sharp, right on time for the morning visiting hour. Manu couldn't figure out how Maoru walked the long distance before day break, but knowing her, there were some things that were difficult to explain about her.

As soon as she came, she knelt beside the bed, her tears falling silently onto the sheets, and Manu reached out, placing a comforting hand on her shoulder. Bubu Naris held her hand and let her sob silently. Bubu Pellie quickly grabbed their plates and went to the eatery to get their share of breakfast.

In that moment, surrounded by love and sorrow, Manu knew that no matter the outcome, they would face it together, bound by connection and love, and the enduring spirit of Bubu Naris; her kindness and strength.

On Monday evening, the doctor arrived with the results of Bubu Naris's tests. He explained to Bubu Pellie that the growth had already spread through the lymph nodes around her neck, making surgery too dangerous. Since Bubu Naris couldn't eat, they had inserted a drip feed into her left arm. Every morning, lunchtime, and afternoon, the nurses came to check on her.

On Tuesday, Manu didn't want to go to school; he had endured a particularly bad dream that left him shaken. In his dream, he was swimming in the Bumbu River when the water began to rise. As he struggled to escape, a dark torrent surged from nowhere and swept him away. He fought against it, cried out, but his body felt heavy, and no words came out. Suddenly, he woke up gasping for air, tears streaming down his face.

Bubu Pellie heard Manu sniffing and his brow furrowed with concern, touched Manu's shoulder; both of them laying on the floor below Bubu Naris' bed at the hospital.

"Did you have a nightmare, my boy?" he asked softly, sitting up beside Manu.

"Bubu, I had a bad dream," Manu replied, his voice trembling. "I don't want to go to school today. I want to stay with you and Bubu Naris."

Bubu Pellie placed a comforting hand on Manu's shoulder, sensing the fear in his heart. "I understand, Manu. Bad dreams can feel so real, can't they? But you need to be brave. Bubu Naris needs us to be strong."

"But what if something happens to her while I'm gone?" Manu's eyes welled with tears again. "I don't want to miss a moment with her."

Bubu Pellie sighed, his own heart heavy with worry. "I know it's hard. But staying at the hospital is important. We can support each other here. Your presence will mean a lot to Bubu Naris. She needs to feel our love and strength. Yes, my boy. It's best if you stay with us. We'll face this together," Bubu Pellie replied, his voice steady and reassuring. "School will always be there, but moments like these we cannot afford to miss."

Bubu Naris sat up in bed and whispered to Manu to bring her bilum. Manu reached to the side of her bed, retrieved the bilum, and handed it to her. She took out a bar of bath soap and asked Bubu Pellie to help her to the bathroom.

When they returned, she sat on the bed, reached into her bilum, and pulled out a tightly wrapped red piece of cloth. She handed it to Manu.

"For you. Open it later when we go home," she said in her normal voice. Manu looked up at her, his heart swelling with gratitude and love.

"Bubu Pellie, help me lie down, please," she said softly. Bubu Pellie quickly moved to her bedside, making her comfortable with gentle care.

Manu had never heard his grandparents shout or scream at each other. Bubu Pellie was a kind and soft-spoken man who always listened to his wife's suggestions and plans. Bubu Naris, in turn, always showed respect when he spoke. They never complained about the life they led. They poured all their love and care into raising Manu, ensuring he attended Omili Primary School, even though the school fees were K200 and they had to gather more driftwood to chop into firewood.

In addition to selling firewood, Bubu Naris always sold kaukaus and tapioca, earning a little extra to give Manu K1.00 each day for his lunch. With that, he would buy a 50t cup icy pole and either a scone or a doughnut. It was love that kept them tightly bonded, and now, seeing them struggle brought tears to Manu's eyes.

At noon, the nurses called out for lunch, their voices echoing through the hospital corridors. Bubu Pellie stood up, stretched his weary limbs, and got their three plates. He planned on getting some soup Bubu Naris can swallow bit by bit while he and Manu would need nourishment to face the challenges of the day together.

As he approached the eatery, the familiar aroma of rice and stew filled the air. He spotted Ruth, a devoted member of their church, bustling behind the counter, her hands skilfully dishing out food to the patients and their families.

"Bubu Pellie!" she called, her face lighting up with a warm smile. "It's good to see you! How is Bubu Naris holding up?"

Bubu Pellie sighed, his expression a mixture of hope and sorrow. "It's been tough, Ruth. She's fighting, but the illness is taking its toll. We're doing our best to support her."

Ruth nodded, her eyes filled with empathy. "You're a good man, Pellie. The whole community is praying for her. You know that, right?"

"Thank you, Ruth. It means a lot to us," he replied, his voice steady but tinged with worry. "Manu is badly struggling with the situation but everything is in God's hands."

"Children often feel the weight of such things," Ruth said thoughtfully. "It's good for him to stay with you here and not attend school for a bit. It helps him process what's happening."

"Can you serve some soup for Bubu Naris please," Bubu Pellie asked her.

"Of course, Bubu Pellie. Give me her bowl please," she answered smiling.

"Thank you, Ruth. Your kindness means more than you know," Bubu Pellie said, a grateful smile breaking through his worry.

He gathered the plates and made his way back to Manu and Bubu Naris.

When he returned, he saw Manu wiping tears from his eyes, as he patted the crisp sheets around Bubu Naris bed.

Bubu Pellie gently leaned over Bubu Naris, softly calling her name. "Bubu Naris, it's time to have your soup," he urged, his voice filled with warmth. However, she simply lifted her hand and waved him off, her eyes still closed in a restless sleep.

With a heavy heart, Bubu Pellie sighed and turned to Manu. "Looks like she's not ready for soup just yet," he said, settling down on the floor beside his grandson. He placed the warm bowl of soup between them.

Manu looked at the bowl, then back at his grandfather. "Do you think she'll be okay, Bubu?" he asked, his voice barely above a whisper.

Bubu Pellie nodded, trying to project confidence. "She's a fighter, Manu. You know that. But right now, she needs her rest. We can't rush her."

As they began to eat, the comforting aroma of the soup filled the air, but Manu's eyes remained fixed on Bubu Naris. "I wish she would wake up. I want to tell her about my dream," he said, his voice heavy with concern.

"She always has an explanation for the type of dream I have" Manu continued pausing to eat.

"She does Manu," Bubu Pellie sighed sadly as he ate the food placed on the floor in front of them.

After lunch, a nurse entered the room, her expression focused, and approached Bubu Naris's bedside. Gently, she placed her hand on Bubu Naris's palm, feeling for a pulse. As her fingers searched, a wave of dread washed over her—there was nothing. No faint rhythm, no sign of life.

The nurse's breath caught in her throat, her instincts kicking in. She quickly straightened, urgency sparking in her eyes as she turned on her heel. "Doctor! I need you immediately!" she called out, her voice steady but laced with tension.

In moments, the doctor rushed into the room, his expression shifting from casual to alert as he took in the scene. The nurse stepped aside, her face a mask of concern. "No pulse, doctor."

With a swift nod, the doctor moved to Bubu Naris's side. The atmosphere in the room shifted, heavy with anxiety as the reality of the situation settled in and Manu grasped Bubu Pellie's arm.

On that cold, overcast Tuesday, Bubu Naris passed away peacefully in her sleep, just after four and a half days in the hospital. The sterile scent of antiseptic hung in the air, contrasting sharply with the warmth of the love that enveloped her family. Manu and his grandfather wept inconsolably, their hearts heavy with grief. The nurses, while kind, could not fathom the depth of the bond that tied this small family together—an invisible thread woven from years of shared laughter, whispered secrets, and unspoken understanding.

Manu knew when Bubu Naris sensed something was amiss; her knowing gaze often lingered on him, filled with a quiet wisdom that transcended words. She never voiced her fears, though—just like her, always protecting her loved ones from worry. Yet, in the last few days, the ailment revealed its cruel grip, stealing her away when they had barely begun to prepare for the unimaginable.

The vibrant stories she once told, the laughter that echoed through their home, now would feel like ghosts haunting the empty spaces she once filled. The world outside continued to spin, oblivious to the heartache that had struck Manu and Bubu Pellie, leaving them in profound sorrow.

As soon as they heard the news, Maoru, Pius, his wife Loretta, Rebeka from their church, and Stephen, Bubu Pellie's old friend, rushed to the hospital. They gathered around the bed where Bubu Naris lay and cried openly.

Pius then called his brother Luka to come pick him up in his vehicle. Together, they drove to Papindo Department Store to buy necessities. When they returned, Bubu Naris was carefully carried to a ten-seater vehicle, placed on a mattress that Pius had bought. They waited for Bubu Pellie to collect some paperwork from the doctor, and as soon as he arrived, they set off for Bumbu Settlement.

When they arrived at Bumbu settlement, neighbours came from every corner of the settlement, weeping for the loss of Bubu Naris, who had touched their lives with her humble, kind and forgiving spirit.

Maoru had cleaned their hut and prepared everything for Bubu Naris's return. She filled all the water containers, chopped bundles of firewood, and placed them neatly under the house. Outside, she had laid out dried coconuts, kaukaus, bananas, and other garden foods on the bench.

The men gently carried Bubu Naris and placed her on the bed, which Maoru had made beautifully. That night, neighbours and church members came to pay their respects. The church group sang hymns and prayed together, while the community shared stories of how Bubu Naris had helped them throughout the years.

Maoru cried uncontrollably, her eyes swollen with grief. Manu understood why she wept so deeply; she had often been seen as a "half-wit" due to her limp and struggles with understanding. Yet Bubu Naris had seen her for who she truly was, caring for her since they first met at the roadside market. It was clear to everyone how much Maoru loved Bubu Naris, treating her as if she were part of their family.

That night, Manu sat beside Bubu Pellie, who sobbed softly near the fireplace. The good women from their church brought an abundance of food, ensuring everyone was fed. But Bubu Pellie didn't touch a single bite. Maoru insisted Manu eat a plate of food earlier, as he sat on the bench outside their hut, comforted by some of the boys from the settlement who sat beside him.

The following day, at 10 o'clock, the church women gathered with solemn purpose. Their hands moved gently as they dressed Bubu Naris in a beautiful white meri blaus, the fabric soft and flowing, a final tribute to her grace. They placed her in a wooden coffin, polished to a soft sheen that captured the dim light, reflecting the love that surrounded her.

A heartfelt funeral service was held at their little church down the road, a sanctuary that had been a cornerstone of Bubu Naris's life for so many years. Its walls echoed with songs of farewell, a testament to the community's love for her. The air was thick with emotion, as friends and family gathered, their faces revealing grief and gratitude, each one sharing in the profound loss.

After the service, Bubu Naris was laid to rest in the Bumbu Cemetery. As they lowered the coffin into the earth, a wave of realisation washed over Manu—his beloved Bubu Naris was gone forever. The finality of it struck him like a cold, icy wind from the Bumbu River on a rainy day.

Pius, his wife Rebeka, and Maoru stayed behind with Manu and Bubu Pellie. They cleaned the hut, while Maoru swept the yard, tears streaming down her cheeks. Eventually, she sat near the flower hedges, overcome with grief, and let out a loud, heart-wrenching lamentation.

Bubu Pellie sat under the guava tree, gazing out at the Bumbu River, lost in thought. Time slipped away, and before he knew it, it was 10 o'clock at night. Pius gently took his hand and led him back to his hut, offering silent comfort in their shared sorrow.

Manu lay down on the bed next to the fireplace and drifted off to sleep. At 2 a.m., he woke up and sat up, glancing around the room. Everyone else was sleeping on makeshift beds spread across the floor. He gently shook Maoru awake.

"Yes?" she responded, alarmed, thinking something was wrong.

"Maoru, I had a dream," Manu whispered, tears welling in his eyes.

"Tell me," she said, grabbing both his hands with a concerned look. Then she noticed something he was holding in his right hand.

"What is that?" she asked quietly, gently touching his hand.

"Bubu Naris gave this to me at the hospital. I won't open it until I'm ready," he replied, showing her the tied-up piece of red cloth. Maoru's eyes filled with tears, and she wiped them away with her work-worn hand, lined with the marks of hard labour.

"Yes, open it whenever you're ready, dear," she whispered, sniffling.

"Maoru, I had a strange dream. I dreamt I was sitting under a tree somewhere. Then I heard a noise and looked up. I saw a bird with beautiful white feathers. It looked like a mother bird because it was quite plump. It came down from the tree gracefully, using a ladder, and I noticed a golden crest on its head. As it stepped onto the last rung, I found myself standing beside it. The bird reached beneath one of its wings and pulled out a book. It held the book out to me, and just as I reached for it, I woke up," Manu recounted, and Maoru's eyes widened in fear.

"I don't know, Manu. I've never been to school, but I think a white mother bird that gives you a book is a good sign," she said, touching his arm gently.

A few days later, everyone worked together to tidy up the yard. Rebeka went to her garden, harvested fresh vegetables, and brought them to Manu and Bubu Pellie's hut. Pius chopped bundles of firewood, while Loretta and Maoru cleaned the little garden near their hut, planting vegetables and tapioca.

Afterward, they gathered for a meeting with Manu and Bubu Pellie, assuring them that they would come back to visit from time to time. If they needed anything, they should not hesitate to ask. Bubu Pellie thanked them all, and they left, except for Maoru, who decided to stay for a few more days.

Manu recognised that Bubu Pellie would never ask anyone for help again. Everyone had been so kind, contributing to Bubu Naris's funeral expenses, and he knew Bubu Pellie was not the type to intrude on others' lives or homes.

As the days wore on and the last of the mourners left for their homes, Manu found himself lost in thought, as he sat under the guava tree. He contemplated how he could best support Bubu Pellie during this difficult time. The weight of responsibility settled upon his shoulders, and in that quiet moment, a profound realisation emerged: he was now in charge.

The realisation stirred something deep within him—a sense of purpose. He understood that he had to step into a role of strength and compassion, to be the anchor for Bubu Pellie as he navigated his grief.

Finally, the sun dipped below the horizon, casting a warm golden hue over the Bumbu River, just like any other day but today, it was a special reminder that he would carry forward the love and lessons imparted by Bubu Naris, ensuring that her spirit lived on not just in memory, but in the action he would take to uplift those he loved. The journey ahead would be challenging, but he was ready to embrace it, for Bubu Naris's legacy was now his guiding light.

3

Bubu Pellie

ubu Pellie was never the same after his beloved wife passed away. The vibrant, diligent man he once was seemed to fade, replaced by a fragile shadow haunted by loss. He often fell ill with pneumonia, and on many days, sat outside their hut with a distant, forlorn look in his eyes—as if searching for memories that had slipped just beyond reach. The energetic, active spirit that Bubu Naris had cherished was now a distant memory, replaced by a quiet sorrow that spoke volumes in his stillness.

During their searches for driftwood along the Bumbu River, Bubu Pellie often had tears welling in his eyes, his tiredness evident in every slow, trembling breath. Manu soon found himself burdened with the task, dragging the heavy wood alone and chopping it with their old, battered axe.

He laboured under the scorching sun, tirelessly, seeking respite in the cool embrace of the river—diving in to wash away his fatigue. Meanwhile, Bubu Pellie sat quietly in the shade, his gaze fixed on Manu with a heavy, mournful heart, burdened by grief and memories that refused to fade.

Manu soon understood that Bubu Pellie needed him more than ever. Every afternoon after school, he would seize his old axe and run down to the Bumbu River, determined to chop wood—his small way of easing the heavy burden on his shoulders. While Manu laboured by the river, Bubu Pellie sold bundles of firewood at the roadside market, his tired hands carefully arranging each bundle. This simple routine became their shared bond, a silent act of support and gratitude—an unspoken promise that Manu would stand by the man who had showered him with love and guidance through life's hardest times.

Bubu Pellie arrived in Lae in his early twenties, originating from Nonambaro village in the Eastern Highlands Province. He made his living as a butcher for Burns Philp, a steady but modest existence.

One fateful day, he met Bubu Naris, an orphan from the rugged mountains of Bougainville's Buin District. She was quietly babysitting for a Salvation Army officer when their paths crossed at the Bumbu Bridge.

Carrying an overloaded bilum brimming with fresh vegetables, she paused on the side of the bridge to catch her breath. As Bubu Pellie passed by, he greeted her with a friendly nod, and she responded shyly with a faint smile. As their eyes met, he noticed how much she struggled to lift and carry the heavy load. Without a second thought, he turned back, gently lifted the bilum from her grasp, and offered to carry it for her. That small, kind gesture marked the beginning of a profound relationship—one founded on respect, love, and quiet steadfastness, that would grow stronger with each passing day.

After Bubu Pellie resigned from his butchering job, he received his final pay check, along with his superannuation benefits. With this, he was able to build a, permanent house—a comfortable home for their family. They always had enough food, and their days were filled with simple contentment and genuine happiness. Bubu Naris left her babysitting duties behind and started her own stall along Kamkumung Road, selling fresh produce. Together, they thrived in their hard-earned stability.

Their deepest joy came with the arrival of their only daughter, Nasila; who, in time, became Manu's mother. She was their pride and joy, growing up in a loving Christian home filled with laughter and hope.

Her parents, kind and devoted, valued education deeply. They enrolled her in a good school, believing that a bright future was within her reach. Through their love, faith, and hard work, they built a life rooted in hope and the promise of brighter days.

Nasila excelled in her studies, winning awards for her academic achievements. But when she reached grade 8, her world changed— she became pregnant with Manu. This news shattered their hearts, filling their home with a mix of joy and sorrow, hope and worry. Despite the pain, they loved her dearly and supported her as best they could.

Manu's father, meanwhile, was already married and could only visit intermittently, often caught up in his own family obligations and responsibilities, leaving a sense of longing and unfulfilled promises in their life.

When Manu was just two years old, his mother fell gravely ill with malaria—fierce and unforgiving. It affected her brain, plunging her into a coma. A few days later, on a bright, sunlit Monday, she passed away suddenly, leaving a gaping void in their hearts.

Bubu Pellie and Bubu Naris were shattered by their loss, their grief heavy and raw. Yet, amid the ache of sorrow, they found solace and renewed purpose in their grandson, Manu. They treasured him deeply, believing he was a precious gift—sent to them as a beacon of hope and love in their darkest hour, a living reminder of life's fragile beauty and the enduring power of family.

By the time Manu turned four, tensions escalated into a violent ethnic clash between rival groups in the settlement areas. As chaos erupted and people began fleeing, opportunists roamed the streets, setting fire to homes. Bubu Pellie and Bubu Naris's house was consumed by flames, along with everything they owned. They salvaged what they could from the ruins and managed to build a small hut on their land.

Two months later, Manu's father came to their house late one evening and told them that he was relocating to another province with his family, severing the last threads of their once-close ties. The weight of this news hung in the air, a heavy reminder to Pellie and Naris of how swiftly life can change.

Meanwhile, Bubu Pellie searched diligently for another butchering job, his heart brimming with hope to provide for his family once more. Yet, the cruel hand of time had taken its toll; he was now deemed too old, lacking the energy and vigour that had once fuelled his labour.

The world outside continued to move forward, but he found himself standing still, caught between the ache of nostalgia and the uncertainty of what lay ahead.

As hunger began to set in, desperation compelled them to scavenge along the banks of the Bumbu River, collecting driftwood that had washed ashore. They chopped it up and sold it at the Kamkumung roadside market, doing whatever they could to survive.

In the midst of this struggle, Bubu Naris tended to her yard garden. She cultivated a variety of greens, kaukau, and tapioca, which not only provided sustenance for them but also served as a source of income. Her hands worked tirelessly as she focused on Manu and his well-being.

"It's a harsh life, but life was never meant to be easy," Bubu Naris would often say, her voice steady yet warm. "Good times don't last forever, Manu. And bad times don't last either. But we must learn how to navigate both."

These wise words echoed in Manu's mind like a guiding mantra, each syllable infused with her warm and kind spirit. He could almost see her, kneeling in the garden, sunlight glinting off her silver hair as she tended to the plants.

"Remember, my boy," she would add, a twinkle in her eye, "it's the storms that teach us how to dance in the rain. Embrace the struggle; it shapes who we are."

He understood now that life's challenges were not merely obstacles, but opportunities to grow stronger and wiser, just as she had taught him.

Bubu Naris's story was nothing short of extraordinary. "I was an orphan, Manu," she began, her voice steady yet filled with emotion. "I left my home stowing away on a ship after walking hundreds of miles from my remote village." It sounded unbelievable, yet every word was true.

"I was the youngest, and after my parents passed away, my siblings were married off, leaving me alone. A widowed old man with seven grandchildren wanted to make me his wife. I couldn't bear the thought, so I ran away, living in various villages for months until I finally reached a seaside town.

"When a crowd gathered to board a ship, I slipped in unnoticed. We arrived in Lae, and as we disembarked, I saw Salvation Army workers preaching near the wharf. I approached one in a white uniform and asked if I could work for his family. He agreed, and that's how I found my way to them until I met Bubu Pellie."

Manu struggled to picture his quiet, kind Bubu Naris trekking over mountain trails, spending restless nights in different villages. She must have truly despised that old man who sought to marry her, preferring to risk everything rather than live that fate. In that moment, Manu realised that when people find themselves in desperate situations, they often do the unimaginable to reclaim their freedom and dignity.

He felt a deep sense of gratitude that Bubu Naris had left her homeland to be with Bubu Pellie. Memories of her flooded his mind—how she would smile in the darkness, her white teeth shining brightly against her rich, dark complexion. He recalled the intricate baskets she wove from coconut fronds, a craft that set her apart from the other women who knitted bilums with wool.

Maoru was the only woman Bubu Naris had taught the art of basket weaving. The patterns they created together were unique and vibrant; Bubu Naris would boil the coconut leaves in water and then dip them in various natural dyes made from local plants. Once the shredded fronds were hung on the clothesline to dry, she transformed them into beautiful works of art. Each basket was not just a functional item but a testament to her creativity and skill, filled with the colours of the earth and the spirit of her heritage.

Manu had never once heard his grandparents raise their voices in anger at each other. Bubu Pellie always treated Bubu Naris with care and respect. In stark contrast, their next-door neighbour constantly fought with his wife, belting their grandchildren, swearing, and chasing everyone out of their home.

"Marisu acts like a madman," Bubu Pellie remarked one day, exasperation creeping into his voice as the commotion repeated for the third time that week. "He shouldn't chase his family like that. As the head of the household, he should know how to resolve matters peacefully."

"Pellie, mind your own business," Bubu Naris replied softly, glancing at her husband with a warm smile. Bubu Pellie returned her gaze, his eyes sparkling with affection.

One day, curious, Manu asked Bubu Pellie if Bubu Naris ever yelled at him like Marisu's wife screamed and cursed.

"Oh, Manu," Bubu Pellie chuckled, "we don't do that kind of yelling. No, your Bubu Naris would never raise her voice like that. And you know," he added with a smile, "if she did, I wouldn't say a word. She is a woman from a faraway land, sent by fate all this way for me."

Bubu Pellie and Bubu Naris were steadfast in their faith, embodying the principles of good Christians not just in words but through their humble actions. Everyone in the Bumbu settlement admired them, feeling welcome to stop by their hut whenever they needed dry coconuts or wanted to pick up bundles of firewood, promising to pay later. Even when neighbours took firewood without settling their debts, Bubu Pellie and Bubu Naris held no grudges, simply letting it go.

"Food and water are things we must never be selfish about," Bubu Naris would often remind Manu and Bubu Pellie. "We sell firewood, and we know there are widows and families struggling. If they can give just a K1, we should give them a bundle." Their firewood was priced at K2 per bundle, but their generosity knew no bounds.

Bubu Pellie always listened attentively to his wife, even when he didn't completely agree with her. He patiently waited for her to finish speaking before responding gently, explaining his perspective with care. This mutual respect and understanding ensured that there was never any yelling in their home, creating a peaceful and loving atmosphere for their family.

Even when their only daughter faced challenges, Bubu Pellie and Bubu Naris felt a deep sadness, their hearts heavy with concern. She was such a clever student, yet they never scolded her or used harsh words. Instead, they offered her love and support, ensuring she remained happy and secure. When Manu's father came to visit, they welcomed him warmly, embracing the complexities of family life.

"Life is funny, Manu. We are here today and may be gone tomorrow," Bubu Naris often reminded him. "Never let your anger set with the sun. You never know what tomorrow might bring."

"Everyone is raised differently, Manu," Bubu Pellie added one day after a neighbour boy had sworn at him on his way home from school. "No one has the same upbringing. It's important to try to understand a person's background before passing judgment on their behavior."

Their wisdom instilled in Manu a sense of compassion and understanding, guiding him through the ups and downs of life.

"Kali's parents always belt him and swear at him, Manu. Don't worry about the words he used on you. Try to form a friendship with him, and you'll see—he can become a great friend." Bubu Pellie's words proved true, as Manu and Kali grew to be close friends.

When Bubu Naris passed away, Kali showed his support by bringing six fresh Kulaus to Manu's home. He settled in beside Manu, the weight of grief evident between them, yet they found comfort in each other's presence. They reminisced about the days spent helping Bubu Naris in the garden, laughing as they climbed the breadfruit tree. They recalled lighting a fire to cook the breadfruit and enjoying it with fresh coconut.

As the sun dipped lower in the sky, casting a golden hue over the Bumbu River, they shared silent moments of comfort, the kind that spoke volumes without words. They talked about their plans for the future, the adventures they dreamed of embarking on—fishing at the river, exploring the hills, and learning new skills together.

As dusk settled in, and shadows began to stretch across the yard, Kali finally rose to leave. With a firm handshake and a promise to return, he left for his house, leaving Manu with the warmth of companionship and the assurance that he was not alone in his sorrow.

$$4$$

Hello Manu

anu grew strong and fit—his body tough and toned, a testament to hard work and resilience. His muscles rippled beneath his sun-kissed brown skin as he pulled heavy pieces of wood wedged between the stones on the riverbank. Dawn had barely broken when his day began—a time when most people still lay in sleep—but he was already on the move.

With practiced ease, he descended the steep cliff to the Bumbu River. The air was cold and crisp, and the sharp rocks and pebbles felt gritty beneath his feet. He used Bubu Pellie's old axe to chop and split the logs, tossing them onto the stony banks. It was gruelling, demanding work—backbreaking, even—but Manu knew this was to provide for both himself and Bubu Pellie.

Manu came to realise that every piece of wood he collected told a story. Some were gnarled and twisted, remnants of storms that had battered the area, while others were straight and sturdy, their smooth surfaces glistening with moisture. Manu learned to appreciate the uniqueness of each log, imagining how they would burn in the homes of families seeking warmth and comfort. The rhythmic thud of the axe against the wood became a form of meditation exercise for him, a way to clear his mind of worries and focus on the task at hand.

As he worked, he developed a keen eye for the best pieces of wood. He knew which types were favoured by customers, often selecting dense hardwoods that were a rare find and would last longer in the fire. His knowledge grew with each passing day, and he began to experiment with different techniques to split the wood more efficiently. He discovered that a well-placed strike could split a log in half with ease, saving him time and energy for the next load.

In school, Manu shone as a bright student, excelling beyond expectations and earning impressive grades. By the end of the year, he had topped all three Grade 7 classes, receiving the coveted Dux Award Certificate along with a Collins Dictionary and twelve 96-page exercise books. This achievement sparked a rare, radiant smile from Bubu Pellie, his eyes glistening with a mixture of pride and sadness as they walked home after the school closing.

As December rolled in, Bubu Pellie worked tirelessly to save enough money for Manu to continue to Grade 8. Each day, he sat at the market, his weathered hands sorting through the firewood, while Manu chopped driftwood down by the Bumbu River. Yet, despite his efforts, Bubu Pellie often found himself drained, fatigue etched into his features like lines on an old map. The weight of worry hung heavily on him, manifesting in the furrows of his brow and the deepening shadows beneath his eyes. He frequently turned to Manu, his voice thick with regret, apologising for their struggles and the burden he felt he was placing on the boy.

"I'm sorry, Manu," he would murmur, his gaze distant. "I wish things were different."

Though Manu was focused on his studies, his grandfather's sorrow gnawed at him like a persistent ache. Bubu Pellie appeared increasingly unhappy and lost, spending his mornings beneath the coconut tree, gazing out at the Bumbu River before dawn. He stared intently at the rising sun, as if seeking answers or solace from its golden rays. Manu observed this haunting ritual for weeks, each sunrise casting a deeper shadow over his heart, his concern deepening with each passing day.

A shiver coursed through him; he feared his grandfather might be losing touch with reality. The thought clung to him like a damp fog, heavy and unyielding. Driven by a sense of urgency, Manu resolved to take action before it was too late. He couldn't bear the thought of Bubu Pellie succumbing to despair.

With determination firm in his heart, he walked into the school and approached Mr. Lance, the Headmaster, who always seemed to embody an air of authority mixed with a genuine kindness.

"Sir, I need to talk to you," he said, his voice steady but filled with a quiet resolve. "I won't be returning to Grade 8 next year. I want to ask if you could hold a spot for me the following year. My grandfather isn't well, and I need to take care of him."

Mr. Lance raised an eyebrow, concern lining his forehead. "Are you sure about this, Manu? Education is important. It opens doors."

"I know, Sir," Manu replied, his resolve unwavering, bolstered by the love he felt for his grandfather. "But I can't let him struggle to sell firewood just to pay for my school fees. I'll save up and return in the following year. I need to be there for him now."

The Headmaster studied him for a moment, the silence stretching between them like the distance between hope and despair. Finally, he sighed, the weight of understanding shifting his expression.

"Very well, Manu. I will hold a spot for you. But remember, education is a gift. You can always return to it."

Gratitude flooded through Manu, but it was accompanied by an equal measure of anxiety. He left the Headmaster's office with a mix of relief and apprehension, knowing that his choice was driven by love but also by uncertainty. As he walked home, he glanced at the sky, the sun casting long shadows behind him, and he felt the burden of his decision settle heavily on his young shoulders.

Manu felt the weight lifted off his shoulders when he left the school. He was relieved that Bubu Pellie wouldn't have to bear that burden alone.

When he got home, he found Bubu Pellie sitting under the coconut tree, gazing out at the Bumbu River.

"Good afternoon, Bubu. How are you feeling today?" Manu asked, settling beside him.

"Aaah, there you are, my treasure. Where did you go?" Bubu Pellie replied softly, almost as if he were whispering a secret.

"Bubu Pellie, I've decided to withdraw from school so I can help you more until you're better," Manu said with a smile, trying to lighten the mood.

In that moment, Bubu Pellie broke down, tears streaming down his face as he embraced Manu tightly against his frail chest. "Oh, my boy," he sobbed, overwhelmed with emotion. Manu felt the warmth of their shared struggle, realising he had made the right choice. In that embrace, they both cried, understanding that together they could endure the harsh realities of life that lay ahead.

"Every day is a gift, Manu," Bubu Pellie whispered, pulling back slightly to look into Manu's eyes. "You have such a bright future ahead of you. Don't let me hold you back."

"But Bubu," Manu replied, his voice firm yet gentle, "you are my priority. We can find a way through this together."

Bubu Pellie nodded slowly, his expression a mixture of gratitude and concern. "I worry for you, my boy. The world is tough, and you're so young. You should be learning, not toiling away."

Manu smiled softly, "And what better lesson is there than taking care of family? I've learned so much from you already."

As the sun began to dip lower in the sky, casting a golden glow over the river, Bubu Pellie sighed. "I wish I could provide more for you. This market... it seems to grow more difficult each day."

Manu glanced at the pile of firewood beside them, barely touched.

"We'll make it work, Bubu. Maybe we can find a way to make this wood more appealing to the buyers. Perhaps a little creativity could help."

"Creativity?" Bubu Pellie raised an eyebrow, intrigued despite his fatigue. "What do you have in mind?"

"We could bundle it differently, or maybe even add some fragrant herbs for aroma. People are drawn to the unique," Manu suggested, his eyes lighting up with hope.

Bubu Pellie chuckled softly, that sound like a gentle breeze. "Ah, my clever boy. I see your mother's spirit in you. She would be proud."

"Let's give it a try tomorrow," Manu said, his heart swelling with determination. "We'll wake up early and prepare everything."

Manu watched helplessly as Bubu Pellie's strength waned each passing day, marked by a slight tremor in his hands and a weariness carved into his face. The vibrant stories that once flowed from his grandfather became whispers, leaving a void that echoed in their small hut. Manu devoted himself to caring for Bubu Pellie, ensuring he took his medicine and rested, while desperately trying to make ends meet.

He continued chopping and selling firewood, but soon realised that the dried wood he gathered from around the Bumbu River simply didn't appeal much to the customers. They preferred the robust, long-burning hardwood that provided a reliable flame; woods from the forestlands. Each trip to the market brought a new wave of disappointment as he watched potential buyers started going past his piles of wood, their eyes searching for something more substantial, straight out of the forests.

Determined not to let his grandfather down, Manu began to experiment with his collection methods. He ventured further along the riverbanks, scouting for better quality wood, even climbing steep hills to find fallen branches from sturdy trees. Yet, the effort left him exhausted, and the sun's relentless heat seemed to weigh down on his spirit.

In quiet moments, he would sit beside Bubu Pellie, as he sat gazing out at the river.

"Bubu, I'm going to find a way to get us the best wood," Manu promised one afternoon, his voice firm yet filled with uncertainty. "I'll make sure we have enough to sell every day."

"You're a good boy, Manu," Bubu Pellie's eyes shimmered with a mix of pride and worry. "But remember, it's not just about the quantity. Quality matters too. You must choose wisely."

"I know, Bubu. I'm learning," Manu replied, his brow furrowing with thought. "I've been watching the way the buyers look at the wood. They want sturdiness and a good scent. I'll make sure to find both."

Bubu Pellie smiled faintly. "You have the heart of a true provider. Just don't push yourself too hard. The river will always flow, but you need to take care of yourself as well."

"I will, I promise," Manu said, though doubt flickered in his mind. "But what if I can't find enough? What if we continue to struggle?"

"Then we will find another way," Bubu Pellie assured him, placing a weathered hand on Manu's shoulder. "Sometimes the best solutions come when you least expect them. We must have faith."

Manu nodded, feeling the warmth of his grandfather's reassurance. "I just want to make things better for us, Bubu. I don't want you to worry."

"Oh, my dear boy," Bubu Pellie chuckled softly, "you carry the weight of the world on your shoulders. But remember, it's okay to share that weight with me. We are a team."

"Always a team," Manu echoed, his heart swelling with determination. "I'll bring back the best wood tomorrow. You'll see!"

As they sat together, the sun dipped lower, painting the sky in hues of orange and pink. Bubu Pellie turned his gaze to the horizon. "You know, Manu, when your mother was young, she had the same fire in her eyes. She would chase her dreams with such passion. It's a gift you've inherited."

Manu smiled, feeling a connection to his mother's spirit. "I wish I could have known her better. I want to make her proud, just like you."

"You are already doing that, my boy," Bubu Pellie said, his voice rich with love. "Every day you show strength and kindness. That's what matters most."

"Then I'll keep going, Bubu," Manu replied, determination igniting within him. "For you, for her, and for us. We can overcome this."

One afternoon, Manu sat beneath the coconut tree, staring down at the Bumbu River, the gentle flow mirroring the turmoil in his heart. The sun cast shimmering reflections on the water, but all he could see were the shadows of their struggles, a constant reminder of the challenges that loomed over them. He pondered his next steps, feeling the weight of their hardships pressing down on him like a heavy stone, each thought heavier than the last.

Manu began to brainstorm possibilities, his mind racing with ideas. What if he could gather and sell handmade crafts made from the scraps of wood? Each piece could tell a story, capturing the beauty of their surroundings. Or perhaps he could start a small delivery service for firewood and other goods, reaching customers who might appreciate the convenience. The thought sparked a flicker of hope within him, igniting a vision of a more stable future.

Yet, as he sat there, reality dawned on him like a cold wave crashing against the shore. He couldn't ignore the fact that there were far more established firewood sellers in the market, their businesses booming while he struggled to attract buyers. He felt a pang of frustration, the competitive landscape daunting and overwhelming.

But instead of allowing despair to take hold, Manu took a deep breath, reminding himself that every challenge presented an opportunity. He could differentiate himself by offering something unique, something that others weren't providing. Perhaps he could combine his love for the river and the land with his entrepreneurial spirit, creating a niche that would set him apart.

5

Empty Tins, Orchids, Golf Course

The next morning, as the sun crested the horizon, golden rays simmered across the landscape, covering nature in a warm embrace. Manu had resolved before daybreak to gather bottles and empty soda cans, intending to sell them at the depot for some quick cash.

He stood beneath the guava tree and stretched his arms and savoured the sun's gentle warmth on his skin, soaking in the freshness of the new day. "Every little bit helps," he murmured, recalling Bubu Pellie's sage advice about resourcefulness.

Inside their hut, the bamboo shelf was bare; their rice, tin fish, noodles, tea, and sugar had dwindled to nothing. He needed to earn money quickly to replenish their kitchen.

There were empty cans littered all over the streets of Lae city, a treasure trove of opportunity just waiting to be claimed. If he could gather enough, it would mean easy money.

He left Bumbu Settlement with a determined heart and stepped out into the blistering sun, the heat already radiating fiercely off the pavement. As he wandered through the busy streets of Lae town, each step was heavy and slow, the long walks exhausting without a bite of breakfast in his stomach.

The sun beat down mercilessly, making the pavement shimmer and shimmer beneath his feet.

His stomach rumbled with hunger, gnawing relentlessly, while his throat grew dry, parched by the heat. Still, Manu pressed on, his resolve untiring. He scoured the streets with keen eyes, searching for discarded cans and bottles and carefully, placed each find into the black trash bag slung across his shoulder.

He often found himself lingering near the taverns, where discarded bottles were plentiful. But the rowdiness and drunken brawls unnerved him, and he quickly opted to avoid the area, sticking to the quieter roads as he searched for his bottles and cans.

The task was grueling and each day left him weary, his body aching from relentless searching. When he returned home each evening, fatigue washed over him as he caught sight of his grandfather.

Bubu Pellie's frail figure stood as a silent reminder of their harsh circumstances. Every time Manu looked at him, a wave of deep sadness and helplessness washed over his young heart. The harsh reality of their struggles pressed heavily on him, like an unrelenting weight that refused to lift.

One cold morning, Manu woke up early, the chill in the air urging him to move quickly. He set off toward Top Town, determination in each step, his breath visible in the crisp morning air. As he passed the Huon Gulf Motel, a voice called out to him.

"Hey, boy! Over here!" The security guard waved him over.

Manu hesitated for a moment but then walked over to him.

The guard leaned against the railing, looking down at Manu with a knowing smile.

"Got some cans for you," he said, reaching behind the rubbish bin and pulling out a tightly packed plastic bag filled with empty soda cans. His eyes softened, and a warmth spread across his weathered face. "Keep at it, young man. You're doing good."

Manu's face lit up with gratitude. "Thank you, sir! Every little bit helps," he replied, his voice filled with sincerity.

The guard nodded, his expression turning serious. "I see a lot of young folks give up too soon. But you… you've got the grit. Just remember, it's not just about the money. It's about building something for yourself."

Manu absorbed the words, feeling a surge of motivation. "I know. I just want to make sure there's food on the table."

"Then keep pushing," the guard encouraged. "The world needs more hard workers like you."

Manu thanked him again and continued on his way, the bag of cans swinging at his side.

He walked across the field and found a spot in the shade of the trees beside Freddy's Famili Stoa. He settled down and began smashing the cans with a stone as he looked around randomly, watching the people walk by.

Suddenly, Manu's small moment of peace was shattered. Shadows from the drain flickered as two older boys slipped out swiftly, their eyes gleaming with mischief. Without warning, they rushed at him, their faces hard and determined.

"Move, kid!" one barked, shoving him roughly aside.

The other reached out swiftly, snatching the plastic bag filled with soda cans before Manu could even react. A rush of shock and fear surged through him as the boys disappeared into the shadows, leaving him stunned and empty-handed in the cold morning air.

"Hey! That's mine!" Manu called out, voice trembling, but they were already gone, swallowed by the darkness.

Manu was bruised in body and shattered in spirit as he stumbled away, each step heavy with grief. The weight of his loss bore down on him like an unending shadow, dragging him under the relentless scorching sun. The searing heat seemed to mock his pain, the sweat stinging his eyes as he struggled forward, his heart aching with a deep despair.

When he finally reached the Bumbu River, he collapsed to his knees, trembling as he cupped the cool water in his hands. The brief sensation of relief was tiny but precious, a fragile respite from the torment inside him. As he splashed the water onto his face, tears blurred his vision, the bitter taste of salt mixing with the river's coolness—reminders of his helplessness, of hopes lost in an instant.

Manu felt exhausted beyond words and quietly sank against the gnarled roots of an old tree trunk, seeking refuge in its quiet shade. His body sagged, tears threatening to fall again, as he allowed himself a rare, silent moment of solitude—lost in thought and loss, overwhelmed by the ache of surviving another day in a world that seemed to give and take everything in an unforgiving whirl.

Later that afternoon, he returned home, but he kept the painful encounter to himself. He didn't want to burden Bubu Pellie with his troubles; instead, he tucked the experience away, hoping to find a way to face the challenges ahead without adding to his grandfather's worries.

The next day, Manu rose early, the morning light filtering through the trees. He checked on his grandfather, who was still fast asleep, his chest rising and falling gently.

He slipped out quietly and made his way down to the river. Following the banks upstream, he spotted four beautiful tree orchids and carefully collected them, their vibrant colours a small spark of hope in a challenging life.

As the sun began to climb higher, Manu set off toward Lae Town, determination in his stride. Today, he planned to sell the orchids for K3.00 each. With each step along the Bumbu road, he felt lighter, whistling softly to himself.

He envisioned the moment he would sell the flowers, eager to buy some fresh fruits for his grandfather from the main market. They had been living off kaukaus for a week, and the blandness of it had become unbearable. Their sugar and tea had long run out, and there was no soap to wash their clothes. It felt as if all the blessings had vanished with Bubu Naris.

But he shook his head, refusing to let despair take root. No, he couldn't think that way. He had to push through for his grandfather's sake. To keep the dark thoughts at bay, he began to sing a song from church, letting the familiar melody wash over him.

He walked past the FODE Centre, and hurried by the YWCA and then Lae Christian Academy, his voice rising softly with each step. He sang until he reached the Court House, then continued past Food Mart, the rhythm of his song blending with the sounds of the bustling town. Each note felt like a reminder of hope, keeping his spirits high as he focused on the task ahead.

Manu walked to SVS Plaza, his heart racing with anticipation. As he approached, he noticed a group of boys standing nearby, each clutching their orchids. They spotted him and immediately turned hostile.

"Hey, you! What do you think you're doing here?" one of them shouted, stepping forward menacingly.

Manu hesitated, his palms sweating. "I—I'm just trying to sell my orchids," he replied, trying to sound confident.

"Not in our territory, you're not!" another boy sneered, crossing his arms. "You better scram before we make you regret it."

"Yeah, go on! No one wants your ugly flowers!" the first boy added, shoving Manu lightly.

Feeling the humiliation wash over him, Manu lowered his gaze. "I'll just go," he mumbled, backing away slowly.

"Good choice! Don't come back, loser!" one of the boys called after him, laughter ringing in the air.

Manu felt embarrassed and defeated, as he turned and headed down the hill toward Eriku, the weight of their taunts heavy on his heart.

As he walked past Angau Hospital, then the Huon Gulf Motel and the Fire Station, he tried to shake off the encounter. But the memory lingered, and he felt a knot of shame tightened in his stomach.

When he reached Papindo Department Store, he saw boys his age eagerly selling their orchids to shoppers. His gaze caught an old man sitting by the entrance, begging for money. The sight struck a chord deep within him, reminding him too much of his grandfather.

In that moment, embarrassment flooded over him. 'I look just like him,' he thought, bowing his head in shame. He lifted the orchids, ready to toss them into the drain, when a voice interrupted his thoughts.

"Hey, how much for those orchids?" a kind voice called out.

Manu turned to see a motherly-looking woman approaching. "I don't know. Here, you can have them," he said, shoving the orchids into her hands, desperate to escape.

"Pssst, wait! Here, take this!" the woman exclaimed, holding out some money.

Manu turned back, eyes downcast, and without meeting her gaze, he grabbed the cash, muttering a thank you before fleeing around the corner.

Once he was out of sight, he glanced at the money she had given him—four five-kina notes, totaling twenty kina. The gratitude he felt was beyond words.

He walked briskly, with Bubu Pellie on his mind and headed to the Tucker Stall at Bumbu Settlement, ready to buy what they needed.

That evening, he cooked rice, a tin of fish, and noodles, filling their bellies for the night. They went to bed satisfied, the warmth of a full stomach easing the weight of the day's struggles.

Manu woke up early the next morning, the dawn light just beginning to break over the horizon. He set off toward Bumbu River, the cool air refreshing against his skin. As he walked, he spotted Kaia taking a shortcut to Kamkumung market.

"Kaia! Good morning! Where are you off to?" Manu called out, waving enthusiastically.

"Hey, Manu! My main boy! Nice to see you!" Kaia beamed, turning back to chat with a wide grin.

"I'm heading to the riverbank to look for tree orchids to sell in town today," Manu replied, feeling the excitement of the day ahead.

"What? Come on! All the boys around here are selling orchids. Why not join me at the Golf Course? You could be a caddie for the white folks!" Kaia suggested, his eyes sparkling with enthusiasm.

"What's a caddie?" Manu asked, puzzled yet intrigued.

"A caddie is a boy like us, hired to carry a golfer's clubs and help find the balls when they hit them," Kaia explained, his enthusiasm infectious. "It's a great way to earn some cash, and you get to meet interesting people!"

"Okay, let's go!" Manu shouted, adrenaline surging through him at the prospect of a new adventure.

Kaia was older than Manu but had a youthful spirit that drew him to boys who were Manu's age. He was funny, quick-witted, and always knew how to lighten the mood. Yet beneath his playful exterior, Kaia was also serious and levelheaded, often providing guidance and encouragement when needed. His presence was reassuring, and Manu admired his ability to navigate challenges with confidence.

As they walked together, Kaia shared stories of his experiences caddying, painting vivid pictures of the golfers he met. Manu listened intently, feeling inspired by his friend's adventures, eager to experience what Kaia was telling him about.

The two friends walked quickly to the Golf Course, their anticipation building with each step. The sound of their footsteps echoed in the quiet morning, mingling with the distant chirping of birds.

When they arrived, they stood in the car park, scanning the area for potential golfers. Soon, an expatriate couple pulled in; the man parked the car while his wife stepped out. She was stunning, dressed elegantly, a straw hat perched on her head, and her fingers adorned with shiny rings that caught the sunlight.

"Good morning, boys!" the woman greeted them warmly, her bright smile radiating friendliness.

"Good morning!" Manu and Kaia chimed back, their voices filled with enthusiasm.

"This is my husband, Blake, and I'm Wanda. Would you like to be our caddies for today?" she asked, her eyes sparkling with kindness.

"Absolutely!" the boys exclaimed in unison, excitement bubbling over as they exchanged eager glances. Kaia added, "We'd love to help! We've been looking forward to this."

Wanda nodded approvingly. "Wonderful! We could use some energetic caddies. Are you ready for a fun day on the course?"

"Ready as ever!" Manu replied, grinning from ear to ear.

Blake, who had been quietly observing, smiled at the boys. "You two look like you're up for anything. Just remember, it's all about teamwork out there."

Kaia nodded earnestly. "We'll make sure to keep everything organised and help you both enjoy the game!"

"Fantastic!" Wanda said, her enthusiasm infectious. "Let's get started then!"

As they moved toward the golf carts, Manu felt a rush of excitement. This might be the opportunity he had hoped for—a chance to earn some money to keep on looking after his Grandfather.

Kaia pushed Blake's trolley while Manu carefully carried Wanda's golf clubs, their eyes glued to the couple as they walked. They listened closely to the instructions, and like sponges, they soaked up the names of the different clubs.

Manu watched everything Kaia did, eager to learn the ropes of being a caddie. Whenever the couple called for the white balls, they quickly scurried to collect them, Kaia beaming with pride as he showed Manu the ins and outs of the job.

As they roamed the Golf Course, they chatted with other caddies while Blake and Wanda chatted with a tall guy they called the Coca-Cola manager in Lae.

"Yo, check this out! Yesterday, I caddied for a golfer from Australia. Dude bought me lunch and dropped K50 in my pocket! Best day ever!" Taia boasted, puffing out his chest.

"Pfft, that's nothing! I used to caddy for Paul and Leslie before they bounced back to New Zealand. They always tossed me K100 after three days and bought me lunch every time! Took me to their crib too!" Mori jumped in, relishing the spotlight.

"Yeah, but they were gonna take him to New Zealand, but their house got half-burnt! Crazy stuff!" Taia added, his tone turning serious.

"No, no! Their house got claimed by the bank, bro," Kaia corrected him, shaking his head.

"How can a house get claimed? I think Taia's right!" Lumba interjected, brows furrowing in confusion.

"Lumba, you dupe! If you take out a loan from the bank to buy something—like Paul and Leslie did with their house—and then you don't keep up with the payments, the bank can swoop in and take it all back. They can take your house!" Kaia explained, his voice firm as he laid down the facts.

"Yeah, that's real," Manu added softly, trying to back Kaia up.

"Who's this guy?" Chay asked, eyeing Manu with a frown that highlighted the scars on his face.

"Oh, this is my main boy. His name's Manu. He's from my Settlement," Kaia replied, introducing him with pride.

The other boys nodded in acknowledgment and reached out to shake Manu's hand, welcoming him into their circle. "Nice to meet ya, bro! You ready to hustle with us?" one of them grinned, and Manu felt a rush of belonging.

For a week, Manu and Kaia worked tirelessly as caddies, their days stretching from dawn until dusk. The local golfers, however, only tipped them K2 or K5 after a long day of hauling clubs and fetching balls.

"I wish more golfers would come from overseas," Kaia grumbled as they walked home, the sun dipping low on the horizon. "They always pay better. I'm tired of carrying stuff for these local guys who don't appreciate our hard work."

Manu nodded, feeling the weight of the day in his legs and the disappointment in his heart. It was exhausting walking around the golf course from 7 AM to 6 PM, and he couldn't shake the feeling that their efforts deserved better rewards. The promise of a better life seemed just out of reach, and he was lost in thought as they made their way home.

"I know it's tough, but at least we're making something," Manu said, trying to lift the mood. "Maybe we can find a way to attract more tourists. They'd pay more for good service."

Kaia raised an eyebrow, his brow furrowing. "You really think so? How do we do that? We're just a couple of kids out here."

"Yeah, but we've got the skills! We're friendly and know the course. What if we spread the word? Talk to other caddies, maybe even the golf shop?" Manu suggested, his voice brightening with excitement.

"Hmm, that could work," Kaia replied, considering it. "But we'd need to make sure we stand out. Maybe we could offer a little extra— like cleaning the clubs or giving tips on the best holes."

"Exactly! We can show them we're not just caddies, but part of the experience!" Manu exclaimed, his enthusiasm infectious.

Kaia chuckled, shaking his head. "Look at you, dreaming big! I like it. But we gotta keep it real too. What if they just stick with the usual guys?"

"Then we'll just have to be the best! Show them we're worth it," Manu said with determination.

"Alright, let's give it a shot," Kaia agreed, a grin spreading across his face. "Together, we'll make this happen!"

As they walked on, the fading light painted the sky with hues of orange and purple, and for the first time that day, hope flickered in their hearts.

For a week, Manu and Kaia worked tirelessly as caddies, their days stretching from dawn until dusk. Each morning, they would rise before the sun, the promise of a new day fueling their determination.

They arrived at the Golf Course by 7 AM, ready to haul clubs and fetch balls for the local golfers.

As the sun climbed higher, the heat bore down on them, but they kept their spirits up. They chatted with each other while waiting for golfers to arrive.

"Manu, you ready to show these guys what we've got?" Kaia joked, flexing his muscles playfully.

"Always! Just hope they tip better today," Manu replied, wiping the sweat from his brow.

But as the days passed, the tips remained disappointingly low. After long hours of hard work, local golfers would often hand them K2 or K5, barely enough to cover a meal.

"Ugh, this is getting old," Kaia grumbled one afternoon as they walked home, the sun dipping low on the horizon. "I wish more golfers would come from overseas. They always pay well. I'm tired of carrying stuff for these local guys who don't appreciate our hard work."

Manu nodded, feeling the weight of the day in his legs and the disappointment in his heart. "It's exhausting, man. We're out here from 7 AM to 6 PM, and it feels like we're getting nowhere."

On another day, while taking a break under a palm tree, Kaia sighed dramatically. "Remember last week when that tourist tipped me K20 just for getting him a cold drink? Those are the days I live for!"

"Yeah, I remember! What happened to those tourists? They should come back!" Manu replied, frustration creeping into his voice.

"Exactly! We need to attract more tourists," Kaia suggested, his eyes lighting up with mischief. "But they don't come all the time! You know we live in a rough town, and we're just two hardworking good guys trying to make a living. Sometimes, I even think of organising the caddies to rob that Chinese shop at Kamkumung corner!"

Manu stopped in his tracks, his jaw dropping. "What?! You're joking, right? You can't be serious!"

Kaia doubled over, laughing uncontrollably. "Come on, Manu! Picture it! We'd burst in there, all sneaky-like, and I'd be like, 'Hands up! This is a caddy takeover!'" Kaia blurted, speaking like a Chinese man.

"Yeah, right! And then what? We'd end up with a bag of chips and a couple of soy sauces!" Manu shot back, trying to hold back his laughter.

Kaia rolled on the sidewalk, his laughter echoing. "Exactly! We'd be legendary! 'The Caddy Bandits—robbers of snacks and cold drinks!'"

Manu chuckled, shaking his head. "Only you would think of something like that. But seriously, we'd get caught before we even made it to the door!"

"True," Kaia admitted, wiping tears of laughter from his eyes. "But hey, a guy can dream, right? Besides, it would make one heck of a story!"

That's what Manu loved about Kaia. He took each day as it came, always ready to find humour in the toughest situations, making their struggles feel a little lighter.

By the end of the week, Manu and Kaia found themselves exhausted yet motivated. As they walked home one evening, Kaia turned to Manu and said, "You know, even if the tips aren't great, at least we're learning."

"Yeah, and we've got each other's backs," Manu replied, a frown creeping onto his face.

As they neared the end of the junction, Manu slowed, his steps becoming hesitant. He looked down for a moment, weighing his words, then spoke softly, "I won't be working as a caddie tomorrow."

Kaia's eyes flicked over to him instantly, eyebrows shooting up in surprise. "Why not? Are you getting married?"

They both burst into laughter, their voices echoing so loudly that they startled the girls walking in front of them.

"I need some time to think about what to do next," Manu said, trying to regain his composure.

"Yes, of course! Do you think we'd carry golf clubs forever? Nooo, man! What would our grandkids think of us?" Kaia launched into his usual antics to get a laugh.

"Bubu Manu and Bubu Kaia! Are you off to the golf course to carry golf clubs?" Kaia imitated a child's voice, and they doubled over in laughter, leaning against the coconut tree next to the track.

"Aaah, Manu, my main boy," Kaia said, his voice a mix of affection and playful teasing. "And what about the caddy job?"

Manu chuckled softly, forcing a lightness into his tone. "I'll take some time off and think. Don't fret… you bos tumas ya," he said, laughter bubbling up as he slapped Kaia's shoulder warmly.

Kaia returned the slap, a grin spreading across his face. "Keep me in the loop, my main boy!" he chuckled as they split into smaller paths leading to their homes, the banter still lingering in the air like a sweet aftertaste.

6

Mark My Trees

The next morning, Manu stirred awake at 5:00 AM, and silently opened the door of their hut. He stepped onto the patapata beneath the guava tree, looking out over the Bumbu River. The world around him was wrapped in a gentle hush, while morning birds chirped in a respectful tone, warming up their unorthodox choirs before the first rays of sunlight.

The air was crisp and still, pulling him deeper into thought as he gazed across the glimmering waters of the Bumbu River. It stretched before him, calm and glassy, its surface shimmering subtly in the early light. The water seemed to breathe, inviting him into a world of quiet reflection. He knew that each morning, the river revitalised itself—the banks cleaned and polished, the pebbles in the shallows turned and scrubbed, while the deeper currents roared with a powerful energy.

As golden rays spilled over the landscape, the birds transformed their quiet tunes into lively chatter, filling the air with a joyful cacophony. The sunlight bathed everything in a warm, amber glow, flickering like firelight against the gentle hills.

Amidst the symphony of dawn, a cheerful song drifted through the air—the sweet, lively call of a Willie Wagtail. Its melody danced delicately against the louder chorus of birds chasing after worms. The Wagtail reminded him of the simple, natural beauty that thrived amidst the chaos humans had created.

Manu paused, listening intently, feeling the coolness of the morning seep into his bones. Peacefulness filled his heart, even as thoughts of yesterday's struggles lingered quietly in the back of his mind.

After a while, Manu rose slowly, shaking off the remnants of sleep and jogged over to their hut. He stepped inside and lit a fire, as the crackling flames bring warmth and life to the space. He set the kettle on and the aroma of sweet tea was soon wafting through the air. He reheated some leftover kaukaus from the night before and started eating right away.

As he ate his breakfast, the sound of raspy coughing pulled him from his thoughts. His grandfather, Bubu Pellie, stirred awake, and sat up.

"Morning, Bubu," Manu greeted, a smile breaking across his face.

"Ooooh, good morning, my treasure. You're always up so early," Bubu Pellie replied weakly, his eyes still heavy with sleep.

"Bubu Pellie, I've been thinking," Manu declared, determination shining in his eyes. "I'm going up to the mountains to chop down a strong tree so we can sell better firewood. I'm tired of wandering around the city every day like a loser."

Manu had made up his mind: if he had to endure suffering, struggling with hunger and thirst, he would do it out of sight, alone in nature. He was done with serving people and receiving far less than his efforts deserved. It was time to take control of his destiny and carve out a path that truly reflected his strength and ambition.

"My grandchild, be careful out there," Bubu Pellie cautioned, his voice a croaky whisper filled with concern. "Most of the trees are claimed by woodcutters already."

Manu's heart sank slightly at the reminder of their struggles, but he shook his head, resolute. "I'll find a way, Bubu. I promise. We need to make a change, and I'm ready to work for it."

Bubu Pellie studied his grandson's face. "You have the heart of a warrior, Manu. Just remember to respect the land. It provides for us and we must treat it kindly."

With a nod, Manu finished his breakfast, feeling a mix of excitement and apprehension.

"I will go beyond the Blue Mountains," Manu declared, determination shining in his eyes. "I might be there for a week or two to claim some trees and prove I can be just like all the other hardworking wood cutters. Bubu, I'll ask Maoru to look after you while I'm away."

"But my grandson," Bubu Pellie said, his voice heavy with concern, "the woodlands are dangerous. Bad criminals in Lae hide in the mountains when they run from the police."

"If I see them, I'll hide," Manu assured him, trying to calm his grandfather's worries. "And there aren't any criminals in the Blue Mountains."

"Yes, but the Blue Mountains are full of Masalais. That's why woodcutters, criminals, and hunters avoid them. It's a forbidden place; no one can survive there," Bubu Pellie emphasised, his eyes reflecting a deep-seated fear.

"There are Masalais because no one is brave enough to explore further into the woods and the Blue Mountains," Manu countered, excitement bubbling in his chest. "I want to see what's really up there."

"And Manu, if you claim your trees and cut them down, how will you carry them back?" Bubu Pellie asked softly, concern etched on his face.

"I'll come back and ask Kaia and his brother to help me. I'll figure it out," Manu replied with unwavering determination.

Bubu Pellie sighed, glancing out toward the distant mountains.

"Well, there are stories told of 'beings' that roam those woods, my child."

"Yes, I've heard about the half-people," Manu chimed in, intrigued. "They jump around and can only be seen during the mountain mists."

"Those are the ones, but there are also stories about the 'changing beings,'" Bubu Pellie whispered, his voice trembling slightly.

"Changing beings? What do they do?" Manu asked, curiosity piqued.

"They can change into whoever they want, depending on the human who enters their land," Bubu Pellie explained, his tone serious. "This being might transform into a beautiful young woman if a young man is wandering nearby. They can entice him, muddling his thoughts until he jumps off a cliff to his death."

"Really? That's terrifying!" Manu exclaimed, wide-eyed. "I'll remember that."

Bubu Pellie nodded, a mix of pride and worry in his gaze. "Just be cautious, my boy. The world is full of wonders and dangers. Trust your instincts and keep your heart true."

"I will, Bubu. I promise," Manu said, a smile breaking through his earlier apprehension. The adventure awaited, and he felt ready to face whatever came his way.

Manu set off to find Maoru, eager to share his plans with her. She had a small stall next to the firewood sellers, where she sold kerosene and other essentials. Maoru was known in the community for her warmth and generosity, always ready to lend a helping hand.

As he approached her stall, the familiar scent of kerosene mixed with the earthy aroma of firewood filled the air. Maoru looked up with a bright smile, her weathered face lighting up at the sight of Manu.

"Ah, Manu! Good to see you, my boy!" she greeted him, wiping her hands on her apron. "What brings you here today?"

"Maoru, I need to talk to you about something important," Manu began, his voice steady. "I'm planning to go beyond the Blue

Mountains to claim some trees for firewood. I'll be gone for a week or two, and I wanted to ask if you could help look after Bubu Pellie while I'm away."

"Of course, I'll take care of him!" Maoru replied instantly, her eyes gleaming with kindness. "Your grandfather is like family to me. You don't need to worry about him."

"Thank you, Maoru. That means a lot," Manu said, relief washing over him. "You've always been so good to us."

Maoru chuckled softly. "Well, we all look out for each other, don't we? Remember when I helped you plant kaukaus and tapiocas in your little garden? It was a joy to see those plants grow. You're becoming quite the gardener yourself!" Manu smiled, recalling the afternoons spent with her, digging in the soil and learning the ways of nurturing life. "I've been trying my best. Bubu Pellie loves the fresh vegetables."

"Just keep tending to that garden," she encouraged, her voice warm. "It will provide for you both. And don't forget to bring me some firewood when you return. I could always use a good supply."

"I will try! If I can," Manu replied, his determination rekindled.

"Now, go and be careful out there, okay?" Maoru advised, her tone turning serious. "The mountains can be unpredictable."

"I will, Maoru. Thank you again!" Manu replied, feeling grateful for her support.

As he turned to leave, he felt a sense of purpose swell within him. With Maoru's help and Bubu Pellie's support, he was ready to face the challenges that lay ahead. The adventure beyond the Blue Mountains awaited, and he was determined to prove himself.

While Manu set off to find Maoru, Bubu Pellie settled down on a weathered log outside their hut, lost in thought. His heart swelled with a mix of pride and concern as he reflected on his grandson. How had this boy, only twelve, grown to be so strong, determined, and brave? It was a question that lingered in his mind like the gentle ripples of Bumbu River.

Perhaps it was the harshness of their life, the endless struggle for survival that had forged Manu's resilience. There were days when a mere morsel was hard to come by, and yet Manu faced each challenge head-on. Bubu Pellie marveled at the boy's unique spirit, a flicker of light in a world often shrouded in darkness.

His thoughts drifted to the day Manu had topped his grade 7 class at Omili Primary School. Pride washed over him, but it was quickly overshadowed by bittersweet memories. Tears welled in his eyes as he recalled the laughter of Bubu Naris, who had guided them through many a hardship. Those afternoons spent wandering the banks of Bumbu River, collecting wood to sell, seemed like a lifetime ago. They had done it together, each step bringing them closer to Manu's school fees and brighter futures.

'Maybe the boy is right,' Bubu Pellie mused quietly to himself. *'Maybe he feels a calling he needs to answer. If I try to stop him, it could shatter his dreams of adventure.'*

He thought of the stories they had shared, tales of bravery and exploration, and how they had ignited a fire in Manu's heart. Bubu Pellie knew that every generation must carve its own path, and perhaps this was Manu's moment to step into the world and embrace his destiny.

With a heavy heart and a deep breath, Bubu Pellie resolved to support his grandson's journey, no matter how daunting it seemed.

As the sun rose higher in the sky, casting golden rays over the land, he felt a sense of hope. This was not just a boy's adventure; it was a chance for Manu to discover who he truly was, to become the man he was meant to be. And as much as it pained him to let go, Bubu Pellie understood that sometimes, love meant allowing someone to chase their dreams, even into the unknown.

Bubu Pellie recalled the heart-wrenching day when his daughter, Nasila, transformed from a lively fifteen-year-old girl into a shadow of her former self. She had gone quiet and withdrawn, her vibrant spirit dimmed.

It was around 11 AM when Bubu Pellie and his wife returned from the bustling main market, their arms laden with fresh produce. As they approached their home, he caught sight of Nasila sitting under the house, her eyes were swollen and red, as if she had been crying for hours.

"What happened, lewa?" her mother asked gently, kneeling beside her. "Did someone do something to you at school?"

Pellie had stepped back, allowing Naris to take the lead, trusting her intuition to navigate their daughter's distress. He busied himself plucking the feathers from the chook they had bought, trying to distract himself from the worry gnawing at his heart.

An hour later, Naris stood before him, her eyes shimmering with unshed tears. "Pellie, please brace yourself," her voice quivering with dread.

"Of course, Naris," he replied, looking up and forcing a reassuring smile, though his stomach twisted with concern.

Naris hesitated, her silence heavy with unspoken fears. Finally, she managed to find her voice, though it trembled.

"What happened?" Bubu Pellie asked, his brow furrowing, sensing the gravity of the moment.

"Our daughter has a problem, dear," she quivered, her voice barely above a whisper.

"A problem? Did someone offend her?" he questioned, standing up, the chook forgotten.

"Yes, dear, someone did," Naris replied, tears spilling down her cheeks.

"Stop crying and tell me, please, Naris," he urged, his heart racing as he braced for the worst.

"She… she is with child, dear," Naris whispered softly, her words hanging in the air like a storm cloud.

Bubu Pellie's world shifted beneath him, the weight of her revelation crashing over him like a tidal wave. His heart ached for his daughter, for the innocence that had slipped away too soon. But within that pain, he also felt a surge of protectiveness.

They sat there in silence, their hearts heavy, exchanging sad glances that spoke volumes. The weight of their shared concern hung in the air like a storm cloud, thick and palpable. Finally, after what felt like an eternity, they spoke quietly, their voices barely above a whisper, contemplating the path ahead before moving to see their daughter.

As they approached her, Pellie's heart broke at the sight of Nasila. Her eyes were badly swollen, her face a small, fragile shadow of the vibrant girl she once was. She looked so small and helpless, a stark contrast to the spirited young woman who had filled their home with laughter. In that moment, Pellie's heart melted; he loved his only daughter more than anything in the world, and seeing her in pain felt like a dagger to his soul.

Gently, they sat Nasila between them, the warmth of their presence enveloping her like a protective shield. Pellie reached out, brushing a stray hair from her forehead, while Naris took her hand softly in hers.

"Lewa," Bubu Pellie began, his voice tender and soothing, "we're here for you. No matter what happens, we will always love you just the same."

Naris squeezed Nasila's hand, her eyes filled with empathy. "You are our precious girl, and nothing will change that. We want to help you through this."

Nasila looked up at them, tears glistening in her eyes. The love and support radiating from her parents began to break through the fog of her despair. "But I messed up," she whispered, her voice trembling.

"No lewa," Pellie said firmly, his heart aching for her. "You are not defined by this moment. We all stumble; what matters is how we rise afterward. We will face this together."

Naris nodded, her voice steady. "We will find a way to navigate this, as a family. You're never alone, Nasila."

She was radiant the next day, her spirit lifted, and throughout the nine months that followed, joy enveloped their home until Manu was born. Pellie never regretted how he had treated Nasila on that fateful day, for she had passed not long after, leaving a void that could never be filled. He was grateful, however, that he had showered her with love and care during her final days, cherishing every moment they had together.

Now, with Manu in his life, Pellie felt truly blessed. It was as if Nasila had left him a precious gift, a piece of her spirit living on in their son. Yet, as he reflected on these bittersweet memories, a deep sadness washed over him. Manu's recent announcement about going to the mountains to chop firewood weighed heavily on his heart.

Why would a child of twelve think like a man? Pellie pondered, his brow furrowing with concern. What had happened to the little boy he once knew, the one who scavenged for scraps around Lae city to feed them both? Now, this same child was ready to take on the world, believing he could shoulder responsibilities meant for grown men.

The thought of Manu marking trees and wielding an axe filled him with dread. How could he allow his grandson to venture into the mountains, a place fraught with danger and uncertainty? Pellie's heart ached at the thought of his boy facing such risks, yet he couldn't shake the feeling that Manu was driven by a deep desire to provide and protect.

Is this what it means to grow up? he wondered, feeling a mix of pride and fear. The boy had transformed into a young man before his eyes, eager to carve his own path, but at what cost?

Bubu Pellie sighed, torn between wanting to shield Manu from harm and recognising the fierce spirit within him. Perhaps this was a crucial step in his grandson's journey, a chance for him to discover his own strength and resilience. But the thought of sending him off into the unknown filled him with apprehension. He knew he had to find a way to support Manu's ambitions while ensuring his safety—a delicate balance that weighed heavily on his heart.

Finally, Bubu Pellie made up his mind: he would go with Manu. Together, they would mark the trees and chop them down. The thought of his grandson venturing into the unknown alone filled him with unease. *What lies beyond the mountains?* he pondered, determined that Manu should not face it alone.

"Hey Bubu, don't worry! Maoru will take care of you. She'll come to live here while I'm gone for a few days," Manu said cheerfully, a bright smile lighting up his face as he approached.

"That's not necessary, dear. I'm coming with you," Bubu Pellie replied, his voice firm.

"Bubu, you're unwell! You can't come with me," Manu asserted, his tone suddenly strong, a hint of defiance in his youthful eyes.

"But how will you cut the trees? Yes, you can mark them, but cutting is difficult, dear," Bubu Pellie exclaimed, his worry deepening. He imagined the dangers lurking in the shadows of the Blue Mountains, the very place that had haunted his thoughts since Manu had shared his plan.

"Okay, Bubu, during this first trip, I won't cut any trees. I'll just mark them all and come back straight away," Manu declared, a mix of determination and youthful enthusiasm in his voice.

"I cannot let you go on your own," Bubu Pellie emphasised sternly, his heart racing as he thought of his beloved daughter and the fear of losing Manu too. The Blue Mountains were no place for a twelve-year-old boy; they were steeped in legends and dangers that he could hardly comprehend.

"Bubu, I need to prove myself," Manu said, his eyes shining with a mixture of hope and resolve. "I want to show you I can be strong, just like you taught me."

Bubu Pellie's heart ached at his grandson's words. He admired Manu's spirit, but the thought of his safety consumed him. "Strength is not just about bravery, my boy. It's also about knowing when to seek help and who to trust."

"Please, Bubu Pellie, I need to do this on my own. I need to prove my worth. I want to do this on my own. I feel that I must do this on my own," Manu implored, desperation lacing his voice as he tried every possible way to express the longing he felt to take this trip.

For the umpteenth time, Bubu Pellie realised that the boy had grown overnight. This child had fed him, taken care of him, and now there was a calling he felt deep within. He must not hold him back.

"Okay, my grandson. I trust you and know that you will take care of yourself, as that is the only thing I am worried about," Bubu Pellie told Manu in a strong voice, a mixture of pride and concern settling in his chest.

Manu packed the axe and knife, gathered four big kaukaus, filled a one-liter container with water, and grabbed a box of matches, placing them on the little bench in their hut.

"I am going tomorrow morning, Bubu Pellie. Today, I will clean the hut and the yard outside. I will also build a better patapata for you to sit on when the hut gets too hot."

"Thank you, my grandchild," Bubu Pellie choked back tears, overwhelmed by emotion and unsure of what else to say.

After their evening meal, Bubu Pellie and Manu sat together for a long time, engaged in heartfelt conversation. Bubu Pellie shared many things about the forest, each word steeped in wisdom.

"The forest is a home to many creatures, both seen and unseen. The trees provide shelter for animals, birds, and reptiles alike. When one cuts down a tree, one may displace a family, and worse still, that family may be killed when the tree falls with force on the ground. Trees are living beings that give us life, one hundred percent."

"Trees are our life, Manu, and we must protect them. A dead tree may lack leaves, yet it can still stand tall because of its roots. Try to mark the trees that are dead but still standing," Bubu Pellie advised him, his voice steady, imparting the wisdom of generations.

Manu knew that birds-built nests in the trees and possums live in the hollow trunks of trees. Bubu Pellie was right, when a tree is cut down, a family is displaced, because a tree is a house for many kinds of living things.

Human beings are very selfish, always thinking of themselves first and do not consider that there are other species of living things, whether it be trees, animals or birds, that we share this earth with.

"Though they do not converse in our languages, all species of living things, have a way of understanding each other," Bubu Pellie told Manu.

"They have their own kind of intelligence, deeply rooted in secrecy which didn't change for thousands of years; while Human Beings keep on changing their knowledge and technologies throughout the years. Trees are the victims of humans. We chop them down and use them in our technologies, without really caring that they are a species that take in water and food through their roots and breathe air out through their leaves that we breathe in," Bubu continued.

"Yes Bubu Pellie, you are correct. We must take care of our trees and other plants," Manu agreed as always.

Manu knew that both his grandparents possessed a wealth of knowledge about forestlands and trees. Growing up, he would sit at their feet, listening intently as they shared stories of their origins in the mountain forests, vibrant with life and rich in tradition. Though they came from islands apart, he believed that the indigenous knowledge of the land was a common thread woven through cultures worldwide.

Bubu Naris would often say, "The trees speak if you listen closely," imparting wisdom about the medicinal properties of plants and the delicate balance of ecosystems."

Bubu Pellie, with a twinkle in his eye, would recount tales of ancient paths through the forestlands, teaching Manu to respect nature's rhythms and cycles. These lessons instilled in him a profound appreciation for the environment and a continuous desire to learn more about the natural world around him.

Manu had always felt a deep connection to the land, realising that the wisdom of his ancestors was not just relevant to their home but resonated universally. He cherished the belief that, regardless of where one stood on the globe, the bond with the earth and its resources was a shared heritage, waiting to be honoured and preserved.

"Manu, foreign loggers are coming into our Country and are cutting down trees, because they want money. But they do not care about the imbalance they are causing in the environment. They are ignorant to the fact, that when they cut down trees, they destroy homes for forest dwellers," Bubu Pellie's voice had an edge to it and Manu knew, he was always vocal about the logging companies that cut trees from Papua New Guinea and ship them all to their Countries.

"I remembered a story your Bubu Naris told me," Bubu Pellie began, his voice low and serious.

"In her homeland, loggers were cutting down trees from forests that were sacred to the villagers. The villagers warned them, sharing stories about how these trees were forbidden, but the foreigners just laughed and kept on chopping."

"What happened next, Bubu Pellie?" Manu asked, leaning in, curiosity lighting up his eyes.

"Well, strange things started happening," Bubu Pellie continued, his tone becoming more mysterious. "Every night, the villagers heard sounds coming from the forest—children crying, men yelling, and women singing lamenting songs that echoed through the darkness."

"Did they ever find out who was crying?" Manu whispered, his voice barely audible.

Bubu Pellie shook his head slowly. "They didn't dare venture into the woods. They knew those were the bush people, displaced from their tree homes, mourning their loss."

Manu's brow furrowed. "And what about the loggers?"

"At their campsite, a few men kept having terrible accidents— three of them died in horrific ways. The villagers said they'd seen these men speaking to mysterious women who lingered around the site," Bubu Pellie explained, his eyes narrowing with intensity.

"Who were the women?" Manu pressed, his heart racing.

"Bush people, my boy. The ones who had lost their homes, roaming the night, filled with anger and seeking revenge for their fallen kin," Bubu Pellie revealed, his voice heavy with gravity.

"Are these just legends, Bubu?" Manu asked, a hint of skepticism creeping in.

"Definitely not, my grandson. These are real stories, passed down by your Bubu Naris," Bubu Pellie stated, his seriousness unmistakable.

"Well, what's the moral of all these stories?" Manu asked, eager for the lesson.

Bubu Pellie leaned closer, his voice softening.

"When we respect the forest and all that lives within it, no harm will come to us. Always remember that, Manu. All living things are connected, and mutual respect must be practiced at all times. Even when we need to chop down a tree, we must ask it out loud, express our need, and thank it for its sacrifice."

"Do woodcutters really talk to trees before chopping them down?" Manu asked, his eyes wide with wonder.

"Some do, and some don't," Bubu Pellie replied, rising to his feet. Manu followed him into their hut, the weight of the stories hanging in the air, a reminder of the deep bond between humanity and nature.

7

Up, Up, Up

efore daybreak, Bubu Pellie walked slowly with Manu to the edge of the cliff overlooking the Bumbu River. Manu's heart was heavy with sadness, at leaving his grandfather behind without much food in their kitchen. But he trusted that Maoru would never let them down.

"When you walk, do not look back and blink," he advised, his voice steady despite his worry.

"I will not look back. And even if I do, I won't blink," Manu assured his grandfather, respect and love shining across his face.

"Always find a fallen tree to sleep under at night. Do not sleep between tree trunks," Bubu Pellie cautioned, the wisdom of indigenous knowledge and experience woven into his words.

"I will not sleep between tree trunks. I'll find a fallen tree and rest beneath it," Manu repeated, ensuring his grandfather knew he understood.

As the first light of dawn broke over the horizon, Manu bid farewell to his grandfather at the top of the cliff, the weight of their parting lingering in the air.

He descended the narrow cliff with cautious steps, the rocky path beneath him crumbling slightly with each movement. He crossed the Bumbu River, the cool water swirling around his ankles like a gentle embrace, invigorating him for the journey ahead. Then he started climbing up the winding cliff, feeling the thrill of adventure suddenly rising, making him smile.

Suddenly, he encountered a man struggling under the weight of a humongous load of firewood, the burden making the man's muscles ripple beneath his skin. Sweat dripped down his brow as he took short, laboured breaths, pausing for a moment to regain his composure. Manu quickly stepped aside, instinctively understanding the need to give way.

The man looked up, his expression a mix of exhaustion and gratitude. "O o o," he greeted, a breathy sound that echoed through the trees.

Manu responded with an equally earnest, "O, o, o," their voices merging into the stillness of the forest.

He walked on, climbing through the thick forest, the air rich with the scent of damp earth and fresh foliage. As he navigated the tangled undergrowth, memories of a story he had read titled *Jungle Boy* surfaced. In this tale, the boy was raised by animals in the wild. Is that truly possible? He found it hard to believe and decided to ask a classmate named Leo whether a human could be raised by animals.

"No, that is not possible. A human baby feeding from a wolf or dog's breast milk will die," Leo replied matter-of-factly. Yet Manu remained unsatisfied; the question gnawed at him, stirring a curiosity that wouldn't fade.

Later, he went home and shared the story with Bubu Naris.

"This world is mysterious," she told him thoughtfully. "In my culture, it is believed that there was a time when humans and animals lived side by side as brothers and sisters."

"Really, Bubu Naris?" he exclaimed, stunned and astounded. Her words opened a door to a realm of mystery, filled with contrasting theories: the learned perspective from western education and the wisdom of the indigenous, who lived in harmony with nature.

"Yes, even if you need help, animals will assist you. Your aura must be kind and connected. Animals are more intertwined with the Earth than we are. What we are doing to Mother Earth is destroying her. Animals simply exist upon her and survive," Bubu Naris replied, her voice resonating with the weight of ancient knowledge.

As Manu trudged on, he noticed that the trees around him were marked with two short strokes and the white initials WP. *They must belong to someone whose initials start with WP,* he thought, curiosity piqued. Just then, he heard the rhythmic chopping sounds ahead, each strike echoing through the trees like a call to adventure.

As he rounded the bend, he spotted a muscular man swinging an axe with practiced ease. He looked closely and realised that he was the same man who sold firewood at the corner of Kamkumung Road.

"Hey, morning!" the man shouted, dropping his axe and striding over to Manu, with a friendly smile.

"Good morning!" Manu called back, a sense of familiarity washing over him.

"You see all my marked trees? All WP, short for Willie Petrus," he explained, a broad grin spreading across his face, revealing two missing upper teeth.

"I replant as soon as I cut down one," he continued, gesturing at the nursery on the left side of the road.

"Yes, you have a lot of trees here," Manu replied, admiration lacing his words as he looked over at the smaller trees ready for planting.

"Yes, pine trees from Bulolo Forestry," Willie announced, as he continued to smile.

"The front side of this mountain is marked with WP," Willie beamed, pride shining in his eyes.

"Yes, you are very lucky. Your trees are closer to town, Willie," Manu smiled back.

It suddenly clicked in Manu's mind that this man's firewood was in big demand. Manu had seen a lot of people buying firewood from him.

"Yes, I have been doing this for over 15 years. So, you want to mark some trees?" Willie asked, his tone shifting to one of curiosity.

"Yes, I'm trying to find some trees," Manu replied softly, a hint of uncertainty creeping in.

"Yeah, there might be some trees up the second mountain. Do you have paint to mark your trees?" Willie inquired, his brow furrowing slightly.

"Aaagh, no Willie, I forgot to find some before I started walking this morning," Manu realised, shock coursing through him. He felt unprepared, as if he had set out on a journey without the right tools.

"No worries, boy! Come over here, and I'll give you some powdered paint. You can mix it with water to make any colour you want when you find your trees," Willie explained, his voice warm and reassuring as he rummaged through the boxes and tins in his little hut.

Willie returned with a small plastic bag of powdered paint, an empty paint tin, and a paintbrush, handing them to Manu.

"Thank you so much, Willie. I really appreciate it," Manu said genuinely, feeling a wave of gratitude washed over him. This unexpected kindness ignited a spark of determination within him, fuelling his resolve to honour the forest and the friendships he was forging along the way.

"Come and eat rice with me first before you start walking," Willie invited, moving ahead with a friendly smile.

Manu felt a thrill at the offer, eager to share in Willie's lunch. He knew he would learn valuable insights from someone with over 15 years of experience as a woodcutter.

As they settled on a log, Willie served rice alongside some Ox & Palm and brewed a pot of coffee. The rich aroma filled the air as they began to eat.

"Willie, what's the most important thing to remember when working in the forest?" Manu asked, his curiosity evident.

Willie paused, considering the question. "Respect the trees, Manu. They are alive, just like us. Always take only what you need and make sure to plant new ones in their place."

Manu nodded, absorbing every word. "What about the animals? How do I keep them safe?"

"Ah, that's a good question. Be aware of your surroundings. If you see a nest or a den, avoid it. The forest is their home too," Willie explained, his eyes thoughtful. "If you're kind to the forest, it will be kind to you."

"Thank you, Willie. I'll remember that," Manu replied, feeling a deeper connection to the land.

The trees along the banks of the Bumbu River and up the cliffs were marked with WP, a clear sign that Willie had claimed nearly every tree near Lae town. Manu couldn't help but wonder if there were any trees left on the mountain to stake his own claim. His curiosity urged him to venture forward; after all, he yearned to explore the Blue Mountains.

He pondered whether Willie Petrus was making a fortune selling hardwood firewood from these slopes. Yet, the sheer labour involved struck him. Claiming trees, painting initials, felling them, chopping the wood, drying it under the sun, and tying it into bundles—each step was a gruelling task.

Then carrying those heavy loads on his shoulders, navigating the steep descents with his knees knobbly and legs shaky, he imagined crossing the Bumbu River and then climbing up the narrow, rocky cliff road to stack the firewood behind his hut. The thought of hauling it all to the roadside markets for a mere K2 per bundle felt overwhelming.

Manu couldn't help but admire the resilience required for such work. Each bundle represented not just wood, but the sweat and determination of a man who laboured tirelessly, transforming nature's gifts into a means of survival.

It was clear: this was real hard work, and his grandfather understood the toll it took on a person. Manu felt a wave of respect wash over him for those who toiled in the forest, their sweat and effort, all to feed their families.

As he climbed the first mountain, Manu noticed several woodcutters labouring tirelessly, their axes striking rhythmically against the marked trees. Among them, he recognised old man Moiku, a figure of strength and resilience, known for being as strong as a bull. He was renowned for selling the most sought-after firewood at the markets.

So, this is where he gets his wood from, Manu thought, watching Moiku skilfully chop into a sturdy, large tree.

Manu recalled a time when Moiku had generously gifted them a bundle of firewood. He and Bubu Pellie had burned that wood, and to their delight, it produced a smokeless fire that not only cooked their meals to perfection but also enveloped their home in a warm, comforting glow. The memory lingered vividly in his mind, evoking Moiku's exceptional skill and the remarkable quality of his wood. Even now, a profound sense of gratitude washed over Manu for the old man, whose kindness he still remembered. It became clear to him that being a good woodcutter was not just a trade but a true art form, one that Moiku embodied with time and dedication.

Manu kept climbing until he reached the top of the first mountain, and then paused to drink from his water container. The water didn't taste good, perhaps overwhelmed by the fresh air and the beauty of his surroundings.

Suddenly, he realised it was already dusk. He had been climbing this mountain all day, navigating through the thick forest, completely unaware that the sun had slipped away.

His legs ached from the continuous trudge up the steep incline. All the trees on this mountain were marked; there were no unmarked trees in sight, a clear proof of how heavily claimed the trees had become.

He sat down beneath a stunning tree, its oval leaves shimmering in the fading light and its slender white trunk standing tall. The branches were clustered closely together, resembling a mushroom with a vibrant green canopy. As he rested, he was struck again by the realisation that dusk had fallen; he had been walking for hours, lost in the beauty of the landscape. The world around him transformed as shadows lengthened, wrapping him in a serene twilight.

Suddenly, he heard the rhythmic sound of someone chopping wood and decided to follow the sound to his left. The trees on this side of the forest were all marked with an X and adorned with three bold red strokes. As he walked past the trees, he entered a clearing that revealed a vibrant garden filled with corn and bananas swaying gently in the breeze.

Curious, he made his way through the garden and approached a small hut with wisps of smoke curling from above it. As he drew closer, he saw a man and a woman working diligently, chopping firewood and stacking it neatly into orderly piles. The warmth of their labour contrasted with the coolness of the evening air, creating a sense of home amidst the wild surroundings.

"Hey, young man! Good afternoon, please come," the tall, slender woman greeted him warmly, her smile inviting.

"Good afternoon, ma'am. Thank you," replied Manu, approaching them with a friendly grin.

They shook his hand and gestured for him to sit on a log outside the hut. The stout man introduced himself as Zinix, while his wife was Noia.

"Our trees are marked with an X, but we don't have many, as this forest is heavily claimed by woodcutters," Zinix explained, a hint of concern in his voice.

"The trees here are excellent for fires. They burn longer, and you only need two sticks to cook your food. It's truly the best firewood you can find," he continued, pride shining in his eyes.

"And where do you sell your firewood?" Manu asked, intrigued by their operation.

"We sell our firewood at various roadside markets all around Lae town," Zinix replied, gesturing expansively to emphasise their reach.

After Noia cooked the rice, she served three generous plates topped with tinned fish, and they all gathered to eat together, chatting about their day. Manu, close to starving, gratefully devoured every grain, savoring the simple yet hearty meal.

"So, are you going to mark some trees?" Zinix inquired, his curiosity piqued.

"Yes, I will go up to the last mountain and see if there are any unmarked trees," Manu answered softly, determination in his tone.

"I heard there will be a bigger firewood market soon. New houses are being designed with chimneys to keep warm in the colder weather," Zinix said, stretching out comfortably on his mat.

"As woodcutters, we always make it a point to replant the trees we cut down," Zinix continued, his passion for sustainability evident.

"Yes, I've heard that woodcutters only take down trees that are dead but still standing," Manu replied, nodding in agreement.

"That's correct. However, we still mark new trees. You know how it is; woodcutters are hesitant to cut down healthy trees unless they are already dead," Zinix explained.

"That's why we sometimes skin the trunk of certain trees to make them dead before cutting them down. Other ancient trees, as you've seen in the forest, are left untouched. We target specific trees only," he elaborated, his voice steady with conviction.

As night fell, Manu was given a cosy spot in the corner to sleep. He thought of his grandfather and offered a silent prayer for him, feeling grateful for this unexpected companionship. He chatted with Noia and Zinix for a while, enjoying their warm conversation, before they all settled in for the night.

Manu woke to the crackling sound of fire dancing on hard, dried wood outside, the warmth beckoning him from his dreams. With a stretch and a yawn, he stepped outside into the refreshing morning air and was greeted by the sight of Zinix and Noia already gathered around the fire. They were sipping steaming cups of tea and savouring bananas roasted over the open flames, their laughter mingling with the sounds of the forest.

Manu felt the fatigue from the previous day's climbing and trudging settle into his bones. He was immensely grateful for having met Zinix and Noia, who had offered him shelter and companionship for the night.

"Come and have a cup of tea!" Zinix called out, his voice warm and inviting.

Noia handed Manu a mug that had clearly seen its fair share of bush adventures, but he didn't mind. The tea was hot and comforting, a perfect companion to the sweet, smoky bananas he devoured, their soft flesh melting in his mouth.

"We're expecting our three sons and their cousins to come today. They'll help us carry the firewood down to Lae," Noia explained, a bright smile lighting up her face.

"That's wonderful! You have excellent helpers," Manu replied, genuinely impressed.

Noia beamed and handed him a bundle of roasted bananas wrapped in leaves. "You'll need this for your trek. You'll be hungry walking around again today."

"Thank you, Noia," Manu said, looking at her with deep gratitude. The warmth of her kindness filled him with a sense of belonging.

"Oh, and Manu, if you happen to come by and we're already gone, feel free to sleep in our hut and eat from our garden," Zinix offered, his tone sincere. Noia nodded in agreement, her eyes twinkling.

"That is incredibly kind of you. Thank you so much," Manu replied, touched by their generosity. "I truly appreciate everything you've done for me."

"Take care, and we hope to see you again," Zinix farewelled as they all shook hands, the bond between them grew stronger in that simple gesture.

As Manu prepared for the day ahead, he felt a renewed sense of purpose. The forest awaited, and with the warmth of their kindness still in his heart, he stepped into the woods, ready to explore through the trees that stood before him.

8

It's Dangerous Out There

Manu walked cautiously through the towering trees, their trunks reaching high above like ancient sentinels. The air was thick with the earthy scent of moss and damp soil, blending with the soft rustle of leaves whispering secrets.

As he ventured deeper, the X markings began to change—first to TP, then RR—marking the names of woodcutters. He kept on walking as sunlight filtered through the canopy, casting dappled patterns on the ground, where ferns and a variety of shrubs thrived in the quiet embrace of nature.

The atmosphere was serene, untouched by the madness of the outside world. Birds sang sweetly above, and a gentle breeze carried the distant sound of a bubbling brook. Manu felt a connection to the land, as if the forest itself was alive, watching and guiding him along a path woven with stories long forgotten.

Suddenly, as he rounded a gnarled black trunk, he spotted a wild pig with her piglets rooting through the earth, grunting merrily as they dug for roots. Manu was totally intrigued, and began to creep silently around the trunk, hoping to observe them without disturbance. But the mother pig, with her beady, watchful eyes, was already aware of his presence.

With a sharp grunt, she stomped her right hind foot, a clear warning, and charged straight for him. Manu's heart raced as he realised he had encroached upon her territory. He quickly weighed his options: to retreat or confront this unexpected encounter. The forest, once a tranquil haven, now pulsed with the thrill of impending danger as the wild pig charged toward him, fierce and determined.

Manu sprinted through the trees, his heart pounding wildly as he stumbled, barely aware of where he was heading. The empty tin rattled and swayed against his knapsack, a frantic soundtrack to his escape. He ran and ran, driven by instinct, not daring to stop until he was certain he had put as much distance as possible between himself and the wild pig and her piglets.

Finally, breathless and trembling, he collapsed onto a flat rock with cool surface which was a welcome relief. As he panted heavily, he recalled the chilling stories he had heard of wild boars attacking people, leaving them severely injured or worse. The pig that had chased him had been impressively large, its powerful frame moving with surprising speed. Even with its size and weight, it had charged at him like a bolt of lightning, a fierce reminder of the untamed nature surrounding him.

As he sat there, catching his breath, he realised just how close he had come to danger. The forest, once a place of beauty and serenity, now felt like a wild labyrinth, filled with both wonder and peril.

He recalled a man he had seen at the hospital when Bubu Naris was admitted. This man was a mechanic at a Lutheran High School, located just outside of town. One morning, around 9 AM, as he was walking to the workshop, he encountered a wild pig that had wandered onto the school grounds, uprooting flowering plants in a reckless manner.

The mechanic, standing a few metres away, attempted to shoo the creature away, but the wild pig had other intentions. With a sudden charge, the wild pig barreled straight toward him as he turned to run, but the pig was relentless. It leapt up, tusks glinting menacingly, and viciously ripped into his buttocks.

The man barely escaped with his life, nearly bleeding to death from the attack. Fortunately, he was rushed to the hospital just in time to receive emergency treatment. The memory of that incident told to him by the man's wife sent a shiver down Manu's spine, a stark reminder of the raw power and unpredictability of wild animals.

Manu looked around, taking in the overpowering calmness of the forest. The sun hung high in the sky, its golden beams filtering through the leaves, creating a dappled pattern on the ground that danced with life. He took a long drink from his water container, feeling the cool liquid revitalise him, and then he began to climb again, a renewed sense of caution guiding his steps.

As he ascended, his mind raced with thoughts of what lurked in the shadows. He recalled a chilling story from a boy who lived on the next road at Bumbu Settlement. The boy had claimed that wild dogs were far more dangerous than any other creature in the forest. Unlike wild pigs, which charged and then retreated, wild dogs roamed in packs, and when they attacked, they tore their prey to shreds, leaving nothing but mayhem in their wake.

A shiver ran down Manu's spine at the thought, and he scanned the forest floor silently, acutely aware of every rustle and whisper around him. The tranquility of the forest now felt layered with a tense undercurrent, as if the very trees were holding their breath. Each step became a careful negotiation between his curiosity and the primal instinct to stay alert, reminding him that he was not alone in this wild expanse.

Manu hiked on, moving with deliberate silence, aware that wild animals roamed these woods, fiercely guarding their territory against any intruders. Unlike human beings, who could greet each other with a simple "hello," or domesticated animals accustomed to human presence, the wild creatures remained alert and wary, their instincts finely tuned to the slightest disturbance.

As he trekked higher and into deeper forestlands, a thought crept into his mind: perhaps there was a real monster lurking in these mountains. He recalled a terrifying movie he had glimpsed through a neighbour's window, the haunting screams of the audience echoing in his ears. In that film, a monstrous creature resided in a cave, and a group of village boys, foolishly curious, ventured inside to provoke it. When the monster emerged, the children screamed, and even the adults watching were gripped by terror.

Manu shook his head, trying to dispel the chilling images, reminding himself that such things were just fiction. He paused for a moment, allowing the breathtaking scenery to wash over him. Each new climb revealed stunning lush greenery, towering peaks, and the gentle rustle of leaves in the breeze. He took a deep breath, grounding himself in the beauty around him, letting the worry of monsters fade as he embraced the majesty of the forest.

The sun blazed directly overhead as Manu began his ascent up the second mountain. He spotted a few woodcutters scattered about, axes striking rhythmically against the trees, but he chose to steer clear of their path, valuing his solitude. Carefully, he climbed down a rocky drop, and there, nestled within the mountain's embrace, he discovered a cold spring bubbling merrily from the rocks.

He knelt, drinking deeply until his thirst was completely quenched, then filled his water container with the crisp, refreshing liquid. Satisfied, he sought refuge beneath the gentle shade of bush palms, grateful for their shelter, covering him with cool mountain air.

He took out his roasted banana and peeled it slowly, savouring the anticipation. The bittersweet taste of the charred bits melded perfectly with the soft fruit, and he found comfort in the simple pleasure of eating. Just as he settled into the moment, relishing each bite, a new sound pricked at his ears.

Instinctively, he slipped into the dense shrubs, hidden from view, banana still in hand. His heart raced as he sat quietly, every sense heightened as he waited, straining to discern the source of the noise that had disrupted his restful moment. The forest was alive, and he was keenly aware that he was not alone.

Suddenly, Manu's eyes caught movement. Two men were creeping through the underbrush, more like wounded animals than anything else. They glanced nervously over their shoulders, their movements calculated and silent. The plain blue shirts adorned with a red stripe across their chests betrayed their identity: escapees from Buimo prison. Yes, those were unmistakably prison clothes.

Manu's heart pounded as he crouched low, holding his breath to avoid detection. The men slinked past him, their furtive glances revealing the fear coursing through them, as if the entire police force were hot on their heels. They approached the spring and drank from its clear waters, exchanging hushed words that Manu couldn't quite make out as their voices were low and tense.

The men exchanged a silent glance, then turned and disappeared into the dense rainforest, their figures swallowed by the shadowy underbrush, leaving Manu alone with the heavy burden of what he had just witnessed. The air thickened around him, infused with the earthy scent of damp soil and the distant calls of unseen creatures. The forest felt transformed, charged with a palpable tension; every rustle of leaves seemed to whisper secrets, and the sunlight filtering through the canopy cast eerie dancing patterns on the ground. He couldn't shake the unsettling sense that danger lurked just beyond the shadows, watching and waiting, ready to pounce at the slightest chance or disturbance.

Manu recalled the news that had been broadcasted last week on FM 97.4. The radio announcer reported that three notorious escapees from Buimo Prison were on the run. These prisoners were serving time for serious crimes, and the entire community of Lae was urged to remain vigilant. The three men were described as dangerous, and authorities warned that anyone who encountered them should exercise extreme caution.

He particularly remembered a harrowing story from the settlement area about one of the prisoners named Kaias. He had brutally murdered a woman who was fishing along the Bumbu River. Approaching her under the guise of asking for a lighter to light his cigarette, he caught her off guard as she rummaged through her bilum for the item. In a sudden and violent act, he attacked her, beating her with a piece of driftwood.

Others fishing on the opposite bank heard her screams and rushed to help. However, by the time they reached her, Kaias had already fled into the dense bushes. The kind-hearted fishermen hurried the woman to the hospital, but tragically, she succumbed to her injuries just a day later.

The police launched a manhunt for Kaias and eventually captured him just three houses down from where Manu lived with his grandparents. He was incarcerated in Buimo Prison, but now he was on the run again. The community was once more on high alert, with warnings to be cautious in their movements and to remain vigilant for any unfamiliar faces.

It was also warned that anyone harbouring escapees would face imprisonment unless a hefty K5000 fine was paid.

Bubu Pellie often lamented that the settlement areas were notorious for sheltering prison escapees and criminals.

"One day, the Police Task Force will come and burn every house down in this settlement," he would tell Manu repeatedly, his voice heavy with concern. "Unless we change our ignorant attitudes and begin to abide by the laws of this country. We must start doing the right thing," he urged.

"The change begins with individuals, and only then can communities be positively influenced," Bubu Pellie emphasised to Manu as they peeled the kaukaus together, his words resonating deeply in the quiet moments they shared.

In that moment, Manu resolved to always report any crimes he witnessed. If he ever learned of anyone harbouring prisoners, he would call the police immediately. He couldn't comprehend why some men would murder women. After all, women are the ones who bring us into the world. Perhaps some men are so twisted in their minds that they forget to respect others, losing sight of the sanctity of life and the nurturing role women play in society. His determination to stand against such violence only deepened in his heart.

Suddenly, a chill ran down Manu's spine, causing him to shiver as he glanced around nervously. He took a bite of his banana, trying to steady himself.

Then he cautiously stood up from his hiding place and peeked out from the shrubs. There was no one in sight. Relieved, he crept out and began to navigate around the mountain. Once he felt assured of his safety, far from the criminals, he resumed his climb.

He reached the summit, breathless and exhilarated, only to find the area eerily deserted—no woodcutters, no signs of human life, though the flora and fauna was alive and vibrant. A quick glance revealed the trees standing untouched, their bark unmarred by initials. As he looked toward the distant Blue Mountains, curiosity sparked within him, stirring thoughts he had tried to set aside. He was there to mark trees, yet the mountains beckoned, presenting him with a choice: stay and fulfill his task or venture into the unknown.

Without a second thought, he chose the latter, leaving the unsettling encounter behind. The allure of the Blue Mountains called to him, pulling him forward with an irresistible pull. In that moment, his worries about claiming the trees faded, replaced by a sense of adventure and possibility.

9

The Blue Mountains

*H*e climbed for a while, only to realise that the sun had dipped below the horizon, and a light drizzle began to fall. The forest was now shrouded in a misty chill as he trudged through the trees, searching for a fallen tree, just as his grandfather had instructed. Worry gnawed at him as darkness was closing in fast, and the rain was picking up.

With each step, the urgency to find shelter for the night grew stronger. The cold moisture seeped into his clothes, making him shiver as the shadows deepened around him. He quickened his pace, every rustle in the underbrush heightening his sense of unease. The forest, once a place of adventure, now felt daunting and unfamiliar as he pressed on, determined to find a safe haven before night fully enveloped him.

He felt a shiver of fear as eerie sounds echoed through the forest, especially the crickets' strange song that rose from a low note to a medium monotone, then culminated in high-pitched shrieks. He had never encountered such noises back in Bumbu settlement; perhaps the crickets there had forgotten their traditional night chants, their little voices silenced by the encroachment of civilisation. In contrast, the crickets of the forest seemed untouched by time, still chanting their lullabies before surrendering to sleep for the night.

He couldn't help but wonder if it was truly crickets, he heard, or if other wild and dangerous creatures were lurking nearby, mimicking their calls in the darkness. The thought sent another wave of unease through him as he pressed on, the forest alive with sounds both beautiful and haunting.

He shivered from a combination of cold and fear, his teeth chattering as aches coursed through his body. His feet felt heavy and weary. Just as he was about to settle between the trunks of closely growing trees, he spotted a fallen tree to his right. Half of it rested against a massive boulder, while the other half was embedded in the ground.

Relief flooded over him as he dashed to take cover from the relentless forest rains. He removed his backpack, along with the tins and paintbrush, and set them aside. Although it was wet and cold, the shelter under the tree trunk kept him dry. He quickly scuttled around, using his hands to flatten the soil and rearrange a few stones into a makeshift bed.

Trembling uncontrollably, he dared not look into the gloomy darkness around him, filled with unfamiliar forest sounds that sent shivers down his spine. The massive uprooted tree provided him refuge for the night. Before drifting off to sleep, he ate a roasted banana and sipped from his water container, grateful for the small comforts.

His legs felt dead and numbed from the day's climb. He laid a piece of cloth on the ground, bowed his head in prayer, and then curled up, folding himself into a tight ball as he succumbed to exhaustion, the forest's eerie symphony lulling him into a restless sleep.

Suddenly, at around 2am, he woke up to the sound of hooting right above him. He sat upright in fear, scanning the forest floor, realising the rain had long stopped.

He was terrified as he watched the fireflies twinkling like tiny stars scattered through the darkness, their flickering light casting eerie shadows across the trees. His imagination raced, conjuring images of half-people lurking just beyond the trunks, leaping silently through the dense underbrush. Were they up and about, moving in the dark forest, watching him?

'No, they move and float with the mist,' he thought to himself, trying to calm his racing heart. *'They are not of darkness.'* He recalled the stories he had heard as a child—tales of spirits carried by the mist, beings that danced in the twilight, not to harm but to guide lost souls.

He soothingly reminded himself that these ethereal creatures were part of the forest, and he was just passing through, not causing any harm or being a menace, destroying their tree homes.

Suddenly a thunderous hoot went off. The hooting seemed to rip his ears apart, as it came from the inside of the uprooted tree, he was sleeping under.

An owl, he realised had its home, right above where he was sleeping for the night. He felt like an intruder taking solace at the entrance of a home that belonged to a forest dweller.

The owl felt his presence moving below and flew off into the night.

Manu felt cold, so he pushed his hand into his backpack and got a shirt and covered himself. There were all sorts of weird, creepy jungle noises, but he closed his ears, covered his face and went to sleep.

Manu awoke to a symphony of new sounds, each more beautiful than the last. The birds filled the air with their cheerful chirping and lively chatter, but it was the haunting whistle of a particular bird that truly captivated him. Its song floated through the morning like a gentle breeze, wrapping around him in a warm embrace.

As he sat there, listening to the melody unfold, it was a smooth high note that lingered with delicate vibrations, returning again like a whisper in the wind. The soothing, wolf-like whistle rose and fell, each note resonating deep within his soul, the vibrations echoing like wind chimes dancing in the air.

This was an experience he knew would stay with him forever, as he had never heard anything like it in his life. It dawned on him that if he tried to explain it to Bubu Pellie, or perhaps Kaia and Chay, they would never understand. The sound he heard was rare, and he realised at that moment the bird—or whatever animal it was—desired to remain unseen while letting its unique sound rule the forest.

He wondered what creature it truly was and if it knew that Manu had spent the night there. Wow, imagine being awakened like this every day, he thought. It was an experience of a lifetime.

Manu felt a surge of awe as his eyes scanned the forest floor, revealing a breathtaking transformation into a lush expanse of greenery—so different from the darkness he had trudged through. The vibrant colours and life around him filled him with a sense of wonder and relief.

He marvelled at how the forest had come alive, bathed in the soft light of morning. But as he noticed the tree trunk dangling precariously over a boulder, teetering on the edge of a steep drop, a wave of anxiety washed over him knowing that he had slept under that trunk.

He stood up, stretching and shaking his hands and feet, invigorating his body after the cold, cramped unrest of the night. Though a chill still coursed through him, it was overshadowed by a surge of excitement, ignited by the forest's breathtaking beauty. Sunlight filtered through the leaves, casting dappled patterns on the ground, while the vibrant colours of the foliage pulsed with life. Birds flitted overhead, their joyful songs mingling with the rustle of leaves, creating a magical world that only a fortunate few ever witness. The air was filled with a clean, vibrant energy that evoked a sense of purity and renewal.

As he inhaled the fresh, earthy scent of the forest, he felt an undeniable connection to this enchanting place. It was as if the very essence of the surrounding wood was awakening something profound within him, urging him to explore further.

The air was cold, yet the beauty of nature enveloped him. He noticed wild orchids blooming abundantly on the unmarked trees, their delicate petals adding splashes of colour to the landscape. Memories flooded back of the days he spent selling ordinary riverside orchids on the bustling streets of Lae Town. But these orchids were something extraordinary—uniquely rare and breathtakingly vibrant. He could imagine their value; each one would fetch K20 or K30 if he were to sell them. The thought filled him with a sense of wonder, recognising the treasure that surrounded him in this untouched paradise.

The unmarked trees towered majestically above him, their trunks adorned with a stunning array of colors. Some stood proud in brilliant white, while others displayed rich shades of brown and deep black. Among them were unique specimens with scaly, rough barks that added character and intrigue to the forest.

Even the birds and other wild creatures watched him with keen curiosity, their eyes bright and inquisitive. It was as if they were pondering, *who is this stranger in our midst?* That thought danced in Manu's mind, bringing a warm smile to his face as he absorbed the beauty around him.

Two hornbills perched on a low branch; their beady eyes fixed intently on him. Manu waved, but the birds remained unbothered, their watchful gazes unwavering. Captivated, he returned their stare, noting that this couple was clearly guarding something precious. *Maybe they're about to build a nest,* he mused, a smile spreading across his lips at the thought.

Meanwhile, other lively birds flitted about on the vines, performing acrobatic somersaults and hanging effortlessly from one leg or their beaks. *'Come on!'* Manu laughed heartily, delighting in their playful antics as he sank down onto the forest floor. *'This is so cool!'*

In that moment, he wished Kaia were with him, imagining how he would conjure something hilarious to lighten the mood, sparking laughter that would reverberate through the trees.

The thought of sharing this adventure with him filled Manu with joy, but he also recalled that Kaia was busy earning money to court some lady—a detail he had heard Maoru mention. He never pressed Kaia about it, respecting he was older than him and because of the bond they shared.

Then right in front of him, he saw a white baby possum with a long bushy tail and round glassy eyes. Manu carefully picked up the possum and then gave it a bit of the roasted banana. The possum poked its long tongue out, tasted it and then got the banana from Manu with its front paws and nibbled at it. Manu saw how undisturbed the nature was. It was awesome to see animals at close range without any fear of humans.

Then he realised something.

He was already in the Blue Mountains.

He walked quietly through the forest and started climbing up the elevation again with the possum on his shoulder. Not long after his little friend went to sleep and Manu tucked it into the side pocket of his knapsack.

He climbed and climbed, but soon fatigue began to set in. His legs felt heavy, each step becoming a struggle as weariness crept in. In a moment of clarity, he decided to change his approach. Instead of continuing upward, he would go around the mountain. As he shifted direction, a sense of relief washed over him; this path felt far more promising than the grueling ascent.

He walked on and on and then he stopped and sat down on a flat rock and rested. He took the possum out, but the little guy was still sleeping so he put it on his lap and rested. He drank his water and ate the last banana that was in the other pocket of the knapsack. He felt quite tired and decided to lie down and have a nap.

He woke up to the sunbeams right above him, playing hopping games on his face. He sat up, rubbed his eyes and then drank some water from the container. He looked down at the little fellow, but the ball of fur was curled up, fast asleep.

He stood up, stretching his arms high above his head, feeling the tension melt away. After carefully placing the sleepy possum in the side pocket of his backpack, he secured the straps and adjusted the weight comfortably. The forest around him seemed to come alive, the rustling leaves and chirping birds urging him onward. As he walked, he felt a renewed sense of purpose, ready to embrace whatever adventures awaited him on this winding path.

10

The Golden-Haired Woman

$\mathcal{H}$e walked through the forest, enjoying the unique fauna and flora that one cannot see in the forests familiarised by human beings. He noticed the wild unusual flowering orchids on a couple of trees, and where one doesn't have to climb too high to get them.

The serenity in the forest was truly sacred, with the animals, plants and trees living in perfect harmony. It felt peacefully lonely, in a sense that the peacefulness indulges the mind, making one realise that a very few humans have set foot in that part of the forest.

The trees looked so powerful. They were like tall calm giants, who owned the mountains and were not fearful of anything. There were different kinds of trees, rarely seen in the low forestlands. The vines twined possessively around the trees and hung loose in certain places, as if on purpose, so that that possums and birds can sit there and enjoy the beauty of the forest.

The branches and leaves were so high on the huge trees so that they blocked the sunlight, except for the few rays that pass through the gaps. The rays bounced on the forest floor, like small fluttering yellow butterflies and gave the serenity a glow of contentment.

The noises of birds screeching didn't erase the tranquillity of the forest. It added a wild primitive chant that was truly rare.

The birds munched away on the wild seeds and fruits. Their eating was noisy and messy, without any etiquette, but here, there were no tables to show manners. Manu smiled at the thought of birds, eating the way they pleased, sitting on branches, hanging upside down and holding food with their feet. He also smiled at the thought of birds using forks and spoons to eat seeds and fruits. He soon realised that he was smiling, so he stopped and looked around.

The trees produced the food and the birds and animals enjoyed every yield without any boundaries and Manu understood as he stood behind the trees, that nature was truly beautiful.

He walked through the shrubs, avoiding mountainous sharp rocks and boulders that seemed to hang against the trunks of the trees and on the slopes. He looked up to a lower branch and saw a large green tree snake waking from a long slumber and uncoiling itself slowly. He stood there quietly and watched in awe, as the snake untwisted itself and move along the branch.

It was green on the top, but its belly was tinted yellowish white. Its eyes were a slanted diamond shape and it focused on Manu, as it flicked its tongue. Manu quickly turned and started walking again.

As he looked across, he spotted a gigantic tree trunk on the other side of a flat rock that spanned three metres across, appearing to be an inviting resting place. As Manu approached, he noticed leaves and flowers scattered across the surface, sending chills down his spine. Why were they here? Who had placed them? He hesitated, unsure whether to walk over the rock, and instead chose to circle it cautiously, his heart racing as he contemplated the mystery surrounding this eerie scene.

A sense of dread crept in. *Maybe the changing beings use this rock for their rituals. Perhaps they heard me coming and are hiding behind the tree trunks, waiting to materialise and take control of my thoughts,* he pondered silently as he navigated around the stone.

Suddenly, he felt something moving above him and looked up.

His breath caught in his throat. A figure descended on a rope, wearing leaves around her waist and a singlet covering her chest. She carried a basket brimming with beautiful flowers.

Manu watched, entranced, as she glided down the rope. She was Caucasoid, unlike any Melanesian he had ever seen. In the midst of the dark forest, she radiated like a beacon of light. Her hair shimmered with golden rays, illuminating her presence.

She was a changing being, and he felt himself hypnotised by the flowers on the rock and those adorning her chest. With a magical allure, she seemed to be descending to whisk him away to an unknown fate. He tried to move his feet, but the spell she cast held him captive.

She appeared so real, so tangible. As she reached the flat rock, Manu turned to flee, but a man's voice suddenly called from high above in the mother tree.

"Sherina, you left the Canon camera!"

Manu looked up, spotting a treehouse nestled among the thick canopy of leaves.

"Ron, there's a boy down here!" the golden-haired woman shouted, a smile breaking across her face as she stepped down from the rope ladder onto the flat rock. She walked over to him, her demeanor warm and inviting.

Bending down, she scattered the flowers around and picked up a Nikon camera near Manu.

She looked so real.

Manu stood frozen at the edge of the flat rock, his breath caught in his throat as he stared at the golden-haired woman. She seemed to radiate warmth, her presence both enchanting and bewildering. Reaching out her hands, she smiled and said,

"Good day, I am Sheri. That is my husband Ron up there."

"Good day, I am Manu," he replied quietly, his voice barely more than a whisper, as if he were speaking in a dream. The world around him faded into a blur, leaving only her luminous figure in sharp focus.

Sheri's eyes sparkled with curiosity and kindness, drawing him in further.

"What brings you here, Manu? This forest can be quite mysterious." Her voice was melodic, wrapping around him like a comforting embrace.

Manu shook Sherina's outstretched hand and felt the warmth of a genuine human connection, grounding him amidst the surreal surroundings. *Maybe I've somehow walked into another world,* he thought, his mind racing. *Perhaps I've stepped into a dimension that has whisked me away to a land of Caucasians.* His thoughts spiraled wildly, grappling with the implications of his unexpected encounter.

But the woman before him was undeniably real. Sherina's voice broke through the haze of his thoughts as she spoke, her words laced with a melodic quality that seemed to resonate with the very essence of the forest. Yet, despite her enchanting presence, his head buzzed with questions, each one colliding into the next.

Why would a white woman and her husband be in the Blue Mountains? What brought them to this remote jungle, and what were they doing here?

11

The Tree House

"**B**ring him up, Sheri!" a man shouted from above, his voice echoing through the trees and shattering Manu's swirling thoughts.

"Would you like to visit our Tree House, Manu?" Sheri asked, her smile bright and inviting.

Manu nodded, confusion mingling with curiosity. *What is happening here?* he wondered. *What are these people doing in the Blue Mountains?*

Sheri took his hand and led him to a rope ladder. As they climbed, it felt as though they were being lifted by some unseen force into the heart of the Mother Tree. They reached a wooden balcony seamlessly integrated into the tree's embrace.

Breathless, Manu gazed out over the breath-taking expanse below. Every tree seemed tiny, dwarfed by his elevation, with only the thick branches of the Mother Tree shielding him from the open sky.

He turned and noticed a man standing nearby. He was tall and slender, with greying hair, he emanated a calm presence.

"Ron, this is Manu. Manu, this is my husband, Ron," Sheri introduced them and gently patted him on the shoulder.

"Welcome to our Tree House," Ron said with a warm smile as he shook Manu's hand.

Who are these people? Questions raced through Manu's mind like a whirlwind. *Are they the changing beings, evolved into something new?*

Why were two foreigners living in a tree house in the haunted Blue Mountains? *Are they Masalais?*

The torrent of thoughts made him dizzy, and he nearly fainted, as Ron quickly guided him to a nearby chair.

Manu barely registered Ron's words; he was overwhelmed by confusion and fear. Just that morning, he had been hiking through these mountains, and now, under the midday sun, he found himself in a tree. *Why? Did they know I was coming? Who are they?*

He desperately scanned the area for the ladder. His eyes fell upon it, coiled around the third branch of the Mother Tree, impossibly out of reach. *How did it get there? What have these people done to me?*

"Please, don't be scared. Here, have a cold drink," Sheri smiled, touching his arm gently and handing him a large glass of orange juice filled with ice cubes.

"Who… who are you people?" Manu asked, setting the glass on the bamboo table beside him.

Sheri and Ron exchanged glances, concern written on their faces. They could see the fear in Manu's eyes, sensing he might leap over the balcony in a moment of panic.

"We are Americans. We study birds and photograph wildlife. Actually, Manu, you've hiked all the way to the mountains of Nubak," Sheri explained, her smile softening the edges of his fear as she handed him the glass again.

Manu's attention drifted to the tree house that Ron and Sheri had crafted. It was unlike anything he had ever seen—completely hidden from view by the thick branches, a true sanctuary. The house was built from bamboo, the structure sat atop the largest branches of the Mother Tree, surrounded by a balcony-like veranda. A table was laid out with cameras and various instruments, including a telescope at the end, pointing toward the horizon. Manu recognised the telescope; there had been one on the balcony of the club at the golf course.

Manu was stunned.

He stood there, his mouth agape, immersed in the breathtaking sight and the unexpected presence of such sophisticated equipment high in the trees.

"We study birds and insects and photograph wildlife," Sheri repeated, taking his hand and leading him further into their home.

Inside, he felt as if he were in a dream. The house was perfect, with two bedrooms, a kitchen, a bathroom, and even a darkroom where Ron developed photographs. Life-like images of birds and insects adorned the walls.

He glanced at a computer in the cosy sitting area and saw photographs of three handsome young men.

"Those are our boys," Sheri said with a proud smile.

Sheri poured him another glass of cold juice and offered him biscuits as they sat together on the balcony. The height of the tree house was only a distant thought amidst the warmth of their hospitality.

"Manu, where are you from?" Sheri asked, her smile encouraging.

"I hiked all the way from Bumbu Settlement in Lae. I started up the first mountain beside the Bumbu River until I got here. I live on the other side of the river," Manu replied, his voice steadying.

"I slept for two nights in the forest," he continued, a hint of pride in his tone.

"Oh goodness! You're not from the Nubak area. Ron, this boy walked over the ranges. Are you fleeing from someone? Are you in danger?" Sheri asked, concern creeping into her voice.

"No ma'am. I just decided to explore the Blue Mountains. I was looking for unmarked trees to claim and chop down for firewood at the well-known Kamkumung roadside market," Manu explained, his eyes brightening at the thought of his adventure.

"So, Manu, aren't you in school?" Ron inquired, his curiosity piqued.

At that moment, Manu's little friend stirred and poked its head out.

"Ooooh, where did you get that from?" Sheri cooed, her eyes lighting up at the sight of the possum.

"You can have it, ma'am. I found it in the jungle this morning," Manu told her, offering the tiny creature to her.

"Do you have a name for it?" Sheri asked kindly.

"No, I don't," Manu replied with a smile, the warmth of their conversation wrapping around him.

"I'll call her… hmm, I think she's a girl, so her name is Lucky. She's ours, you and me," Sheri declared, her eyes sparkling.

"Okay," Manu agreed, feeling an unexpected sense of connection.

Sheri took the little possum, offered it some water, and placed it in a soft brown basket. Within moments, it was fast asleep.

"A nocturnal creature! Wait until nightfall, and she'll be up and about," Ron laughed, glancing at Sheri and Manu, his mood lightening the atmosphere.

"So, you don't attend school?" Ron asked again, his tone more serious.

"Ron, school hasn't started yet. This is only the second week of January," Sheri reminded her husband gently, her brow furrowing with concern.

"I was in school last year, but I won't be attending this year," Manu replied quietly.

"Why not? You seem like a very bright boy, and you speak so well," Sheri emphasised, leaning closer, her voice softening in an effort to understand.

Manu hesitated, his fingers tracing the rim of his glass. "I was brought up by my grandparents. My grandfather can't afford the fees anymore. He is not well, and my grandmother, who used to save up enough each year for my fees, died last October," he explained, looking down as he spoke.

Sheri's heart sank. "Oh, Manu, I'm so sorry to hear that. Have you thought about what you might do instead?"

"Not yet, but I will surely go back to school next year. That is not my main concern right now. In my culture, family comes first. So, I'm out in the mountains looking for trees to make good wood to sell at the market. I need to take care of my grandfather," Manu explained, aware that they might not fully understand why young people often ventured into the forests alone in the Islands.

Sheri nodded, empathy filling her eyes. "That's a heavy responsibility for someone so young. You're doing a brave thing."

Manu smiled slightly, understanding their concern. "It's just what we do. I hope to save enough to return to school next year. I want to make sure my grandfather has what he needs and that he is well. Grandmother's death hit him hard."

Ron leaned back, a thoughtful expression on his face. "You have a strong spirit, Manu. It's admirable how you prioritise your family."

"Thank you. There's no one else. They are all I've got," Manu replied, realising that sharing his story had made things feel a little lighter.

"So, you say your grandmother passed on in October last year?" Sheri asked again, a bit confused by Manu's recount.

"Yes, ma'am. My grandmother passed away last October. And as I said, her passing hit hard on my grandfather. He's been ill for quite a while, so I won't be attending school this year. I'm going to take care of him," Manu explained softly this time.

"So, you decided to climb these mountains to claim some trees for firewood?" Sheri asked, her concern deepening.

"Yes, ma'am. My folks are woodcutters, so it's only right that I continue the trade," he replied with a faint smile, a sense of pride flickering in his eyes.

"How old are you?" Sheri inquired, her concern deepening.

"I am twelve," he replied, smiling.

"What grade were you in last year?" Ron asked, his brow furrowed with curiosity.

"I was in grade 7," Manu answered, accepting a cold glass of water from Sheri.

"Please, start from the beginning and tell us what led you to climb these mountains in just two days, looking for trees to claim," Sheri urged, her concern now mixed with irritation, wondering if an old, demanding man had sent this boy on such a perilous journey with paint and brush in hand.

Manu then realised that Sheri and Ron did not fully understand the story he was trying to convey through their questions. So, he began from the beginning—how Bubu Naris became ill and how her passing transformed everything into a struggle.

As Manu recounted his story, Sheri and Ron fell silent, disbelief etched on their faces. They could hardly fathom that a boy his age would undertake such a daunting trek. No one had ever traversed the ranges to reach the Blue Mountains before, and the enormity of his journey hung heavily in the air.

Manu paused, deep in contemplation. *I have died in the woods and been taken to the threshold of heaven by a golden-haired angel,* he thought, lost in a reverie. *And now I am being interrogated, as if I must prove my worthiness to enter Paradise.* A flicker of humour sparked within him, reminiscent of Kaia, who always found a way to laugh even in the darkest moments. He began to smile, but quickly suppressed it, glancing over at Ron and Sheri, wondering if they could sense the lightness creeping into his heart amidst the weight of their questions.

"Where do you get your water?" he finally asked, breaking the stillness.

"Come with me, and I'll show you," Sheri smiled, taking his hand once more.

They walked to the back of the house, where three large tanks stood proudly. "They're supported by sturdy posts sunk deep into the ground. Come and see," Sheri suggested, pointing to the posts.

Manu approached the balcony's edge and noticed five large posts that, from the ground, resembled tree trunks. One post had a medium-sized brown pipe attached, which piqued his curiosity. "What is that?" he asked, gesturing toward the pipe.

"Oh, that's the plumbing pipe," Sheri replied, laughing heartily. "And we have solar power too!" she added, showing him how the sun provided their electricity.

The rest of the day sped by as Manu continued to explore the tree house. Sheri and Ron shared more about their life in the forest; their enthusiasm was infectious.

As the sun began to dip below the horizon, casting golden hues across the sky, Sheri started preparing dinner.

"You must stay with us tonight, Manu," she invited warmly. "But first, we'll have to eat."

For dinner, they enjoyed minced meat and rice, followed by ice cream for dessert. As Manu sat on the balcony, he felt as if he were floating among the clouds, with the lights of Lae town twinkling far below. It was utterly enchanting.

"This tree house was built three years ago," Sheri explained, refilling his glass with orange juice. "We usually spend Christmas in Nevada in the USA, and our friend Luka from the Rainforest Habitat comes to look after this place until we return in January. We just got back three days ago."

Ron chimed in, "Morobe Mining helped fund this project by hiring a bamboo builder from the Philippines. Our friend Nikko flew over to Morobe just to construct this tree house without harming the environment. There are some very special species of birds in Morobe that we are photographing and recording for future generations."

Manu felt a pang of discomfort at the thought of humans disturbing the delicate flora and fauna of the Blue Mountains. He had witnessed the untouched beauty of the landscape and developed a profound respect for the forest's inhabitants. Even if he hadn't encountered Sheri and Ron, he would never have marked or claimed trees here.

He would have sought out dead trees, still standing but stripped of their leaves.

"But how do you get your food?" Manu asked, shifting the conversation.

"Maki keeps our vehicle at his little hamlet, just a ten-minute walk from here. We go shopping in Lae town for our supplies," Sheri explained.

"We're going to Bulolo tomorrow. Would you like to come with us?" Ron asked, his eyes sparkling with excitement.

"Oh yes, please! I would love to go. I've never been to Bulolo," Manu replied, beaming at both Ron and Sheri.

In the soft glow of morning, Manu marvelled at the fact that he had slept in the most enchanting room, nestled high within the tallest tree. It felt surreal to reflect on the whirlwind of events that had unfolded the previous day—how he had gone from searching to claim and mark trees to now resting above them, cradled in branches.

When it was time to depart, the three of them stepped onto the rope ladder. Manu noticed it was cleverly operated by a pulley system that gently lowered them to the ground.

"Is this your secret escape route?" Manu joked, glancing up at the majestic tree house.

Ron chuckled, his eyes twinkling. "You could say that! It's our little way of staying connected to the treetops."

Sheri smiled warmly, adding, "And it saves us from a long climb every time we want to go down."

"Can I try?" Manu asked, his eyes sparkling with excitement.

"Of course! Just watch how I do it," Ron replied, pointing the remote control at the ladder with a playful grin.

Once they landed, Ron aimed the remote at the ladder, and with a simple click, it ascended back into the canopy on its own.

Manu's eyes danced with curiosity as he watched Ron. "That's amazing! How did you come up with this idea?"

"It was Nikko's idea," Ron told Manu.

"Oh, Mr. Nikko, the bamboo building expert from the Philippines!" Manu chuckled, imagining the man's expertise.

"Yes! He told us it was easier and safer to go up and down the tree house this way. Or you can be Tarzan and Jane!" Sheri laughed, her voice light with humour.

"Our son Trevor liked the Tarzan idea so much that he kept climbing the huge trunk of the Mother tree," Ron added, shaking his head with a grin. "That boy should live in the jungle!"

With a knowing smile, Ron aimed the remote skyward and pressed a button. The pulley whirred to life, and the rope ladder descended once more. Manu erupted into laughter, the joy infectious, prompting Ron to grin and send the ladder back up again.

"Can it go faster?" Manu asked, excitement bubbling over in his voice.

"Let's see!" Ron replied, adjusting the settings on the remote with a playful glint in his eye.

As the ladder ascended swiftly, Manu's laughter echoed through the trees. "This is the best ride ever!" he exclaimed, feeling a thrill he had never experienced before.

Sheri watched them both, her heart warming at the sight. "Just be careful! We don't want you to float away!" she called out, her laughter mingling with theirs.

"Don't worry, I'll hold on tight!" Manu shouted, still beaming with joy.

12

Off to Bulolo

Sheri and Ron led the way along a narrow track, the air rich with the fragrant aromas of damp moss and wildflowers. Towering trees arched overhead, their leaves forming a natural canopy that filtered the sunlight into shimmering dappled patterns on the forest floor. As they stepped into the open, the path widened into a bulldozer's track, revealing a picturesque village nestled against the majestic backdrop of the Blue Mountains.

The vibrant tropical flowers bloomed in abundance, and the houses, thatched with sago palm, dried grass, and bamboo, exuded a rustic charm. Manu saw smoke curling lazily from some of the homes, mingling with the mouthwatering scent of smoked pork wafting through the air.

Beyond the village, the Blue Mountains range loomed majestically, its peaks kissed by wisps of clouds. The landscape was a breathtaking contrast of deep greens against the azure sky, creating an idyllic scene that felt almost surreal. The gentle sound of a nearby stream added to the tranquility, enveloping the area in a unique serenity, almost a solace.

Suddenly, a short shirtless man came running towards them.

"Hey, good morning, Professor Ronald and Doctor Sherina!" the man greeted, smiling broadly, chewing his buai[4].

"Good morning, Maki," Ron replied, a cheerful warmth in his voice. "It's good to see you. Please meet our new friend, Manu."

Manu stepped forward, extending his hand. "Nice to meet you, Maki."

Maki shook his hand firmly, his smile broadening. "Welcome, Manu! You've come a long way, haven't you?"

"Yes, I hiked from Bumbu Settlement," Manu replied, feeling a sense of pride.

"That's impressive! Not many your age would take on such a journey," Maki responded, nodding in respect. "What do you think of the mountains?"

"They're beautiful," Manu smiled, his eyes lighting up. "I've never seen anything like it."

Turning to Ron, he said "When you come back, my son and I will help you carry your things to your tree house again," Maki offered, his smile warm and genuine.

"Really? That would be great. Thank you." Ron replied.

Maki waved as they began to get into the Land Cruiser. "Drive safely! I'll be looking forward to seeing you again!"

"See you soon, Maki!" Ron called out, as the engine roared to life.

It was quite a long drive, and Manu found himself sitting silently next to the window, mesmerised by the stunning scenery that whizzed by. The vibrant greens and blues blended into a picturesque landscape. Sheri occupied the space between Manu and Ron, her fingers dancing over her iPad as she tapped away, completely absorbed in her tasks.

Meanwhile, Ron drove with a focused intensity, navigating the winding roads at a brisk pace that made Manu a bit nervous. After an hour, though, he realised that Professor Ronald was an experienced driver, confidently handling the curves.

---

4 Betelnut

As they drove, Ron casually mentioned that they were heading to stay with their friend, Doctor Sherf, an Entomologist renowned for his work in butterfly preservation in Papua New Guinea. Sheri eagerly chimed in, her enthusiasm obvious as she explained that Bulolo served as the head office for Butterfly Farming Projects. She talked about the incredible variety of butterflies found in Papua New Guinea.

Sheri told Manu that Doctor Sherf has assisted farmers in starting their butterfly farms, and then continued on explaining the importance of sustainable practices and biodiversity.

Manu listened intently, captivated by the prospect of their adventure and the fascinating world of butterflies in which Doctor Sherf was an expert.

As they approached the little town of Bulolo, the sun hung low in the sky, dimming and weary as it prepared to set. Ron navigated to Doctor Sherf's house, which was conveniently located right next to the airstrip. As they pulled into the car park, Doctor Sherf greeted them, his smile wide and welcoming.

"Doctors, welcome! How are you? My, my, and who is your little friend with a possum on his shoulder? That's a very rare possum indeed!" he exclaimed, stepping closer to examine the creature.

Manu shifted slightly, feeling both proud and a bit shy. "This is Lucky," he said, gently stroking the possum's fur.

Doctor Sherf's eyes widened with curiosity. "My goodness, it's a female! Where did you get this from, son?" he asked, his tone both amazed and playful.

"He found it in the mountains yesterday morning, Doctor," Sheri answered for Manu, her voice warm and encouraging.

"Really? That's quite the adventure." Doctor Sherf said, looking back at Manu. "You must be quite brave to venture out like that. How did you manage to catch her?"

"I found her on the forest floor, in the morning," Manu replied, a hint of pride in his voice.

"Clever boy! You've got a knack for this," Doctor Sherf stated, grinning. "I'll make sure she gets a proper check-up. It's important to keep such a rare creature healthy."

"Very rare species. Wow, this is excellent", Doctor Sherf was truly amazed.

After proper introductions, they all went inside Doctor Sherf's house.

Manu observed Doctor Sherf's house, a captivating space brimming with dried butterflies and insects meticulously arranged in glass cases. The living room and corridors were adorned with these specimens, creating an atmosphere that was both enchanting and oddly fascinating. Each display seemed to tell a story of nature's exquisite beauty and delicate fragility.

As he wandered deeper into the house, his gaze fell upon an ancient-looking gun, distinctly different from the ones carried by the Police Task Forces in Lae. Manu was intrigued, so he stepped closer, examining the weathered surface and intricate details that hinted at a storied past.

"Oh, I found that gun in the jungle once when I went to collect insects," Doctor Sherf remarked, catching Manu's interest.

Manu's eyes widened in surprise. "Really? That's incredible! How did you come across it?"

Sherf chuckled softly, his eyes sparkling with vivid memories. "I was deep in the bush, searching for rare beetles. It was partially buried under some leaves. I couldn't believe my luck."

"Did you ever find out how it got there?" Manu asked, utterly fascinated.

Doctor Sherf nodded. "I believe it's from World War II. The conflict was quite intense here in Bulolo."

"No way!" Manu yelped, completely flabbergasted.

After a delightful dinner of creamy chicken, rice, potatoes, and broccoli, they all settled on the veranda, savouring their coffee as the evening air wrapped around them. Manu was handed a can of soda, its coolness refreshing against the warm ambiance.

Doctor Sherf, who oversaw butterfly and insect preservation in Bulolo, was in his fifties. Despite being divorced, he radiated energy and enthusiasm for life, his well-built frame a testament to his love for the outdoors. Having dedicated the last ten years to his work in Bulolo, he had become a vital part of the community.

As Manu admired the hundreds of books lining the shelves in Sherf's home, he couldn't help but wonder how the doctor found time to read them all. Each volume seemed to hold a world of knowledge and adventure.

Sherf shared his insights about butterfly farming, his passion evident in the way he spoke. He painted a vivid picture of the process, highlighting the importance of sustainability and the delicate balance of nature that fascinated Manu.

"The international demand for tropical butterflies is much greater than is generally recognised. Each year millions of them are caught and sold throughout the world. Many buyers are scientists engaged in research on aspects of systematics, ecology, ethology, evolution, and conservation. Others are individuals who like expensive curios that incorporate butterflies, such as display cases, coffee tables, wall hangings, or other objects. But increasingly, the fragile, iridescent creatures, mounted in plastic or glass, are used to decorate less-expensive items such as purses, trays, platters, screens, and other common objects in Europe, North America, and Japan. In addition, amateur butterfly collecting, which reached a peak in Victorian times, is again becoming popular," Doctor Sherf informed them.

"All this has produced a strong and active market. The current trade is estimated to be between US $10 and $20 million annually, and the demand is rising. Remote regions of Papua New Guinea are benefiting from this burgeoning interest in tropical insects, and several hundred villagers are rearing or collecting butterflies, beetles, and other insects for export. The Papua New Guinea government now considers insects a national resource, and it has made butterfly farming part of the nation's village economic development. At Bulolo, it has established an Insect Farming and Trading Agency (IFTA) to handle the business details of a growing international trade. And Papua New Guinea is the only country so far to specify insect conservation as a national objective in its constitution," he stopped and lit his tobacco and took a long puff, blowing out the smoke like a thick mist.

"Botanical research is the key to Papua New Guinea's butterfly farming program. Local botanists and ecologists have identified the plants that the various butterfly species use during their life cycle. The butterfly farmers then build up their "livestock" by clearing small areas of ground and planting leafy food plants for larvae, together with the nectar-producing flowering plants that adult butterflies feed on. The combination of flowering and leafy plants provides a complete habitat where butterflies find everything they need to grow and reproduce. Therefore, most remain, and the farmer retains his livestock without fences or walls," he stopped and took a sip of his coffee.

Manu was astounded.

Doctor Sherf saw the look on Manu's face. "Hey, Manu boy, are you okay?"

"Doctor, about butterfly farming. You said, you don't need a fence, no money or whatever to start it?" Manu asked the doctor.

"No Manu, you only plant nectar-producing flowering plants and the adult butterflies will come and feed on them. Then they lay eggs and you have butterflies to sell," Doctor Serf explained with a smile.

"You also, need to make sure your plants keep flowering. It's more like a beautiful flowering garden for butterflies, Manu."

"Would you like to see a butterfly farm tomorrow?" the kind doctor asked.

"Oh, yes please," Manu answered enthusiastically.

"Hey, Marvin, the last time we were here. You said that you found an old gold dredging machine?" Ron asked changing the subject.

"Oh, yes, I did. It's at the forestry workshop with Limia, my driver and mechanic. He is looking into it," the doctor said laughing.

"Bulolo used to be a gold dredging centre, eh," Sherina wondered aloud.

"Yes, Bulolo was once a gold dredging centre in the former Territory of Papua New Guinea. Bulolo is situated on the Bulolo River, a territory of the Markham River, about 32 kilometres North-West of Wau and 43 kilometres South of Lae."

"Hey, Marvin, how many town residents are here in Bulolo?" Ron asked again.

"Well, there are about 20 thousand people here, Ron," the doctor answered drinking the last of his coffee and putting the mug on the table.

"Tell us about the gold that was mined here," Sheri asked the doctor.

"Actually Sheri, gold was dredged here in the 1930s. It all begun on 21st March, 1932 with the whole of the 1,100-ton dredge transported to the field in pieces by air from the port city of Lae."

"Such hard work," said Ron as he continued drinking his coffee. Manu listened with interest.

"The largest single part was the main tumbler shaft, 12 feet long and weighing 6, 870 pounds."

"Tsk, tsk…unbelievable," Sheri continued nodding her golden head and clicking her tongue.

"But dredging operations were interrupted by the war in 1941 and were not resumed until six years later. On February 1942, at around 11am, Bulolo was bombed by five twin engine bombers."

"By the Japanese?" Sheri asked standing up to stretch.

"Yes, of course," the doctor answered. "As the gold petered out, the dredges were abandoned and they can still be found along the Bulolo river bed. Like the one I found, a smaller one."

"You said, it's at the forestry workshop? Tell us a bit about the forestry here," Sheri asked the doctor.

"Well, forestry is the major industry, PNG Forestry Product is the main enterprise. Bulolo was the main headquarters of a company formed to exploit the pine forests that grow in the valley. In conjunction with the milling of timber an extensive scheme of re-afforestation was undertaken to ensure perpetuity of suppliers," he explained.

"Marvin, you are very well informed. I truly admire you," Sheri looked up at her husband and they both nodded towards Doctor Sherf.

"I love Papua New Guinea. It is a very unique country. Morobe Province in itself, has very interesting flora and fauna. I am truly privileged to work here in Bulolo. Every day, I congratulate myself for choosing this job," Doctor Sherf stood up and lit his tobacco.

"Tomorrow, my young friend, we will visit a butterfly farm. Now, you all go on and get some sleep. I know the drive up here is rough and tiring," he waved them off, said good night and went straight to the bathroom.

Manu settled into the small room at the far end, the quietness wrapping around him like a comforting blanket. In the adjacent spacious visitor's room, Sherina and Ronald's laughter echoed softly.

As he lay down, thoughts of his Grandfather surged forth, as sadness came crashing over him. He sat up with nostalgia heavy in his heart. He got down from the bed, knelt beside it, bowed his head and whispered a prayer, asking God to watch over his beloved Bubu Pellie until he could return to Lae. The moonlight streamed through the flimsy curtains, casting ethereal shadows that danced around him, enhancing the intimacy of his supplication.

After finishing his prayer, he felt a blend of sorrow and hope, clinging to the belief that love could transcend any distance, knitting hearts together across time and space. Then he pulled up the covers and went off to sleep.

13

The Great Awakening

The next day, Doctor Sherf took Manu, Sherina, and Ronald to Makanda's butterfly farm. The farm was a stunning garden brimming with vibrant flowering plants, creating a variety of colours. Manu was particularly drawn to the creeping vine that gracefully intertwined with the crotons, its lush green leaves providing a perfect backdrop for the vivid blooms.

As they wandered through the garden, Doctor Sherf pointed out various species. "Look at that one!" he exclaimed, gesturing toward a striking orange butterfly. "That's the Papuan Eggfly. They're quite common around here."

Makanda, the farm's owner, joined them with a warm smile. "I'm glad you're enjoying the garden! Each flower is carefully chosen to attract different butterflies."

Ron raised an eyebrow, intrigued. "How do you manage to keep them all here?"

"It's all about creating the right environment," Makanda explained. "We plant specific flowers and maintain the right humidity. Butterflies thrive in these conditions."

Sherina knelt beside a cluster of blossoms. "These trumpet flowers are stunning! Do they attract a lot of butterflies?"

"Absolutely!" Makanda replied. "Their shape is perfect for certain species. You'll see them fluttering around in no time."

Manu watched a bright yellow butterfly land nearby, his eyes wide with wonder. "It's like a living painting! How do you get them to come here?"

Doctor Sherf smiled, enjoying the enthusiasm. "Patience and a little bit of magic. Nature knows how to find its way. And speaking of impressive butterflies, have you heard of the Queen Alexandra's Birdwing? It's the largest butterfly in the world, and it's found right here in Papua New Guinea, especially in Morobe Province."

"Really?" Manu asked, fascinated. "How big can it get?"

"Some can have wingspans of over 10 inches!" Doctor Sherf said with excitement. "They're a true marvel of nature."

As the doctors conversed with Makanda, Manu wandered through the garden, observing everything with keen interest. An exciting idea began to blossom in his mind. He paused to admire the vibrant caterpillars munching on the leaves of a lemon tree when Sherina called out to him, urging him to join the others.

After exchanging warm goodbyes with Makanda, they made their way back to Doctor Sherf's house. As they climbed the steps, Manu turned to Doctor Sherf, his voice filled with eagerness. "Doctor Sherf, please teach me about butterflies."

The doctors exchanged glances, and a smile spread across Doctor Sherf's face. "Of course. I'd love to teach you everything. Come, let's sit out on the veranda."

Once outside, Doctor Sherf retrieved his butterfly books from the shelves, meticulously arranging them on the coffee table. He then began to share his knowledge about butterfly farming, his enthusiasm infectious as he explained the intricacies of raising these beautiful creatures. Each page turned revealed a new world of colour and wonder, igniting Manu's curiosity even further.

"The key to farming butterflies is to establish a garden with plants of the various species needed for their life cycles. The ideal farm area is about 0.2 hectares. This is spacious enough for growing food plants for adults and larvae and small enough to keep the plants watered, weeded, pruned, and generally well-tended. Such a farm can contain about 500 vines, grown like bean plants on poles or shade trees.

"It is important to surround the site with a thick hedge of hibiscus, bougainvillea, xora, poinsettia, or other nectar-bearing plants whose flowers attract adult butterflies and encourage them to remain in the area. The hedges also keep out pigs and other livestock that may damage the leafy plants inside the farm.

"A good way to start a farm is to establish it in a vegetable garden[5]. By the time the vegetables are ready to harvest, the area already has some thriving butterfly food plants and probably some winged livestock as well.

"One of the most successful butterfly food plants in Papua New Guinea is Aristo lochia tagala, a vine on which the larvae of more common birdwing butterflies feed. Another is Evodea—a food plant of the large blue Ulysses swallowtail and many colourful weevils.

"Shade trees also can be food plants for butterflies other than birdwings and for beetles or weevils. Examples are species of Annona (such as sour sop), Citrus (such as lemon), Cerbera, and Graptophyllum. Wallace's Longhorn Beetle feeds on breadfruit (Artocarpus communis).

"Normally, one area of the farm is kept aside for growing seeds or cuttings[6]. In this nursery the butterfly food plants are watered and cared for, and unhealthy ones are easily spotted and weeded out". The Doctor stopped abruptly, got a glass of water and drank it all in one gulp.

Then Doctor Serf drew a diagram for Manu on how to set a butterfly farm.

---

5 Papua New Guinea butterfly farmers often plant butterfly vines between their rows of sweet potato or taro

6 IFTA sells seed of some suitable species.

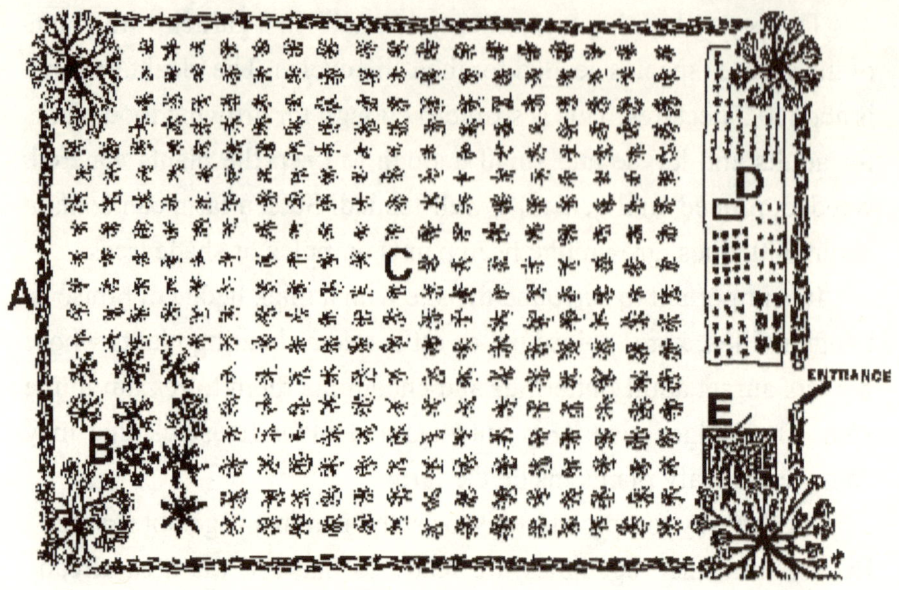

A. Hedge of hibiscus, xora, and poinsettia to keep pigs out and provide nectar.

B. Fruits trees (such as lemon).

C. The aristo lochia vine grown on the branches of others trees (such as leucaena), to feed caterpillar larvae.

D. Nursery area.

E. A hut for tools. [7]

"Okay Doctor, I understand everything you said about farming. But please, tell me about the butterflies and their life cycles" Manu asked.

"Of course," smiled the doctor. "Normally, each butterfly species has a preferred food plant for its larvae. After the female has mated, she searches for the correct plant and lays her eggs on or near it. In a few days the eggs hatch, and the young caterpillars usually eat their own eggshells and begin feeding on the softer leaves and shoots of the food plant.

"As they grow, the caterpillars shed their skins. Each moult is called an instar, and five instars occur before a larva is big enough to

<hr>

7 Diagram courtesy IFTA, Bulolo

pupate. Pupation is a resting stage during which the adult butterfly develops inside the hard, protective chrysalis. For pupation the larva selects the underside of a stem or leaf to protect it from rain and predators." Doctor Sherf, stopped and flipped the pages of a book on the coffee table. Then he continued.

"After 10 days to 3 weeks, depending on the type of butterfly, the pupa[8] case splits open and the adult insect emerges. This usually occurs before 9 o'clock in the morning. The freshly emerged adult then takes from 3 to 4 hours to expand and dry its wings before flying off to feed on nectar and to search for a mate to begin the life cycle once again."

"How are butterflies harvested, doctor?" Manu asked.

"Right Manu," the doctor smiled and continued. "Once the farm is well established, pupa can be collected daily. Ideally, about 50 percent should be left or released. At least as many females as males should be released. Pupae that are too high to reach are usually left to emerge naturally and repopulate the farm. Others are left because they are not quite perfect.

"The farmer can usually see that emergence will occur on the next day, since the pupa becomes darker in colour as the adult wing and body colours develop. He then plucks off the stem or leaf to which the pupa is attached. The soft, new pupa are not touched because this damages the adult," the doctor emphasised.

"He pins the leaf to a board or puts it in a net or in a small cage. Often these are kept inside to protect the pupae against pests and large predators. However, some farmers construct small houses out of bush materials to hold the pupae ready for hatching. Others keep their pupae in the open and count on being able to collect the adults before they have flown away.

"Care is taken to protect the specimens from ants and rats. For example, the legs of the cage are placed in bowls of water to deter ants from climbing up. The pupae are sprayed with water 2-3 times

---

8 the inactive transformation stage of an insect that undergoes complete metamorphosis, such as a butterfly, and is called a chrysalis

a week to speed up the hatching process and to prevent them from drying out. Only a light spray is used; otherwise, the pupae develop mould," Doctor Sherf explained.

"The pupae are best kept in a shady place so the butterflies will remain calm after hatching and will not flap and damage their wings."

"How do they process them?" Manu asked.

"Well, when the newly emerged butterfly has completely dried its wings, it is carefully caught by the thorax and injected with a small amount of a killing agent such as ethyl acetate or boiling water."

"Small butterflies are particularly easily damaged if handled, so they are placed for about 10 minutes in a killing jar containing cotton soaked with a little ethyl acetate. A layer of cardboard is placed above the cotton so that the butterflies are not stained by the solvent.

"The farmer places the dead butterflies in paper envelopes, being careful at all times not to touch or damage the wings. The envelopes are easily made from grease-proof paper, which the agency supplies on request.

"To ensure that the butterflies will not mould, they are placed on a black plastic tray and dried in the sun, in their paper envelopes, for about 4 days. During this time, they are protected from pests such as ants, and the drying trays have a screen on top to prevent the envelopes from blowing away or from being rained on," the doctor clearly explained.

"Once properly dried, the insects, still in their envelopes, are stored in boxes, preferably air-tight to prevent condensation and mouldiness. When enough specimens have been collected, the villager packs them carefully in strong cardboard boxes—which the agency also supplies—with cotton or kapok. A few naphthalene crystals are added to keep away pests, and the box is wrapped and sent here, to Bulolo."

After the engaging lecture on butterfly farming, the atmosphere shifted to one of warmth and companionship as Sherina prepared a delightful lunch. She served a platter of deep-fried kaukau chips, their golden edges crisp and inviting. The aroma filled the room, a tantalising hint of salt and sweetness wafting through the air. Alongside, she presented succulent pieces of chicken, marinated in a blend of local spices and cooked to perfection, its skin crackling with flavour.

The vibrant vegetable salad added a refreshing crunch, featuring freshly picked greens tossed with ripe tomatoes and cucumbers, drizzled with a light vinaigrette that enhanced the natural flavours. To complete the meal, Sherina laid out a colourful array of local fruits—juicy mangoes, sweet bananas, and tangy pineapples—each bite bursting with tropical essence.

As they gathered around the table, the conversation flowed easily.

"Sherina, these kaukau chips are incredible! How do you get them so crispy?" Manu asked, his eyes lighting up.

"It's all in the preparation," Sherina replied, smiling. "I soak them in water first, then pat them dry before frying. It helps to get that perfect crunch!"

Doctor Sherf chimed in, "And the chicken! The spices are just right. What did you use?"

"Oh, just a mix of garlic, ginger, and a bit of chili for a kick," Sherina explained. "I like to keep it simple but flavourful."

Ronald, savouring a piece of mango, added, "This fruit is so fresh! It's like a burst of sunshine in every bite."

"Exactly," Sherina replied, beaming with pride. "There's nothing like local produce. It's the best part of living here in Morobe Province."

As they enjoyed the meal, laughter and stories filled the air.

14

Back To Lae With A Purpose

As the first rays of sunlight streamed through the window, a warm, buttery aroma wafted through the air, gently coaxing Manu from his dreams. The scent of breakfast filled the room, mingling with freshly brewed coffee and the fragrance of steeped tea.

In the kitchen, Doctor Sherf was in his element, skillfully preparing breakfast. The toast crackled as it browned, and the rich scent of melted butter filled the air. He hummed a cheerful tune, adding to the warmth of the morning.

As Manu joined Doctor Sherf, Ron and Sheri at the table, he saw steaming cups of coffee and tea alongside plates of toast with butter.

"Nothing beats a hearty breakfast to start the day," he declared. "The secret is in the butter—always use the best!"

Ron and the others chuckled, knowing that Doctor Sherf had a knack for turning even the simplest meals into tasty delights.

"Let me tell you about the time I learned a lesson the hard way in Poland," Doctor Sherf started, his eyes twinkling with mischief.

"It was a bright Saturday morning, and I had invited some friends over for breakfast. I wanted to impress them with my famous pancakes. I had the flour, the eggs, and of course, the butter—well, sort of. You see, I usually buy the best butter, but that day I was feeling a little thrifty. I opted for this mysterious 'budget butter' I found in the back of the fridge." As he continued, everyone leaned in closer, eager for the punchline.

"I mixed everything together and poured the batter onto the griddle, watching it sizzle. The pancakes were fluffy and golden, but as I flipped them, I noticed something odd. They didn't smell like pancakes; they had an unusual aroma!"

"What did you do?" Sheri asked while Ron and Manu looked on.

"Oh, I soldiered on, of course! I plated them up and served them with syrup, thinking, 'How bad could it be?' But as my friends took their first bites, I saw their faces turn from excitement to confusion. One friend even managed to choke out, 'Is this… butter or a science experiment?'"

Doctor Sherf paused for dramatic effect. "I'll tell you, it was a disaster! Turns out, that 'budget butter' was actually a mix of margarine and some sort of unidentifiable spread. It was like a culinary crime scene!"

The table roared with laughter, and Doctor Sherf continued, "In the end, we all agreed that breakfast was an epic failure. But we couldn't let it ruin the day. So, we turned it into a cooking competition. Everyone grabbed whatever they could find in my kitchen, and we had a 'Pancake-Off' right then and there."

He leaned in closer, lowering his voice. "And you know what? The winner was the one who made pancakes using leftover pizza dough! We called them 'Pizza-cakes', and they were surprisingly delicious!"

By the time Doctor Sherf finished, everyone at the table was in stitches. "So remember," he concluded with a grin, "always use the best butter—or at least check the expiration date in your fridge. You never know when you might end up with a culinary adventure!"

They laughed and shared stories while the little creature Manu had rescued from the Blue Mountains scampered around, occasionally stopping to nibble on a crust of bread.

"Look at him go!" Manu said, pointing. "He's quite the gourmet now."

"Indeed," Doctor Sherf replied with a grin. "He has good taste, just like us."

Manu got up from where he was sitting and went over to Sherina and whispered into her ear. Sherina's mouth, which was full of toast, turned into a huge smile.

"Marvin," she called Doctor Sherf's name.

"Yes Sheri," he looked up from the Post Courier he was reading as he took the cigar out of his mouth

Ron stopped eating and looked at Sherina, then at Manu.

"Manu and I would like to give you, Lucky," she told Doctor Sherf smiling.

"Lucky? Who is lucky?" Doctor Sherf asked confused.

"The possum," Sherina and Manu answered at the same time chuckling.

"Dziękuję bardzo chłopcze!" he exclaimed in his indigenous language.

"Doctor Sherf is muttering in Polish," Ron laughed good naturedly, making Doctor Sherf smile. "Thank you so much, Lucky will keep me company, more like a family in this house, until I take her down to the Rain Forest Habitat at the University of Technology. My friend, Peter works there and they might find a friend for Lucky."

They all climbed into the vehicle, waving goodbye to Doctor Sherf with bright smiles. He stood there, a reassuring figure, promising to visit them in the tree house soon.

"I'll bring some interesting books on insects," he said, his eyes twinkling with enthusiasm. "If you're ever curious or want to learn more, just let me know. I'm always happy to teach you."

Manu felt a surge of gratitude. The thought of learning from Doctor Sherf filled him with excitement, and he could already imagine the fascinating discussions they would have.

As the vehicle pulled away, he looked back at the doctor, who waved again, a warm smile on his face. The promise of new knowledge and adventures ahead made Manu's heart race. He knew this was just the beginning of something special, not only for him but for the entire community.

Manu nodded, his mind alive with possibilities. The support of Doctor Sherf and the excitement of his friends made him feel unstoppable. The journey to Lae Town felt like the first step toward a bright future filled with discovery and joy.

Manu sat in the vehicle between the two doctors and he felt like bursting. Now, he knew what he wanted to do, a very simple thing that he would start and teach his grandfather to manage. He couldn't wait to get back to Lae, to Bumbu settlement and put his great idea into action.

He pictured the plot of land next to their shack. He knew the land belonged to his grandfather, because years back Bubu Pellie, bought this land, built a permanent house, but it was burnt down during ethnic clashes. His Grandfather still has the papers to prove he owned that land.

"Bubu Pellie, how come your papers didn't get burned?" Manu once asked.

"Well, Bubu Naris carried our important papers, money, and other valuables in her bilum, safely tucked away in a secured folder. That's how we didn't lose our Land Right papers."

Manu felt a deep sense of satisfaction—truly pleased—that his grandfather owned a piece of land perfect for his plans. Ideas raced through his mind about how to transform that land, and he envisioned telling his grandfather to fence it off for their new venture. The possibilities seemed endless, and he couldn't wait to get started. He didn't even realise he was smiling as these thoughts bubbled up inside him.

"Hey, big guy, what's that smug smile about?" Sherina playfully punched his left arm.

"Was I smiling?" Manu teased back, attempting to play it cool.

"Oh yes, you were. I'm guessing it must be a girl you're eager to see in Lae," she shot back with a grin.

"Nooooo!" Manu laughed loudly, shaking his head. "I'm thinking of something very important."

"Oh good!" Ron chimed in, shooting him a quick glance as he sped down the road. Everything outside the window rushed by in a blur, adding to Manu's thrill.

"What's making you smile, Manu dear?" Sherina laughed, squeezing his hand affectionately.

What lovely people, Manu thought. How had he been so blessed in such a short time? His mindset and plans had shifted so effortlessly; it felt almost surreal. He still pinched himself occasionally, just to confirm that all of this was real.

"Well, I'm going to start a butterfly farm!" he declared, inhaling deeply and looking straight ahead as Ron accelerated toward Lae Town. The excitement surged through him, filling him with a sense of purpose and joy that he couldn't wait to share.

"A butterfly farm? That sounds amazing!" Sherina said, her eyes lighting up. "What do you plan to do first?"

"I want to begin by preparing the land," Manu explained. "I'll plant native flowers that attract butterflies. It's essential to create a welcoming environment for them."

"That's a great start," Ron encouraged. "How will you keep the butterflies safe?"

"I'll build a small enclosure to protect them from predators," Manu replied, his confidence growing. "And I want to create a habitat that replicates their natural environment as closely as possible."

Sherina nodded, clearly impressed. "Have you thought about how you'll take care of them once they're there?"

"Yes! I'll research the best practices for butterfly care—what they need to thrive. I want to ensure they have everything they require."

"That sounds like a solid plan," Ron said, glancing over with admiration. "I can't wait to see it all come together."

Manu smiled, feeling a surge of determination. "This is just the beginning. I want to make it a place where butterflies can flourish, and I'll learn everything I can to make that happen."

"And remember," Manu added with a grin, "Doctor Sherf said he would always be available to help me, just like he did for Makanda's butterfly farm we visited yesterday. I know I can count on him for guidance."

"Having him in your corner is a huge advantage," Sherina said, her expression encouraging.

The vehicle sped on, and as the sun streamed through the windows, Manu felt a renewed sense of hope. He was ready to turn his dream into reality, and with the support of his friends and Doctor Sherf, nothing could hold him back.

15

Butterfly Farming

At 5pm, they arrived in Lae town and went to the Huon Motel. Manu wanted to walk to Bumbu settlement, but the doctors told him that it would be a good idea to walk to Bumbu Settlement in the morning, after they all go shopping first. They booked into an apartment at the back of the Motel, closer to the Botanical Garden, opposite the War Cemetery.

Manu got the couch downstairs next to the 20-inch flat screen TV. It was awesome, watching a large screen. The movies looked so real, especially when the horses were galloping, Manu thought they were about to come out of the screen and jump over him. It was splendid.

They ordered Room Service; a dinner of fresh salad, rump steak and boiled potatoes. As they ate, the doctors discussed Manu's butterfly farm plan. After discussion, it was settled that the doctors would go back to Bulolo and buy the kinds of 'butterfly alluring plants' from Makanda's farm, while Manu get his plot of land ready, according to all the information he learned from Doctor Sherf.

The doctors retired upstairs for the night and Manu laid down on the couch with a fat pillow and a comfy blanket.

At 3am, Manu suddenly woke up. He lay on the couch and thought of what he was planning to do. He made up his mind then, to work very hard and make sure his butterfly farm was successful. He also decided that after he started the farm, he would ask a professional to come and show him and his Bubu, how to collect the butterflies, because that was a fragile job. He had understood, Doctor Sherf, when he explained it, but he still needed experienced people to come and show him. He knew the Doctors would help him and show him the right things to use to dry the butterflies.

Manu was deep in thought, his brow furrowed in concentration. "I'm going to be the ultimate butterfly farmer!" he declared, puffing out his chest like a proud scientist unveiling a groundbreaking discovery. "No mistakes, no butterfly casualties!"

With a triumphant grin, he grabbed the remote, ready to unwind. He clicked on ABC3, but the movie on screen didn't grab his attention. "Next!" he said to himself dramatically, flipping through channels like a game show host hunting for the grand prize.

Finally, he landed on HBO, where Transformers blared to life. "Whoa!" Manu exclaimed, eyes wide with excitement. Just then, he recalled the moment at the Golf Course Lounge when Kaia's eyes nearly popped out of his head during the preview. "Dude, my main man, I wanna be a machine!" he breathed in deeply, then flopped down on the couch like a deflated balloon.

He dropped the remote on the floor and imagination took flight. He pictured himself farming butterflies, then transforming them into colourful machines. "Yes! Imagine it—fluttering trails of mechanical butterflies zooming all over Bumbu Settlement!" He chuckled at the thought, envisioning a sky filled with vibrant, buzzing contraptions, each one more outrageous than the last.

"People would be like, 'What's that? A butterfly or a robot?' And I'd just say, 'Why not both?'" He smiled to himself, the idea growing bigger and wilder in his mind. "I could start a revolution! 'Join the Butterfly-Machine Movement!'"

Lost in his daydream, Manu couldn't help but laugh at the absurdity. "Who needs a garden when you can have a sky full of fluttering robots? I could even train them to do tricks! 'Watch as my butterfly transforms into a blender for smoothies!"

A giant robot materialised, and to Manu's astonishment, he was the robot—a massive, shimmering butterfly robot!

"Hey, Butterfly-Bot 3000!" Kaia yelled up at him, grinning like a kid on Christmas morning. "You flutter in, transform, and then serve lemonade to everyone!"

Manu laughed, feeling a rush of power. "And then the Golf Course gossips, 'Did you see Manu's butterflies? They've upgraded!'"

Suddenly, bright, colourful butterfly beams flashed right in his eyes, and Manu instinctively squinted. He opened his eyes, only to be greeted by a different kind of light. Sunbeams bounced through the glass windows, illuminating the room where he was sprawled out on the couch. The smell of breakfast wafted in from the kitchen, where the doctors were busy preparing a meal.

Manu blinked, realising he had drifted off to sleep and missed the rest of Transformers. "Darn! I totally missed it and had the weirdest dream about butterflies," he muttered to himself, still half-lost in his fantastical vision.

"Morning, sleepyhead!" Sherina called from the kitchen, her voice cheerful and bright.

"Morning," Manu replied, stretching and trying to shake off the remnants of his dream.

"Did you sleep well?" Sheri asked, her eyes sparkling with curiosity.

"I did for most of the night, but then I had this wild dream," Manu chuckled, folding the bedcovers and tidying the couch as if it would help organise his thoughts.

"What was it about?" Sheri leaned against the kitchen counter, intrigued.

"Oh, you won't believe it! I was this giant butterfly robot, serving lemonade at a golf course!" Manu exclaimed, his hands gesturing animatedly. "Kaia was there, and he was just loving it. Everyone was buzzing about my upgraded butterflies!"

Sheri laughed, shaking her head. "Only you, Manu! Seriously, what's next? A robot that makes breakfast?"

"Hey, that's a brilliant idea!" Ron grinned. "Imagine a Butter-Bot 5000 whipping up pancakes while fluttering around the kitchen!"

Sheri rolled her eyes playfully. "Just don't let it take over the cooking duties, or we'll end up with butterfly-shaped omelets!" They all burst into laughter.

"Go take a shower, then come and have something to eat," Sherina told Manu.

After he showered, he put on green trousers with three pockets on each side. Sherina had bought him new clothes in Bulolo. He didn't know how she managed it, but now he owned three t-shirts, three pairs of trousers, three pairs of underwear, a pair of shoes, and a new knapsack.

"Did you watch some TV late this morning, Manu?" asked Ron, who was reading the paper and sipping his cup of coffee.

"I was watching Transformers, and I don't know how I just fell asleep," Manu replied with a smile.

"The long ride from Bulolo must have worn us all out. I slept like a log, too," he laughed loudly.

"I did, too," chuckled Sherina as she brought beef sausages, baked beans, toast, and a glass of juice to Manu.

"Yes, we drove to Freddie's family store while you were still snoring and bought these," Sherina said with a grin.

"Oh really?" Manu asked, surprised.

"Yes, when we came back, you were still snoring," Ron said, looking at Manu with a kind smile.

"Did I really snore?" Manu asked, shocked.

"Yeah, you did," Ron replied, looking at him seriously.

The doctors both glanced at Manu, then burst out laughing. "Gotcha!" they exclaimed, pointing at Manu. Manu laughed, too, and they all enjoyed a jolly good breakfast together.

At around 10 AM, they pulled into the parking lot of Papindo Department Store. The sun hung high in the clear blue sky, casting a warm glow that made the asphalt shimmer like silver. The lot was alive with activity; cars of every shape and size maneuvered, their engines humming softly as shoppers hurried in and out, bags swinging from their arms.

To the left, a lively group of children played, their laughter ringing out like music, mingling with the distant honking of horns. They chased each other around a weathered concrete planter, bursting with vibrant flowers that swayed in the gentle breeze, their petals fluttering like colourful flags. A few pigeons pecked at crumbs left behind, darting away with a startled flutter as the kids approached.

Nearby, a couple of beggars sat against the store's exterior, their faces show stories of hardship and resilience. One elderly man, with a scruffy beard and tattered clothes, held a small cardboard sign that read, "K1.00 Tasol[9]". His eyes, though tired and sunken, sparkled with a hint of hope as passersby occasionally dropped coins into his outstretched hand.

The air was thick with the scent of fresh produce wafting from the store, mingling seamlessly with the dust kicked up by the busy foot traffic. Vendors set up makeshift stalls along the edges of the parking lot, selling everything from ripe bananas to intricate handmade crafts, their vibrant displays adding a splash of colour to the scene.

Manu stood there, his heart swelling with emotion. It felt like ages ago that he was scaling the streets of Lae, scavenging for soda cans, but it had only been a month or so. It was unbelievable how the universe twists and turns life around. Now, he was the shopper, not lingering outside, waiting for someone to toss out an empty soda can for him to collect.

What astonished him even more was that he was with two strangers from another country. As he and his companions stepped out of the vehicle, the warmth of the sun enveloped them like a comforting

---

9 K1 that's all

blanket, and a few curious onlookers turned to stare, their faces breaking into smiles.

Inside, they filled their cart with essential supplies: two hefty bales of 20 kg rice, a carton brimming with noodles, a carton of tinned fish, and two large packets each of tea, sugar, and salt. They also grabbed a litre of Mama's cooking oil and a 5kg bag of flour.

But it wasn't just the groceries. They ventured into the tools section, where they selected two sturdy bush knives, an axe gleaming with potential, a spade, a hammer, and a packet of nails—everything they needed for their ambitious plans.

As they loaded their haul into the vehicle, Manu couldn't shake the feeling of disbelief. The doctors treating him with such care were strangers—not just unfamiliar faces, but people from a different country altogether. It was overwhelming.

Unable to contain his curiosity any longer, he leaned toward Sherina, his voice barely above a whisper as they drove toward Bumbu settlement. "Why are you doing this?" he asked, his tone trembling with uncertainty.

"Doing what?" Ron, snuggled between them, turned to look at him, confusion on his face.

"You are treating me, as if I am your relative, buying me things and taking good care of me," tears were flowing from Manu's eyes. He couldn't help it.

Life was very unfair to him, for years, and now a turn of events from these two kind strangers, who belonged to another land.

Sherina and Ron looked at each other and then Ron stopped the vehicle next to Phil's motel and Sherina hugged Manu and Ron patted his head.

"We just want to help you out a bit. You are a great person, climbing the Blue Mountains for the sake of love, to take care of your grandfather. We want to let you know, we are here for you and we want to be your friends," Sherina told him in a kind soft voice.

"You need friends like us. You are a unique child," Ron finished off for Sherina. Then he started the engine and they all drove off to Bumbu settlement.

When they arrived at Bubu Pellie's house, he was sitting on the patapata Manu had built for him, cradling a cup of tea while gazing out at the shimmering Bumbu River.

As soon as Manu jumped out of the vehicle, he sprinted toward his grandfather, wrapping his arms around him in a tight embrace. Bubu Pellie was taken aback, his mouth opening in surprise as he processed how Manu had come, especially since he last saw him five days ago, climbing down the Bumbu River cliff.

"Manu? Is that really you?" Bubu Pellie exclaimed, looking at him with wide, incredulous eyes. "I thought you were still up in those mountains!"

"Yes, Bubu! I came back! I wanted to see you," Manu replied, his voice full of excitement. "I've made new friends too! They're here with me."

Bubu Pellie shook his head slowly, still trying to grasp the situation. "I can't believe it! You've been through so much, my boy. It's unbelievable to see you here, so full of life. How did you manage to climb back down so quickly?"

Manu grinned, his eyes sparkling with joy. "It was a bit tough, but I had to hurry back to you. I missed you! And I wanted to introduce you to Doctor Sherina and Professor Ron."

Bubu Pellie's expression softened, a mixture of pride and confusion washing over him. "You always surprise me, Manu. It's not every day that a young man descends from the mountains with friends in tow. You've grown so much."

With a beaming smile, Manu stepped back slightly and gestured to his new friends. "This is Doctor Sherina and Professor Ron. They study wildlife up in the Blue Mountains. And this is my grandfather, Bubu Pellie."

Bubu Pellie's expression softened as he grasped Sherina's hand firmly, his smile radiating warmth. "Welcome to our home, Doctor and Professor. It's a true pleasure to meet you both."

"We're honoured to meet you, Bubu Pellie," Ron replied, his voice warm and inviting as he shook Bubu Pellie's hand. "Please, just call us Sherina and Ron. We've heard wonderful things about you."

Sherina chimed in, her eyes sparkling, "Manu speaks so highly of you. It's clear he loves you very much. You've raised a remarkable young man."

Bubu Pellie chuckled softly, a proud glint in his eyes. "He's a good boy, always looking out for me. It's wonderful to see him with friends like you. Tell me, what brings you to our little corner of the world?"

Sherina exchanged a glance with Ron before answering, "We're conducting research on the unique wildlife in the Blue Mountains, but we also believe in connecting with the local community. Manu's stories about you inspired us."

"Stories?" Bubu Pellie asked, intrigued. "What stories does he tell?"

Manu jumped in, his enthusiasm bubbling over. "I told them about how you taught me to fish in the river and how you always know the best places to find wild fruits. They want to see all the beautiful things you've shown me!"

Bubu Pellie's heart swelled at Manu's words. "Ah, the river has many secrets. Perhaps I can show you both some of those hidden treasures while you're here."

Ron nodded eagerly. "We'd love that! It would be an honour to learn from you."

Soon, a lively crowd gathered around them, drawn by the presence of the newcomers. Sherina and Ron engaged warmly with the villagers, sharing smiles and laughter as they exchanged captivating stories about the vibrant wildlife in the Blue Mountains. Meanwhile, Manu busily carried all the goods into their hut, a sense of determination fueling his every movement.

After the initial excitement settled, Ron and Sherina turned their focus to Manu and Bubu Pellie. They stepped aside for a more private conversation, their expressions shifting to serious yet compassionate.

"Manu," Ron began, his voice steady, "we want to help you and your grandfather. Here's K200 to get you started on your plans."

Bubu Pellie looked at Ron in surprise, his brow furrowing. "You're very generous, but we cannot accept this without understanding your intentions."

"Bubu Pellie," Sherina interjected gently, "Manu will explain what he intends to do." She noted Bubu Pellie's unease and offered a reassuring smile as he apologised for his cautiousness.

Sherina continued, her tone warm. "We believe in what you're doing. Manu, we need you to prepare your plot of land. We'll be back in a week to see how you're progressing."

Manu's eyes widened, a mix of excitement and disbelief washing over him. "You really mean it? You'll come back?"

"Absolutely," Sherina confirmed, her voice filled with encouragement. "We want to see you succeed."

With that, Ron and Sherina enveloped Manu in a tight hug, and he felt a surge of gratitude and hope. "Thank you! I won't let you down." he exclaimed, his heart racing with promise.

Bubu Pellie shook both of their hands firmly, his voice thick with emotion. "Thank you for believing in my grandson. Your kindness will not be forgotten."

As they were about to leave, Maoru arrived, balancing a bundle of firewood atop her head.

"Manu!" she yelled, her face lighting up as she dropped the firewood and rushed to embrace him.

"This is Maoru, my late Bubu Naris's friend. I asked her to look after Bubu Pellie while I hiked up the mountains," Manu introduced smilingly.

Sherina and Ron extended their hands to Maoru, who smiled shyly, her cheeks flushing with warmth at the attention.

With heartfelt farewells, they climbed into their vehicle. Sherina turned back one last time, her voice carrying over the whispers of the crowd. "Take care of each other. We'll see you soon!"

The neighbours crowded around Manu, their faces alight with curiosity. "How did you meet such wonderful people?" one of them asked, leaning in closer.

Manu beamed, his excitement bubbling over. "It's a bit of a long story, but I'll tell you!" He took a deep breath and began recounting his adventure, describing how he met Doctor Sherina and Professor Ron during his climb in the Blue Mountains.

As he spoke, Bubu Pellie listened intently, pride swelling in his chest. The crowd hung on Manu's every word, their eyes widening as he shared the details of his journey and the kindness the doctors showed him.

"Can you believe it?" Manu said, his voice filled with wonder. "They helped me so much and promised to return!"

Karia, an older woman with a warm smile, shook her head in disbelief. "What a miraculous turn of events! Life has a way of surprising us, doesn't it?"

Bamba chimed in, "You're such a brave boy, Manu! Climbing those mountains and meeting them—what courage you have!"

Bubu Pellie nodded, his voice full of emotion. "You have made us all proud, my grandson. Your spirit and determination are truly inspiring."

The crowd erupted into applause, shaking Manu's hands enthusiastically. "Congratulations!" they cheered. "You're a hero to us!"

Manu wished everyone well and thanked them.

Bubu Pellie was immensely proud of his grandson. He held Manu's hand firmly, their fingers intertwined as they walked toward their hut. "I know you are meant for bigger things, Manu," he said, his voice rich with warmth and conviction. "Yahweh has blessed you for being such a kind grandson to Bubu Naris and me. You will see, my grandson, you are destined for greatness."

Manu smiled, feeling the weight of his grandfather's heartfelt words. "I hope so, Bubu. More than anything, I want to make you proud."

Once inside the hut, Manu took a deep breath, excitement bubbling within him like a fizzy drink. "I've been thinking a lot about what I want to do with the land," he began, his eyes sparkling with determination. "I want to start a butterfly farm."

Bubu Pellie raised an eyebrow, intrigued and encouraging. "A butterfly farm? That sounds wonderful! But tell me more about it."

"I envision a place where different species of butterflies can thrive," Manu explained, pacing slightly as he spoke, his enthusiasm palpable. "I'll plant flowers that attract them and provide a safe habitat. It'll be beautiful! We can collect the pupae, dry them, and sell them. Imagine the colours and the joy it will bring!"

A broad smile spread across Bubu Pellie's face, his heart swelling with pride. "That's a brilliant idea, Manu! You have such vision."

"I need your help to mark the boundary around the land," Manu replied eagerly. "I want to ensure there's enough space for the butterfly farm. I met Doctor Sherf in Bulolo, and he took me to Makanda's farm. I learned so much about what needs to be done!"

Bubu Pellie nodded, his eyes gleaming with admiration as Manu continued to explain his plans. "We can make this dream a reality together, my boy. I'll help you every step of the way."

Early in the morning, Bubu Pellie took Manu for a walk around his block of land, carefully showing him the boundaries by marking them with sticks pushed into the ground. "This is not just my land, Manu. This is our land," Bubu Pellie said, smiling warmly at him.

Manu looked around, absorbing the beauty of the surroundings. "But what do you mean, Bubu?"

Bubu Pellie continued as they walked, "The truth is, this land will be yours, Manu, once I am gone." As they marked the boundary, the weight of Bubu Pellie's words hung in the air, and he was filled with hope.

After warm breakfast of tea and crispy fried flour balls, Manu reached for a K100 note and made his way to a stall at Kamkumung Market to exchange it for K2 and K5 notes. With cash in hand, he headed to Omili Primary School, where he purchased 15 bundles of vibrant hibiscus and xora plant cuttings.

He felt satisfied with his acquisitions and strolled over to the bus stop, catching sight of five street boys hanging out nearby.

"Hey, naispla ol bestie yia!" Manu called out, waving his hand. "Who wants to help me carry bundles of fresh cuttings to my land? I'll hook you up with some cash!"

The boys perked up, exchanging excited glances. One lanky kid with a wide grin stepped forward. "You know we're down! How much you givin' us?"

"Let's say K10 each if you help me out," Manu replied, watching their eyes light up with anticipation.

"Sweet deal!" another boy exclaimed. "We need some cash for our rolls, man!"

"Alright, let's do this!" Manu leading them to Omili Primary School. "Just be careful with the cuttings; they're delicate."

"Yeah, yeah, we got this!" the first boy assured him, balancing a bundle on his shoulder. "Lead the way to your land, boss!"

As they walked, the boys chatted and joked, their laughter echoing down the road. Manu felt energised and motivated, ready to work hard and bring his butterfly farm vision to life.

After collecting the bundles, Manu turned to the boys with an idea. "Hey, would you guys be willing to help me clear my land a bit more? I can give you K12 each once we're done."

The boys exchanged eager glances, excitement lighting up their faces. "You know we're in!" the lanky kid replied, nodding enthusiastically. "What do we need to do?"

"First, we need to clear out the weeds and debris," Manu explained, gesturing to the overgrown plot next to his house. "Once that's done, we can dig around the edges and plant the hibiscus and xora cuttings.

It'll make a great boundary for my butterfly farm!"

"Sounds like a plan, boss!" said one of the shorter boys, grabbing a handful of weeds. "Let's make this place look good!"

As they worked, laughter filled the air. "You sure you know what you're doing, Manu?" teased the mischievous boy. "This garden looks like it could use a miracle!"

"Every garden can be transformed!" Manu laughed back. "Just wait and see."

After a while, as they took a break, Manu asked, "By the way, I don't think I've properly introduced myself. I'm Manu. What are your names?"

The lanky kid stepped forward. "I'm Shala. Ready to dig."

"I'm Imaka," said another boy with a bright smile. "Let's make this garden awesome!"

"Doni here" chimed in the third boy, waving his hand. "I'm all about the butterflies!"

"James," said the fourth, nodding. "I can't wait to see how this turns out!"

"And I'm Shan," the last boy added with a grin. "Let's get to work!"

Once the plot was cleared, Manu clapped his hands. "Alright, now let's dig around the edges for the cuttings."

"Digging is our specialty!" Shala shouted, grabbing a spade. "We'll have this done in no time!"

With teamwork, they dug deep holes around the plot while others carefully placed the hibiscus and xora cuttings into the ground.

"Make sure they're close together," Manu instructed, kneeling beside them. "We want a nice, secure fence of plants."

"Like a fortress!" Shala added, grinning as he planted his cutting with care. "No one will mess with your butterflies!"

"Exactly! And it'll look beautiful," Manu replied, feeling a surge of excitement. "Just imagine all the colors when they bloom!"

When they finished, the boys stood back to admire their work.

"Not bad for a day's effort, huh?" Doni said, wiping his brow.

"Yeah! We're like garden heroes." James chimed in, puffing out his chest proudly.

"Thanks for the help, everyone," Manu said, genuinely grateful. "You've made this place come alive. Now, let's celebrate with some food."

Just then, the delicious aroma of lunch wafted through the air. Manu turned to see Maoru and Bubu Pellie preparing a hearty meal of rice with fried vegetables.

"Wow, that smells amazing!" Imaka exclaimed, his stomach rumbling.

Bubu Pellie stepped outside with a warm smile. "We made plenty, boys! Come and get it while it's hot!"

As they gathered around and sat on the patapata, the boys dug in with enthusiasm. "This is the best reward!" Doni said, savouring a mouthful. "You're a legend, Bubu Pellie!"

"Yeah, this is awesome!" James added, his eyes wide with delight.

Maoru chuckled as she served everyone. "You all worked hard today. You deserve a good meal!"

After finishing their plates, Shala leaned back with a satisfied grin. "If you ever need help again, just call us, Manu. We're always available."

"Absolutely!" Shan chimed in. "We love working with you!"

Manu smiled, "I really appreciate that, guys. I know where to find you, and I'll definitely need your help again soon. There's always more work to be done."

"Count us in!" Imaka said, raising his hand like he was taking an oath. "We're ready for the next job!"

Feeling energised by the meal, the boys laughed and chatted, their spirits high. As they finished up, Manu couldn't help but feel grateful for the newfound friendships and the promise to engage them when he needed help with his butterfly farm.

"Thanks again for the lunch, Maoru and Bubu Pellie. You two are the best," Manu said, beaming with appreciation.

"Anytime, Manu. We're here to support you," Maoru replied, giving him a friendly pat on the back.

With their bellies full and hearts light, the boys left as the sun was setting.

During the week, Manu and his grandfather worked very hard, planting hibiscus cuttings all around their land, blocking off any intruders that might want to come into their yard. Bubu Pellie looked much healthier and stronger and for the first time, he was happy. He worked hard, like he used to when Bubu Naris was alive. Manu realised that the sadness that floated around him, was nowhere to be seen anymore. Bubu Pellie whistled a happy tune for the whole week, they worked and planted cuttings of hibiscus, xora and other plants around their land.

Manu went and called the boys to come around and help for a couple of days more, as Maoru cooked their lunch. It was tiring working in the hot sun, but they always ran down to the Bumbu River swam for half an hour and then come back straight to the garden and started working again.

Their land looked quite different. It was developed and organised. Even some of their nosey neighbours kept asking Bubu Pellie, what was going on and he always told them that Manu was developing their land and later they will see, what he was doing. They didn't ask anymore.

During the second week, Manu went around Bumbu Settlement area and looked for plants that Doctor Sherf had showed him at Makanda's farm. He bought a lot of flowering vines. Then he went to the main market and bought citrus seedlings and other exotic plants with juicy flowers.

He came and planted them in the plot of land, he had fenced off with the boys, and then realised there were already, three citrus trees growing on the land, which used to be their garden. He was very pleased indeed. He planted the vines around the citrus and planted the other plant cuttings in an orderly fashion.

He watered the plants and took care of them, like babies every morning and evening. He just loved doing it.

On that Thursday, the doctors arrived with an array of vibrant plants they had purchased from Makanda's butterfly farm in Bulolo. As they approached, Sherina and Ron were truly stunned by the transformation they saw.

"Manu, this is incredible!" Sherina exclaimed, her eyes wide with admiration. "You and your grandfather have done such a fantastic job."

Manu beamed with pride. "Thanks, Sherina. It's been a lot of work, but seeing it come together feels amazing."

Ron bent down to inspect the plants. "These are beautiful! You've really created a special place here. I can't wait to see how it all flourishes."

Sherina nodded enthusiastically. "And I have some exciting news for you! Doctor Sherf mentioned that when you have everything ready, he would love to come down and visit your butterfly farm. He said to invite him."

"Wow, really?" Manu's face lit up with joy. "That's amazing! I am so thrilled."

Sherina smiled warmly. "He believes in your vision, Manu. You've shown so much bravery and hard work. It's inspiring."

"Thank you! I couldn't have done it without the help of both of you," Manu replied, feeling a sense of gratitude.

Ron added, "And don't forget to take care of yourself along the way. A healthy garden needs a healthy gardener!"

"Definitely! I'll make sure to rest and stay hydrated," Manu promised, nodding earnestly.

As they unloaded the new plants, Sherina said, "Let's get these in the ground so they can start thriving alongside the others. Your butterfly farm is going to be a sight to behold!"

With energy and excitement, Manu and the doctors worked together, planting the new arrivals.

16

Manu The Butterfly Collector

Manu and his grandfather created a vibrant garden filled with various plant species essential for the life cycles of butterflies. Their ideal butterfly farm spanned approximately 0.1 hectares, providing ample space for nurturing food plants for both adult butterflies and larvae. This area was sufficient to ensure that the plants were well-watered, regularly weeded, pruned, and meticulously cared for.

Within Manu's farm, they cultivated around 35 vines, which were elegantly grown on poles, reminiscent of climbing bean plants, while strategically placed shade trees offered refuge from the sun. The thoughtful design of the garden not only supported the butterflies but also created a serene environment for all who visited.

They also planted kaukau, tapiocas, aibikas, taros and cabbages all in rows. Such hard work, but Manu was keen to establish a well-set garden that would attract a lot of butterflies. Manu planted Aristolochia tagala, a vine on which the larvae of more common birdwing butterflies' feed. Another he planted was Evodea, a food plant of the large blue Ulysses swallowtail and many colourful weevils. These two plants were provided by the doctors who told Manu that they were very special.

Doctor Sherf had told Manu that the shade trees can also be food plants for butterflies other than birdwings and for beetles or weevils. In the garden there was already a Soursop tree, a Citrus tree and a breadfruit tree.

Manu and his grandfather also built a nursery for growing seeds and cuttings. In this nursery, they always water and care for the butterfly food plants. They place drums around the garden that they covered with fly wire. These drums collected rainwater that they used to water the plants in the garden.

They kept working each day and the different kinds of plants grew. The vines started sprouting leaves and creeping up the trees. The other plants sprouted and grew as well. It was awesome, watching the changes happening in the garden.

After more than three months, the garden had blossomed into a vibrant array of tropical flowering plants. The air was filled with the sweet scent of nectar, and soon, butterflies started fluttering in from seemingly nowhere. One sunny morning, as Manu tended to the blossoms, he spotted a butterfly dancing through the air.

"Bubu! Look!" he called excitedly to his grandfather.

Bubu walked over, squinting against the sunlight. "Where, Manu?"

"Right there! The one with the orange and black wings!" Manu exclaimed, pointing.

Just then, a second butterfly joined the first, followed by a third that flitted close to Maoru, whose yellow hair sparkled like sunshine.

"Whoa, that one almost landed on my head!" Maoru laughed, her eyes wide with wonder.

"Maybe it thinks your hair is a flower!" Manu teased, grinning at her.

As the days passed, the garden became a haven for these delicate creatures. By the end of the week, six butterflies were flitting about, their colors creating a breathtaking spectacle.

Two weeks later, the garden was alive with even more activity. Different kinds of butterflies arrived in numbers, their wings painted in hues of blue, yellow, and purple.

"Look at that one!" Bubu pointed to a striking blue morpho. "It's magnificent!"

"Can we name them?" Maoru suggested eagerly. "I want to call that one 'Sky Dancer' because of its colour!"

"Great idea! I'll name the orange one 'Sunset Flyer,'" Manu added, his heart racing with excitement.

"Let's keep a notebook to record all the butterflies we see," Bubu proposed. "It will help us learn more about them."

"That's an excellent idea, Bubu Pellie," Manu laughed and started counting the butterflies again.

Manu realised that each butterfly species had a preferred food plant for its larvae. He observed that after the female had mated, she searched for the correct plant and laid her eggs on or near it. In a few days the eggs hatch, and the young caterpillars ate their own eggshells and began feeding on the softer leaves and shoots of the food plant.

The caterpillars grew and turned into cocoons, pupae then adult butterflies.

Manu continuously read the notes that Doctor Sherf had given him and watched the butterflies, as they hatched from larvae, to caterpillars and then to adult butterflies. They multiplied in numbers and Manu's garden came alive with fluttering colours.

The doctors had been away at the University of Papua New Guinea, completing a project for the last six weeks, and Manu couldn't help but wish they were there to witness the transformation of his lively, colourful garden.

One sunny morning, as the sun cast a warm glow on the blossoms, Bubu Pellie stood admiring the fluttering spectacle around him. "My grandson, your butterflies are multiplying in numbers!" he exclaimed, a proud smile spreading across his face.

"Yes, Bubu Pellie! It's incredible!" Manu replied, his eyes sparkling with enthusiasm. "Just yesterday, I counted ten different species. I can hardly believe how quickly they're coming."

Bubu chuckled, his voice rich with warmth. "It seems they've taken a liking to your garden, Manu. You've tended to it with such care."

Manu nodded, his mind racing with ideas. "You know, I think it's time to ask Doctor Sherf to come and show us how to dry the butterflies. Imagine having them preserved. We could create a beautiful display for everyone to see."

"Great idea!" Maoru chimed in, her eyes bright. "We could even host an exhibition. People would love to learn about the butterflies and how we're helping them thrive."

"That's right!" Bubu added, his enthusiasm matching theirs. "We can show the community how special this garden is and share the knowledge we've gained."

Manu's heart raced at the thought. "Let's write a letter to Doctor Sherf today! I want him to see how our garden has come to life."

"I'll help you!" Maoru offered, her smile infectious.

"I mean, I can't write but I will speak and you write," Maoru quickly added and they all started laughing.

As the month of May neared its end, Manu felt a surge of excitement; his Butterfly Farm was ready for its first harvest. The hedges stood tall and robust, the garden was impeccably clean, and the plants were bursting with vibrant flowers. Best of all, countless butterflies flitted about, painting the air with their delicate colours.

While it all seemed effortless, Manu knew that significant hard work lay behind this beautiful scene. He diligently weeded, pruned, and watered the garden, ensuring each plant received the care it needed. Fortunately, Lae was blessed with frequent rain, making it easy to collect water in the 44-gallon drums positioned next to the nursery and scattered throughout the garden.

Meanwhile, Bubu Pellie and Maoru busied themselves at the Kamkumung Market, selling kaukau, tapioca, and aibikia leaves, earning money every day. Maoru was a tremendous help in the butterfly garden as well, planting kaukau, tapioca, and taro, and lending a hand with weeding and watering the nursery.

That night, as the stars twinkled overhead, Manu sat at his little table. The soft glow of the kerosene lamp illuminated his focused expression as he penned a letter to Doctor Sherf, eager to share the flourishing progress of their garden and seek guidance for the next steps ahead.

Dear Doctor Sherf

Hello and, how are you?

This is your friend Manu Aneva, whom you taught how to rear butterflies and that you send word with Doctor Sherri and Professor Ron that you are interested to see what I am doing and what I have done.

I am officially inviting you to come and visit my butterfly farm. I would suggest you come this Thursday, so I will wait for you at Anderson's Foodland at 4:30pm and we arrange your visit to my butterfly farm the next day.

Doctor, I believe the butterflies are ready to be harvested, so I am now depending on you to show me how it is done.

Awaiting your arrival with zeal and great excitement.

Your friend

Manu

The next morning Manu woke up very early and worked in the Butterfly Farm. Maoru helped him to weed the hedges and his grandfather planted new tapioca stems.

At around 11:30am, Manu got on a bus and went to the Bulolo Bus Station. He saw an older driver and went over to him.

"Good afternoon *bestie*," he greeted the driver.

"Good afternoon, *nais wan*. Do you want to go to Bulolo?" the driver asked smiling.

"No, I just want to send a letter to Doctor Sherf. Do you know him?" Manu went closer to the driver.

"The butterfly doctor, who lives near the airstrip?" the driver looked seriously at Manu.

"Yes, that's the one. Can you deliver a letter to him please?" Manu asked kindly and smiled.

"Of course, sure I can," the driver replied as he got the letter from Manu.

Manu pushed his hand into his pocket and got a K5 note and gave it to him.

"Buy your Pepsi and flour balls."

"Thank you. Don't worry, I will give this letter to the butterfly doctor, as soon as I arrive in Bulolo", he assured Manu with a big smile.

Throughout the week, Manu, Bubu Pellie and Maoru worked in the garden from morning until around lunch time. The butterflies even sat on Maoru's ginger coloured hair and Bubu Pellie laughed and said, "Maybe they think, it is some kind of flower with nectar."

There were so many butterflies and they made the garden so beautiful, by their silent fluttering, appreciating the flowers everywhere.

On Thursday, Manu woke up around six o'clock and worked in the Butterfly Farm. He weeded around the hedges, pruned the flowering trees, polished up the nursery and whispered to the hundreds of butterflies and told them that a very important man named Doctor Sherf was coming to visit.

Finally, he stood at the edge and admired his colourful garden that he had made with the help of his grandfather and Maoru. *How awesome*, he thought. He was worried a bit that the beautiful butterflies were going to be dried and sold. They were so beautiful, living, breathing and enjoying the nectar of the flowers in the garden. But this was business and all along, he had made this garden to breed butterflies for money, so he can go back to school and take good care of Bubu Pellie. There are so many butterflies in Morobe Province, it's not that I am going to dry them all and sell them, *No*, he reassured himself. *I called and invited these beauties here by slaving to grow these plants and flowers, so it's time to harvest*, he cheered himself and answered his Bubu's call to go and eat his kaukau with a cup of hot tea.

"Thank you Bubu, for this breakfast," Manu sat down as he washed his hands in the drum water.

"You woke up very early today, my grandson. What are your plans for the day?" Bubu Pellie asked as he handed him his breakfast.

"Oh Bubu Pellie, have you forgotten? Doctor Sherf is coming from Bulolo today," Manu smiled and munched his kaukau.

"Oh, that is right. I seem very forgetful these days," Bubu Pellie shook his head and sat next Manu.

"It's okay Bubu Pellie, I forgot to remind you in the morning," Manu smiled at his Grandfather, as he sipped his tea.

"I will go to Anderson's Foodland after 3pm today and wait for Doctor Sherf. Then we will come here and he will see the Butterfly farm," Manu explained to his Grandfather.

"Then after he has inspected the butterflies, he will tell us whether they are ready to be harvested or not. If they are ready, he will show us how to go about drying them and what kind of chemicals we are to use. If they are not yet ready, he will come back at a later date."

"Okay, that is good," Bubu Pellie smiled at his grandson.

"You have worked very hard to make your Butterfly Farm come to reality Manu," Bubu said softly.

"I would not have done it without your help Bubu Pellie and of course Maoru too," Manu was grateful and it was obvious that he had truly appreciated his Grandfather's commitment in helping him grow the Butterfly Farm.

By 3pm, Manu was already waiting for Doctor Sherf in front of Andersons Foodland in Eriku. He looked at the vehicles as they drove into the car park. There were mostly parents who were stopping by to buy late lunches for their school children before driving them home.

As Manu turned to swat an annoying fly, he saw Kaia hurrying over to him smiling.

"Hey Manu, my main boy. What are you doing here? I thought you were out chopping firewood in the mountains," Kaia yelled shaking his hand.

"Ha, ha, ha," laughed Manu. "No, Kaia, I am just at Bumbu."

"You know what?" Kaia slapped Manu on his back. "I've been hired by two Australian Professional golfers. One of them is a close friend of Tiger Woods and they've golfed around the world.

"Hey, that's great Kaia," Manu smiled at him.

"They pay me K50 a day, boy. Come on, I'll buy us two cans of coke and meat pies," and with that he pulled Manu into the shop.

Kaia bought their food and gave a K10 to Manu. He tried to decline but Kaia shoved the K10 into his trousers pocket.

"Hey, very nice trousers with one, two, three, four, five, six pockets. Boy, where did you get this from? And cool sneakers too," Kaia squealed punching Manu's shoulders.

"Thank you, Kaia. It's a long story, where I got these from," Manu chuckled as he munched on the chunks of meat within the pie. He opened the coke and drank a mouthful. All tasted so good after a hard day of work in the sun.

"Hey, you waitin' for a girl or somethin'? Kaia scowled at Manu, talking in his caddie language.

"No. Hahahaha," Manu laughed and pretended to punch Kaia. "I am waiting for Doctor Sherf."

"Doctor Sherf? Who is that?" Kaia asked confused. "Are you dealing with Marijuana, boy?" Kaia looked around eyeing to see who Manu was waiting for.

"No, I am not. Hahaha" Manu laughed until his eyes glistened. They always had great fun when they were caddies at the golf course. Kaia was lively, funny and full of crazy talk and had always lightened up Manu's dull days, back then.

"He is from Poland in Europe. He is coming down from Bulolo to check my butterflies," Manu smiled at Kaia and then drank the last of his coke.

"Whaaaat?" You butterfly keeper now?" Kaia asked in surprise.

"Yeah, I guess," Manu chuckled and then both of them saw a Land Rover, covered in dirt driving into Andersons Foodland car park.

"That's him there," Manu pointed and waved at Doctor Sherf, who waved back at him.

"Wow, you were always too smart to carry golf sticks," Kaia laughed as he followed Manu to the car park.

"Hello Manu. How are you?" Doctor Sherf came out of his truck and greeted him.

Manu smiled at the Doctor. "Hello Doctor Sherf, I am good thank you. Welcome to Lae. I am very pleased that you could come," Manu greeted Doctor Sherf and shook his hand.

"It is truly my pleasure, Manu," Doctor Sherf smiled back at Manu.

"This is Kaia. A friend of mine," Manu pointed at Kaia.

"Hello Kaia. How do you do?" Doctor Sherf shook Kaia's hands and smiled at him too.

"I am very well, thank you Doctor," Kaia shook the doctor's hand and gave a little bow.

They chatted animatedly for a while, with Kaia impressing Dr. Sherf with tales of his time at the Country Club.

"You won't believe it, Dr. Sherf! I was Tiger Woods' caddie last week!" Kaia exclaimed, his eyes sparkling with excitement.

"No way! What was that like?" Dr. Sherf asked, leaning in with genuine interest.

"It was incredible! I handed him the clubs, and he gave me some tips on my swing. I felt like a pro just being there." Kaia replied, grinning from ear to ear.

"Did he hit any amazing shots?" Manu chimed in, his curiosity piqued in a playful manner, laughing softly.

"Oh, absolutely! He sunk a 30-foot putt that had everyone cheering. I swear the whole country club was buzzing." Kaia laughed, clearly reliving the moment.

As the clock approached 4:15 PM, Kaia glanced at his watch. "I've got to run and meet Chay and the other caddies. Catch you later!" he said, giving a friendly wave.

Manu waved back, excitement bubbling inside him as he climbed into Dr. Sherf's Land Rover.

"I am ready to see your farm, boy." Dr. Sherf smiled as he reversed the vehicle.

"Absolutely! I can't wait to show you everything." Manu replied, a wide grin spreading across his face as they merged onto the main road.

"Did he really meet Tiger?" Dr. Sherf asked, glancing over at Manu with a playful smile.

"Noooo, Dr. Sherf! Kaia is full of nonsense just to spark up a laugh," Manu explained, his eyes twinkling with amusement. They both burst into hearty laughter.

"I wouldn't mind a friend like Kaia!" Doctor Sherf mused as he changed the gear.

17

Young Achiever's Award

Dr. Sherf parked his Land Rover outside Manu and his grandfather's hut. As they both stepped out, Bubu Pellie and Maoru came rushing from behind the hedges, panting with excitement.

"Doctor Sherf! You made it!" Bubu Pellie exclaimed, bounding forward. Maoru followed, smiling shyly from behind.

"Doctor Sherf, this is my Grandfather, Bubu Pellie," Manu introduced, beaming with pride.

Bubu Pellie gripped the doctor's right hand with both of his, his face lighting up with warmth. "Welcome to our block of land, Doctor! We're thrilled to have you here."

"Thank you, Bubu Pellie. It's truly my pleasure to be here," Dr. Sherf replied, returning the handshake with a firm grip and a smile that radiated sincerity.

"Doctor Sherf, this is Maoru. She helps us at the Butterfly Farm," Manu continued, gesturing toward Maoru as she stepped forward, giggling shyly.

"Pleased to meet you, Maoru," Dr. Sherf said, shaking her hand gently. "I've heard wonderful things about your work with the butterflies."

Maoru's cheeks flushed as she nodded her head, barely able to contain her excitement. "Thank you! I love working with them. They're so beautiful!"

"I can't wait to see what you've all created here," Dr. Sherf smiled, looking from Manu to Maoru, his eyes sparkling with enthusiasm.

"Let's go show you!" Manu urged, his voice filled with eagerness.

"Lead the way!" Dr. Sherf replied smiling.

Manu led the way around the hedges, with Dr. Sherf close behind, eager to see the butterflies. In no time at all, they arrived at the edge of the garden. Dr. Sherf paused, overwhelmed by the vibrant array of colours fluttering all around him. He stood in silence for a moment, taking it all in, while Manu felt a flicker of worry.

Was something amiss?

"Manu, this is wonderful!" the doctor finally exclaimed, shaking Manu's hand vigorously.

Manu exhaled slowly, a wave of relief washing over him. If Dr. Sherf were a smaller man, Manu would have lifted him off the ground in sheer joy.

"This is one of the best butterfly farms I've ever seen. Unbelievable," Dr. Sherf added, his smile brightening as he began to explore the garden. "How did you manage to create such a vibrant habitat?"

"I've worked hard to create the right environment," Manu replied, beaming. "It took a lot of patience and learning from mistakes."

Dr. Sherf nodded, admiration in his eyes. "Your dedication really shows. It's not easy to cultivate such a rich ecosystem."

Manu grinned, feeling a surge of pride. "I just wanted to make it a place where butterflies could thrive."

"Well, you've certainly succeeded," Dr. Sherf smiled, his gaze scanning the fluttering wings. "I'm truly impressed. Every detail is remarkable."

As they continued to explore, Dr. Sherf paused to examine a cluster of pupae. "These look healthy! You must be doing everything right."

Manu beamed. "Thank you! I really enjoy taking care of them."

Dr. Sherf smiled warmly. "And it shows. Your hard work is paying off, Manu. I'm very pleased with what you've accomplished here."

Manu could see the genuine impression on the doctor's face, and his heart swelled with pride. At that moment, he felt like the happiest person in the world, knowing that Dr. Sherf approved of his butterfly farm.

"Thank you, Dr. Sherf. Your support means so much to me," Manu expressed, his voice filled with gratitude.

"Let's keep exploring!" Dr. Sherf replied, his enthusiasm infectious as they continued their tour of the beautiful garden.

Doctor Sherf asked Bubu Pellie to let Manu go with him that night, because they needed to discuss butterfly preservation.

"That is all right Doctor Sherf," Bubu Pellie smiled, pleased with the positive feedback from him about the Butterfly Farm. Bubu Pellie felt a kind of fulfilment that all the hard work throughout the months was not in vain. He totally believed that his Grandson's idea of rearing butterflies was truly a brilliant one.

They drove on to the University of Technology, to the house that Doctor Sherf usually stayed at, when he came down to work at The Rain Forest Habitat.

After a dinner of rice and tinned beef stew, the Doctor and Manu sat in the living room.

"Manu, I will now give you instructions on preserving butterflies then you can get on with your butterfly preservation."

The Doctor opened his brief case and got out some notes.

"Manu, your farm is well established and you have to collect the pupae daily. Ideally, you have to release and leave about 50 percent. At least as many females and males should be released. Pupae that are too high to reach, I suggest you leave, so to emerge naturally and repopulate the farm. When you see that a pupa is not quite perfect, leave that," the doctor paused and looked at Manu.

"You can usually see that emergence will occur on the next day, when the pupae become darker in colour as the adult wing and body colours develop. You can pluck off the stem or leaf to which the pupae are attached. Do not touch the soft new pupae, because it can be damaged."

Manu looked at the Doctor and nodded.

"Pin the leaf to a board or put it in a net or in a small cage. Keep the pupae inside so as to protect the pupae against pest and large predators. However, you and Bubu Pellie may construct small houses out of bush materials to hold pupae ready for hatching. If you keep your pupae in the open, then count on luck to collect the adults before they have flown away."

"Yes, Doctor Sherf, I understand," Manu told the Doctor, as he sat engrossed in his explanations.

"Care must be taken to protect the specimen from ants and rats. For example, the legs of the cage can be placed in bowls of water to deter ants from climbing up. Remember to spray the pupae with water 2 to 3 times a week to speed up the hatching process and to prevent them from drying out. Only use a light spray, otherwise the pupae develop mould."

The Doctor went to the fridge and poured two glasses of orange juice. He placed two straws into the cup and gave one to Manu.

"Thank you, Doctor," Manu smiled and put his drink on the coffee table.

"Keep the pupae in a shady place, so the butterflies will remain calm after hatching and will not flap and damage their wings," the Doctor took a long sip of his juice and cleared his throat. "Now, on to the preserving bit Manu," he smiled and lit his tobacco pipe. "When the newly emerged butterfly has completely dried its wings, carefully catch it by the thorax and inject it with a small amount of a killing agent such as ethyl acetate or boiling water. Small butterflies are particularly easily damaged if handled, so you can place them for about 10 minutes in a killing jar containing cotton (cotton wool) soaked with a little ethyl acetate. Place a layer of cardboard above the cotton, so that the butterflies are not stained by the solvent."

"I see," said Manu nodding his head.

"Place the dead butterflies in paper envelopes," the Doctor continued, puffing his tobacco. "Be careful at all times, not to touch or damage the wings. The envelopes are easily made from grease proof paper."

Manu looked at the Doctor and nodded.

"To make sure, that your butterflies will not mould, place them on a black plastic tray and dry them in the sun, in their papers, for about 4 days. The drying tray must have a screen on top to prevent the envelopes from blowing away or being rained on or to protect them from pests such as ants. Once properly dried, the insects still in their envelopes must be stored in boxes; preferably an air-tight container to prevent condensation or moulding. When you have collected enough specimens, you can pack them carefully in strong cardboard boxes with cotton or kapok. A few naphthalene crystals can be added to keep away pests and the box must be wrapped and sent to me in Bulolo."

"But Doctor, where will I buy the supplies for butterfly preserving?" Manu asked, a bit confused and worried.

"Aaaah Manu, I have brought you most of the things you will need. I am the boss at the Butterfly Preservation Agency in Bulolo. We supply preserving items to farmers who are ready to harvest their butterflies," the Doctor smiled at Manu.

Manu was so pleased, he stood up and shook Doctor Sherf's hand.

They had a breakfast of toast, coffee and tea and then got into the Land Rover. There was a busy day ahead at Manu's Butterfly Farm.

At 9 am Doctor Sherf and Manu arrived at Bumbu Settlement to the Butterfly Farm. The Doctor showed Manu, the Butterfly Preserving stuff he had brought with him. He unloaded them from under the canvas at the back of his Land Rover. There were jars, four containers of ethyl acetate, a dozen black plastic trays, 6 boxes of paper envelopes, a roll of fly wire, boards were in a carton, a bag of naphthalene crystal and a big green canvas.

"All these are your first supplies. When you run out let me know by sending me a note", Doctor Sherf informed Manu and Bubu Pellie. Then Doctor Sherf practically showed them by hand, the process he explained to Manu that night.

Bubu Pellie, quickly got his hammer and built a long fly screen cage. They placed the cage in the spare room in their hut and with the Doctor instructing, they collected the pupae and placed them in the cage carefully, but firmly.

"This farm is the breeding ground and you have perfect pupae" Doctor Sherf kept repeating.

By 3pm, Doctor Serf had instructed and practically shown Manu and Bubu Pellie the methods of preservation.

"I will be here in Lae for a week working at The Rain Forest Habitat. I will come here at 3pm every day. Manu and Bubu Pellie, keep preserving and I will check each time I come," he instructed them and drove back to the University of Technology.

After Doctor Sherf drove off, Manu talked to Bubu Pellie and Maoru and explained again, how fragile the pupae were. He told them to inform him of pupae sightings so he would be the only one to handle them until both of them had gotten used to the procedure.

The next morning, Manu and Bubu Pellie, built more fly screen cages and cut containers, filled them with water and stood the cages inside them. The spare room in their hut was filled with cages while all the other equipment was stored in the room they slept in.

There were pupae emerging and there were so many beautiful butterflies with many different colours.

Manu carefully caught them by the thorax and injected them with ethyl acetate and then carefully placed them in paper envelopes without touching their wings. He placed them in the black plastic trays and put them in the sun in their papers. The screen on the drying trays protected the butterflies from pests or being blown away or rained on.

At around 3pm each day, for the whole week, Doctor Sherf came and was always tremendously pleased with what Manu had done.

"Excellent Manu. This is excellent," he kept saying, as he looked at the drying butterflies in the paper envelopes.

18

Three Months Later

Published in *The PNG Post Courier,* October 2002

A remarkable achievement has emerged from Bumbu Settlement in Lae, Morobe Province, Papua New Guinea. Twelve-year-old Manu Aneva has been honoured with the prestigious Young Achiever's Award for 2002.

Against all odds, Manu has launched a thriving butterfly farm on his 0.1-hectare backyard. His journey began after a visit to Bulolo, where he learned about butterfly farming from renowned entomologist Dr. Marvin Sherf.

Embracing the art of butterfly farming, Manu dedicated himself to mastering the craft. Today, he proudly owns one of the finest butterfly breeding farms in Papua New Guinea and the Pacific Islands.

"His butterflies are perfect in form, and this young man preserves them expertly. I sell his butterflies to Australia, Europe, and the United States," stated Dr. Sherf, the Director of Butterfly Farming and Manager of the Agency in Bulolo, during an interview with **The Post Courier** yesterday.

In recognition of his outstanding efforts, Manu will receive K20,000 from ANZ Bank to support the growth of his butterfly farm. ANZ Bank annually awards Young Achievers throughout the Pacific Islands, celebrating the talent and determination of youth in the region.

Sherina and Ron returned from the University of Papua New Guinea, having completed their reports on the endangered species of Morobe Province. They gathered outside near Manu and Bubu Pellie's hut, perusing the article in the Post Courier. Bubu Pellie had tears in his eyes, and Maoru sat sniffing on the mat nearby.

"This is a dream come true for a young boy," Ron kept repeating, sipping his Diet Coke as he scanned the pages. "Can you believe how far Manu has come?"

Sherina rummaged through her handbag, her excitement unmistakable. After a moment, she pulled out a small envelope and announced, "Bubu Pellie, I would like to seek your permission for something special. Ron and I have a gift for Manu. After he receives his award tomorrow, we want to take him to Nevada at the end of November to spend four weeks with us."

Bubu Pellie looked thoughtful, then nodded firmly. "Yes, Sherina, you have my permission to take my grandson to your homeland. After all, you were the one who met him in the Blue Mountains and helped him succeed in his butterfly farm," he expressed seriously, without hesitation.

Manu sat there, confused and speechless, his heart racing at the unexpected news.

"Manu, is that okay with you?" Sherina asked gently, patting him on the head.

"Absolutely! Yes, thank you so much, Sheri!" Manu exclaimed, standing up in excitement. He hugged Sherina tightly and then shook Ron's hand with enthusiasm.

Ron smiled, his eyes twinkling with joy. "We can't wait to show you around Nevada, Manu. It'll be an adventure!"

Bubu Pellie wiped his eyes, a proud smile crossing his face. "Enjoy every moment, my boy. It's a wonderful opportunity."

Manu nodded, gratitude filling his heart. "I will, Bubu Pellie. I promise!"

The next day, Manu was awarded a K20, 000.00 Cheque over a formal dinner at Lae International hotel. Bubu Pellie, Doctor Sherina, Professor Ron and Doctor Sherf plus dear Maoru were all there.

Bubu Pellie and Mauro looked primed and articulate in their new clothes. Manu swallowed a lump in his throat, to see his grandfather happy and smiling.

The ANZ Bank Manager, did a short speech about the importance of entrepreneurship, thinking big and believing in your strength and capability, like young Manu Aneva did.

Manu recognised the Coca Cola Manager, who played golf at the Country club. Everyone shook Manu's hand and congratulated him.

The Post Courier and National Newspapers interviewed him and took pictures of him, plus everyone present at the formal dinner.

A well-dressed woman, who introduced herself to Manu as Wanda, who was the ANZ Bank secretary, presented him with a bouquet of fresh orchids, after Manu received his Award.

"For our butterfly boy," she smiled. "Yes, you deserve flowers too."

Manu handed the orchids to Sherina. "For that big bamboo vase up at the tree house," he whispered smiling.

"Oh, splendid idea, Manu," she smiled admiring the beautiful orchids.

Everyone was served like kings and queens by the beautiful smiling waitresses.

Sherina and Ron got into a serious conversation with the 8 Mile Crocodile Farm Manager, so Doctor Sherf drove Manu, Bubu Pellie and Maoru home to Bumbu Settlement, on his way to The University of Technology. "What a fulfilling night, Manu. I will see you all tomorrow." Then he bid them all goodnight and drove on to the university.

Manu, Bubu Pellie, and Maoru gathered around the pupae, their eyes wide with excitement as they observed a dozen butterflies already emerging, displaying vibrant black, blue, yellow, and green wings.

"Look at this one!" Manu exclaimed, pointing to a particularly striking butterfly. "It's beautiful!"

Bubu Pellie smiled, his heart swelling with pride. "I am so proud of you, my grandson. You have worked so hard for this moment."

Manu turned to his grandfather, gratitude shining in his eyes. "I couldn't have done this without you, Bubu Pellie, and of course, Maoru as well. Your support has meant everything to me."

Maoru, sitting cross-legged on the ground, chimed in with a shy smile, "I love helping with the butterflies! It makes me so happy to see them grow."

"Your care and dedication has made a big difference, Maoru," Manu said, giving her a reassuring nod. "We make a great team."

"Just remember to enjoy the moment, Manu," Bubu Pellie advised, placing a gentle hand on his shoulder. "This is your achievement."

"I will, Bubu. Thank you for believing in me," Manu replied, feeling a wave of warmth and encouragement.

Maoru clapped her hands in excitement as another butterfly broke free from its pupa. "Look! It's ready to fly!"

19

Hello Nevada

In the next few weeks, there was a lot going on at Manu's Butterfly Farm. The days were filled with weeding, watering, pruning, and preserving the delicate habitat, while meetings with Sherina, Ron, and Bubu Pellie became routine. The primary purpose of these meetings was to prepare for Manu's trip to Nevada, ensuring that all necessary travel papers were filled out correctly.

One sunny afternoon, the group gathered under the shade of a large tree, with papers spread out on a wooden table.

"Alright, Manu, let's go through these travel documents," Bubu Pellie said, a serious look on his face. "It's important we get everything right."

Manu nodded, looking over the forms. "I want to make sure I have everything I need for the trip."

Sherina smiled, encouraging him. "You'll do great, Manu. Just think about all the amazing experiences waiting for you."

Ron added, "And don't forget to share your journey with everyone back home. They'll want to hear all about it!"

"I will! I want to tell them what I learn," Manu replied, his excitement growing.

As they continued filling out the forms, Bubu Pellie asked, "Have you thought about what you'll say when you meet new people?"

"I want to tell them about the butterflies and how important they are to our environment," Manu replied, determination in his voice.

"That's a wonderful idea," Sherina said. "Your passion for butterflies is inspiring."

Maoru, sitting nearby, chimed in, "And when you come back, you have to tell us everything! I want to hear all about Nevada!"

"Of course, Maoru! I'll bring back stories and maybe some souvenirs," Manu promised, smiling at her enthusiasm.

Doctor Sherf collected all the dried butterflies for the tenth time and went back to Bulolo. Manu's butterfly farm was now registered as a Business under the name, 'Aneva's Butterflies'. All his payment was deposited into 'Aneva's Butterflies' ANZAC Bank Account.

Bubu Pellie was very good with book-keeping and kept all payments, spending and wages up to date.

Bubu Pellie and Manu built a better and modern house with roofing Iron and bamboo walls. The house's plan was drawn and prepared by Manu and he paid Kaia's big brother, who was a carpenter to build the house. It was like a bungalow over-looking the Bumbu River below and the Blue Mountains far beyond. The rooms were wide and airy and the flooring was laid out with timber and then covered with a forest-leaf-design floor mat. The windows had fly screens and curtains. There was a long veranda at the front where Bubu Pellie and Manu entertained visitors who come to visit the Butterfly Farm.

They kept their old hut for the pupae, with Maoru sleeping in their old room. She refused to move to the new house.

"I will sleep here and make-sure the pupae are well taken care of," she told Manu and Bubu Pellie in a serious tone of voice.

Bubu Pellie and Maoru faithfully collected the pupae, injected the butterflies and preserved them. They also tended the garden and made sure that all vines, trees and flowering plants were well taken care of. They obviously enjoyed taking care of the Butterfly Farm and of course, they were all getting enough money from the work they did. Bubu Pellie made sure, there was enough food and all other necessities were taken care of also. He also made sure that each of them was paid some wages at the end of each week.

Above all, Bubu Pellie also made sure some money was saved for Manu's education.

On a beautiful tropical dew kissed morning, as the golden sun rose beyond the Bumbu River, over the Blue Mountains; Manu hugged Bubu Pellie and Maoru goodbye. He hopped on the Airport Transfer Shuttle and was taken to Nadzab airport. When his flight was announced, he boarded the Air Niugini Fokker 28 and flew to Port Moresby to meet Sherina and Ron. They were going for their four weeks holiday in Nevada, USA.

His heart ached deeply for his dear grandfather, but he consoled himself that he would return after four weeks and see him again. He prayed silently that God would keep his Bubu Pellie safe, until they would see each other again.

Ron and Sherina picked him up from Jackson's Domestic Terminal and they all drove to the residential area of the University of Papua New Guinea.

On their way, Manu was in awe, seeing the freeway and the traffic lights, plus the many cars, trucks, buses, vans and there were so many taxis. There was no taxi service in Lae. People rode in PMVs (public motor vehicles) or open backed trucks are hired for K10.00 upwards. The taxis in Port Moresby[10] passed by in striking colours.

"Quite different from Lae, huh," Ron looked over at him smiling as he stopped at the traffic lights in Waigani.

"Yes, very different," Manu agreed with Ron. Manu looked to his right and saw an Asian woman driving a van. Her slanted eyes were focused on the gathering traffic as she maneuvered her way through

---

10 National Capital of Papua New Guinea

the queue. *Wonder if she sees properly*, Manu thought. *Her eyes seem small and narrow. She is very adept.*

After dinner, Ron called Manu over to the computer he was working on.

"Sheri, come over here and let's converse, will you?" Ron called out, as Sheri washed pots and plates in the kitchen.

"I will be there shortly, give me a second!" she answered rather loudly.

"See here Manu, this is the country of USA. There are 50 States in the US. I am from the state of Nevada."

"And which state is Sheri from?" Manu asked, looking closely at the US map on the computer.

"Oh, Sheri is originally from Germany," Ron smiled and waved at Sheri to come over to them.

"Really?" Manu looked at Ron and then at Sheri, who had just joined them.

"Yes, I am from Germany. We met at the University of Bonn, got married and then worked at Senckenberg German Entomological Institute".

Ron continued, "We moved to Nevada when our son Trevor was 5 years old and then settled at my family ranch, while doing research on endangered species, whenever we got hired by Universities and Research Institutions from around the world."

"Wow, that is one splendid story," Manu exclaimed, intrigued by the doctors. They were truly important people, yet they didn't act as if they were.

"Nevada is a Western US State, defined by the great expanses of desert and by the 24-hour casinos and entertainments for which, its largest city, Las Vegas is known," Ron related, as he sipped the hot coffee that Sheri had handed him.

Manu listened intently drinking the hot milo with the cookies that were placed in front of him.

"It's raining heavily outside Ron. Did you lock the front gate?" Sheri asked as she peeked out the window.

"I sure did," Ron informed his wife.

Sheri sat opposite Manu, smiling warmly at him. Manu returned her smile while sipping his milo, his thoughts drifting to Lae. He wondered if it was raining there, too, and if Bubu and Maoru were doing alright.

"It doesn't rain in Port Moresby as much as it does in Lae," Sheri stated, as if reading his mind. "I know that your butterfly farm is in excellent hands and you shouldn't worry. Your Bubu Pellie is busy, occupied and happy," Sheri smiled, as she turned on her laptop.

"Yes, he is happy and busy these days," Manu looked at Sheri and they both laughed.

"I heard the butterflies love Maoru's hair," Ron chuckled. They all started laughing.

"They certainly do," Manu said with a grin. "She dyes her hair in such vibrant colors."

"A moving flower, I'd say," Ron chuckled, laughter bubbling up from deep within.

Manu felt a mix of excitement and nervousness after hearing various stories about Nevada. He had once overheard expatriates discussing Las Vegas at the golf course and began to wonder if it truly was the entertainment hub they described.

"Ron, what's this city called Las Vegas? Is it where all the movie stars live?" he asked.

"Manu, Las Vegas, located in Nevada's Mojave Desert, is a resort city renowned for its vibrant nightlife, featuring 24-hour casinos and a variety of entertainment options," Ron explained, smiling at Manu as he flipped through the Traveller's Guide.

"It must be a hotspot for tourists, right, Ron?" Manu inquired.

"Oh yes, Manu! It's a popular destination for tourists, gamblers, and anyone seeking a bit of worldly fun," Ron explained.

"Of course, Manu! We will visit Las Vegas. You'll see," Sheri added, focused on her laptop.

On a cloudy Tuesday morning, Ron, Sherina, and Manu checked in at Jackson International Airport at 4:30 AM. They boarded an Air

Niugini Boeing 707 flight bound for Changi International Airport in Singapore. After a brief layover, they then took a direct Delta Airlines flight to Harry Reid International Airport in Paradise, Nevada.

The flight across the vast Pacific Ocean felt long and winding. Just a day earlier, Manu had read about the rattlesnake that inhabits the desert terrain. He learned that this snake is highly venomous and produces eerie sounds with the rattle at the end of its tail. While researching Nevada, he had seen pictures of the snake on Google, and they left a lasting impression on him.

The snake looked menacing.

Manu found it difficult to focus on the musical playing on the mini-screen in front of him; his thoughts kept returning to the rattlesnake he had read about.

"Sheri, could you turn off this movie and help me find something to read about rattlesnakes?" Manu asked, glancing at Sheri, who was engrossed in her research on endangered species in Morobe Province, Papua New Guinea.

"Oh, you want to read about rattlesnakes?" Sheri replied, looking surprised. She quickly turned off the movie and began searching for information on the topic.

"Yes, I do. Ron showed me some information about them the other day on his computer, but I was feeling sleepy and didn't finish my reading," Manu explained to Sheri as she scrolled through pictures of strange-looking snakes on the mini-screen.

"Here you go, Manu. Enjoy." Sheri said, ruffling his fuzzy hair before returning to reading on her iPad.

> The rattlesnake is a highly venomous pit viper found throughout the Americas, particularly in the United States, where it inhabits diverse environments from deserts to woodlands (Encyclopaedia Britannica, n.d.). This snake is easily recognised by its triangular head, vertical pupils, and distinctive tail rattle, which it vibrates as a warning.

Rattlesnakes are typically gray, tan, or brown, often featuring diamond-shaped patterns or bands. A unique adaptation is the pit organ located between the eye and nostril, which detects infrared radiation from warm-blooded prey, allowing them to hunt effectively in the dark (Encyclopaedia Britannica, n.d.).

The genus Crotalus includes about 27 species, averaging around 5 feet in length, while the genus Sistrurus consists of three smaller species, typically less than 2 feet long. Crotalus species have small scales on their heads, distinguishing them from the pygmy rattlers that possess larger head shields (Encyclopaedia Britannica, n.d.).

Rattlesnakes have venom glands located beneath their eyes, surrounded by muscles that give their heads a robust appearance. They use hollow fangs to inject venom into their prey, usually rodents or ground birds. When threatened, a rattlesnake will assume a striking position, coil its body, and vibrate its rattle. Most will retreat if not provoked further, but they can strike from any position (Encyclopaedia Britannica, n.d.).

Rattlesnakes give birth to live young, typically in litters of six to twenty-four. Newborns have a small segment, or 'button,' at the end of their tails, which grows with each molt. In the wild, most rattlesnakes have no more than eight to ten segments on their rattles, as they wear down over time (Encyclopaedia Britannica, n.d.).

In the northeastern U.S., the timber rattlesnake (C. horridus) is common, while the pygmy rattler (S. miliarius) is found in the Southeast. The eastern diamondback (C. adamanteus) and western diamondback (C. atrox) are among the largest and most dangerous species, with various others inhabiting the arid Southwest and extending into Mexico (Encyclopaedia Britannica, n.d.).

"Phew," Manu exhaled deeply, catching Sheri's attention.

"Everything okay, Manu?" she asked.

"These rattlesnakes seem like nasty fiends. Even though there are antivenoms available in the U.S., they still scare me," he replied.

"They are definitely frightening, Manu. About ten years ago, Ron and I studied various species alongside a snake-handling expert. We spent months in Mexico observing the habits of the large and deadly Cascabel rattlesnake. It's as ugly as its venom is lethal," Sheri said, playfully popping her eyes wide open.

"Yes, I read about that. I wonder if the indigenous people have their own traditional antidotes, like we do in our country," Manu inquired.

"What a thoughtful question, Manu. Oh yes, they do! We even documented that in our research. We recorded several traditional remedies used in Morobe for wasp stings, snake bites, centipede bites, and other injuries from wild creatures," Sheri explained.

Manu and Sheri continued their conversation for a while, and then he closed his eyes and leaned back. When he woke up and rubbed his eyes, he saw Sheri smiling at him.

"You just slept your way back to Tuesday, Manu," Sheri laughed, noticing the confused look on his face.

"Oh, we're a day ahead in PNG. We left Port Moresby on a Tuesday, and after a day of flying, we arrive back on a Tuesday."

"Aah, so if we fly through a whole day, we end up on Tuesday again. Wow, that's amazing!" Manu exclaimed, glancing at Sheri and then at Ron.

As they flew over the terrain, Manu noticed that it looked nothing like Papua New Guinea. Far below, he could clearly see the stark differences in the landscape. He felt the plane descending and realised they must be flying over the state of Nevada. Instead of lush greenery, there was an expanse of arid desert.

"Goodness, what kind of land is this?" he wondered. "How do people live in such barren surroundings, devoid of trees, plants, and flowers?" Manu thought it was terrible. He couldn't imagine living in a place like this.

"That's Las Vegas, Manu," Sheri said, pointing out the window. Manu looked outside, and the view below took his breath away.

"That is an aerial view of the Las Vegas Strip," Sheri continued. "It never ceases to impress me with its sheer size and lavishness."

"Las Vegas is renowned worldwide for its opulence," she explained. "The city consists of three main areas: the old downtown, where it all began; The Strip, known for its iconic casinos and resorts; and Las Vegas Boulevard, which extends all the way south to Silvertown, home to the massive South Point Casino and Spa. This is where gambling flows like a waterfall."

While Sheri shared her insights, Ron remained engrossed in one of his scientific readings.

After more than 18 hours of flying, they landed at Harry Reid International Airport in Paradise. Manu felt a wave of relief wash over him as he stepped back onto solid ground. He quickly noticed that no one seemed to stare or linger; everyone was in a hurry to get somewhere. This bustling atmosphere was a stark contrast to Lae, where people often stood around, chewing betel nut and spitting without a care.

The airport buzzed with energy, filled with travellers from around the globe, all eager to explore the vibrant city known for its dazzling nightlife and extravagant resorts. Neon lights flickered in the distance, hinting at the excitement that awaited them on The Strip. Manu felt a mix of anticipation and curiosity about what Las Vegas had to offer, from its famous casinos to its spectacular shows. He could hardly wait to experience the city that never sleeps.

As they exited the lounge, a tall, athletic young man appeared seemingly out of nowhere and lifted Sheri up onto his chest, adding to the whirlwind of excitement that surrounded them.

"Muuuuuummmmmm!" he yelled, his voice echoing in the bustling atmosphere.

"Trevorrrr!" Sheri screamed, wrapping her arms around his neck before planting kisses on both his cheeks.

"Trevor, this is our friend, Manu," she said, intertwining their hands with Manu's and bringing them together.

"Heyyyy, Manu! Welcome! So, pleased to meet you, man!" Trevor exclaimed, gripping his hand firmly around Manu's before giving him a hearty slap across his shoulders. Manu instantly liked him; he radiated warmth and energy. At 25 years old, he was lean and clean-shaven, exuding the confidence of a successful financial lawyer.

Manu hadn't noticed his fiancée until he pulled her forward, introducing her with a proud smile, adding to the welcoming atmosphere.

"Mum, Dad, this is Carmelia," he said, beaming at his parents. "Remember, we went to university together, and she was the class president? I introduced her once when she invited me to her youth fellowship."

Sheri and Ron greeted Carmelia warmly, their faces lighting up with recognition. She turned to Manu, extending her hand for a shake. Carmelia was of medium height, with brown hair that framed her face beautifully and a lovely smile that instantly made him feel at ease.

After the introductions, they all piled into the car for the drive to their ranch. The scenery blurred past as they chatted and laughed, the excitement palpable in the air.

When they arrived at the ranch, Manu was introduced to Aunt Tanya. She was a tall, immaculate woman with dark skin, reminding Manu of Maoru, and she had a loud, vibrant personality that filled the space. Her presence was commanding, and she exuded warmth as she welcomed Manu, making him feel like part of the family.

"Welcome, Manu," Aunt Tanya said, holding his hand firmly while looking deeply into his eyes. Her gaze was warm and reassuring, instantly putting him at ease.

"You are in good hands, Manu. We are so pleased to have you here with us," she added with a radiant smile, pulling him into a heartfelt hug.

As she embraced him, Manu felt a wave of comfort wash over him. It was as if he had stepped into a new family, one filled with love and acceptance. Aunt Tanya's presence was both nurturing and vibrant, and he could sense that her enthusiasm would make his stay unforgettable.

"Here at the ranch, we believe in making memories," she continued, stepping back to look at him with sparkling eyes. "We have plenty of adventures planned, from horseback riding to exploring the nearby trails. You'll get to experience everything this beautiful place has to offer."

Her words filled him with excitement, and he couldn't help but smile. Manu realised that this visit was going to be more than just a stay; it would be a journey of connection and discovery, surrounded by people who genuinely cared.

"Let's get you settled in," she said, giving him a playful nudge. "You're going to love it here!"

Manu also met Uncle Hoft and Uncle Ken, two guys who always seemed to head to Las Vegas after Christmas to enjoy the excitement of New Year's Day.

"We don't have annoying or bossy wives, so it's better to spend it all in Vegas!" Uncle Hoft laughed loudly, his voice booming. He was a big, hairy man, reminding Manu of a fuzzy bear pulling fish out of a river on a nature documentary on the NatGeo wild channel. His friendly attitude immediately made Manu feel comfortable, and he sensed a connection with this larger-than-life character.

As they started talking, Uncle Hoft eagerly shared stories of their adventures in Las Vegas—tales filled with late-night fun, lively shows, and great times with friends. Ken added a few funny stories of his own, sharing mishaps that had everyone laughing.

"You see, Manu," Ken said with a wink, "the key is to enjoy the craziness. Las Vegas teaches you to live in the moment and have fun without worries!"

Manu felt drawn in by their lively energy. The thought of spending New Year's in such an exciting place was thrilling, and he could almost hear the distant sounds of laughter and music from the Strip.

"Next time you're in Vegas with us, you'll have to join the fun!" Uncle Hoft said, giving Manu a friendly pat on the back with a hearty laugh that filled the room.

Manu smiled, feeling a sense of belonging as he imagined the adventures ahead, surrounded by this lively family. He realised that this visit would be a chance to reconnect and create memories that would last a lifetime.

For the next few hours, Manu listened intently as Uncle Hoft and Uncle Ken recounted their Las Vegas escapades. Each story was filled with laughter, painting a vivid picture of their adventures in the city of lights.

"I've stayed in so many different places in Las Vegas over the years," Uncle Hoft began, his eyes sparkling with memories. "My old favourite was the now-demolished Stardust. There was something magical about it—the atmosphere, the shows, the excitement. I also enjoyed the Monte Carlo Hilton, which is now rebranded as the SLS. And who could forget Circus? It was a blast when I was younger!"

Uncle Ken nodded enthusiastically, adding, "But for the last several years, I've been going to the South Point Spa and Casino. That's where I attended the trade show to buy accessories for the upcoming boating season. It has everything you need—great food, comfortable rooms, and a fun atmosphere. Plus, the trade show is always a highlight for me. I get to see the latest trends and connect with other boating enthusiasts."

As they spoke, Manu could feel the excitement in their voices, the way they reminisced about the past while eagerly anticipating future trips. Uncle Hoft animatedly described the bustling casino floors, the bright lights, and the thrill of placing bets, while Ken shared stories of late-night adventures that often ended with them laughing until dawn.

"Every trip is a new adventure," Uncle Hoft remarked, leaning back with a satisfied grin. "You never know who you'll meet or what you'll experience. That's the beauty of Vegas!"

Manu felt a surge of excitement as he listened, imagining the vibrant nights filled with laughter and the thrill of new experiences.

"Uncle Ken owns a boating business in Portland, Oregon," Trevor explained to Manu, a hint of pride in his voice. "That's why he's always on the lookout for the best parts he can find at any dealer."

As they all sat around the patio, enjoying the warm evening and each other's company, Trevor continued, "Where is that trade show held?"

Ken chimed in, "The show is at the south end of the Strip, about eight miles from the central area. You take Las Vegas Boulevard north, and along the way, you pass some iconic sights."

He gestured animatedly as he spoke. "First, you'll drive by the famous Welcome to Las Vegas sign, which you've probably seen in countless movies. It's a real landmark! And as you head further north, you enter the airport area, where all the private jets and helicopters line the streets. It's impressive to see, and you can't help but notice the wealth in the air."

Trevor nodded, adding, "It's a sight to behold! The mix of luxury cars and high-end aircraft really highlights the lifestyle of those who come to Vegas. Uncle Ken always says that seeing all those private jets is a reminder of the opportunities out there—especially in the boating industry."

"Exactly," Ken agreed. "The trade show attracts a lot of serious buyers, and it's a great place to make connections. I'm always excited to see the latest innovations in boating technology and find parts that will give my customers the best experience on the water."

Manu listened intently, fascinated by their enthusiasm and knowledge. He could picture the bustling trade show filled with vendors showcasing everything from sleek boat designs to cutting-edge accessories. The camaraderie among the boating community, the thrill of discovery, and the vibrant atmosphere of Las Vegas all added to the allure.

"Next time, you should join us at the show," Uncle Ken suggested, focusing on Trevor, a smile on his face. "It's an experience you won't forget!"

"The sheer size of the Strip and its hotels is astounding," Uncle Holf remarked, his eyes wide with enthusiasm. "You really have to walk into each one to be truly floored by their over-the-top style. It's an experience like no other!"

He continued, "Take the Bellagio Hotel, for example. The iconic water fountain show in front is a must-see. It plays every half hour, and the water shoots hundreds of feet into the air, choreographed to music. It's quite beautiful, whether during the day or at night when the lights enhance the spectacle."

As he spoke, Trevor nodded in agreement, a smirk spreading across his face. "True, huh?" he said, glancing around the table. It was becoming increasingly clear that the alcohol on Uncle Ken and Uncle Holf's side was disappearing fast, and their animated storytelling was becoming more colourful by the minute.

"Every visit to Vegas feels like stepping into a different world," Uncle Holf continued, his enthusiasm infectious. "From the opulence of the Venetian, with its gondola rides, to the vibrant atmosphere of the MGM Grand, each hotel offers something unique. You could spend days just exploring them all!"

Trevor chimed in, "And don't forget about the art installations! The Bellagio has a stunning conservatory filled with seasonal flowers, and there are always incredible pieces displayed throughout the hotels. It's like a gallery that's open 24/7."

The group laughed, enjoying the lively conversation. Manu felt the excitement in the air, drawn into their shared passion for the vibrant energy of Las Vegas. He imagined the dazzling lights, the laughter, and the thrill of discovery waiting around every corner.

"Next time, we'll make sure you see it all for yourself," Trevor promised, raising his glass. "To unforgettable experiences!"

"Vegas can be extremely hot during the summer and cooler in the winter," Uncle Holf began, his excitement palpable. "Summer temperatures are incredibly dry, often reaching as high as 120 degrees Fahrenheit. You really feel the heat, especially with no humidity to soften the blow. In contrast, winter offers a more moderate climate, with daytime temperatures ranging from 60 to 70 degrees. It's rare to see snow on the valley floor, but when it does happen, it creates a surprising and beautiful sight against the desert landscape."

"Forget the weather, Hoffy! Are you kidding me?" Uncle Ken chimed in, his voice slightly slurred by the alcohol. "Listen, the casinos are another thing to behold! The atmosphere is electric; the money flows, and the lights mesmerise you."

He leaned in closer, his eyes sparkling with excitement. "All the slot machines have bright screens designed to draw your attention. My personal favourite game is Craps. It's exhilarating! You throw a pair of dice and aim to hit a seven on the come-out roll to win. If you make a point, the challenge is to roll that number again before hitting seven and losing. There are literally hundreds of ways to place bets on the table, making each round thrilling."

Uncle Ken's passion was contagious as he reminisced about his last trip to Vegas just a few weeks ago. "I had an hour of perfect throws. I was what we call 'in the zone'. I had the arm! I positioned the dice into a chevron with threes up, gripping them just right with my fingertips. I made sure to launch them in an arc, landing flat with minimal bounce, just enough to hit the back wall to qualify."

He paused, taking a sip of his drink before continuing. "I was following a book by Frank Scoblete, the definitive guide on Craps. His strategies have really improved my game. I enjoy it immensely, but I'm also pretty conservative when it comes to gambling. I like to win, not just give my hard-earned money away."

As he spoke, Trevor and Manu exchanged amused glances, captivated by Uncle Ken's animated storytelling. The vibrant energy of the casino, the thrill of the game, and the dazzling lights of Las Vegas came alive in their imaginations, making them eager for their own adventures ahead.

"Next time, you'll have to show me your winning techniques," Trevor said, grinning. "I want to be 'in the zone' too!"

Aunty Tanya appeared with a large tray of beef jerky, placing it in the centre of the table as everyone gathered around.

"Here you go, everyone! A little snack to keep the energy up," she said, her voice cheerful but quickly turning serious. "But let's not get too lost in the glitz and glamour nonsense, Ken. What about the homeless people living in the underground tunnels of Vegas? It's a reality that many prefer to overlook!"

Her words hung in the air, shifting the mood of the conversation. "You see," she continued, her tone earnest, "Las Vegas is not just about the bright lights and extravagant shows. Beneath the surface lies a complex issue of homelessness. The underground tunnels, originally built for flood control, have become a refuge for some of the city's most vulnerable populations."

Uncle Holf nodded, his expression sobering. "I've heard stories about those tunnels. It's estimated that hundreds of people live there, seeking shelter from the harsh desert climate. During the scorching summer months, it can be a lifeline from the heat, and in winter, it offers some protection from the cold."

Aunty Tanya leaned in, her eyes reflecting concern. "Many of these individuals have faced incredible challenges—job loss, addiction, mental health issues. The stigma surrounding homelessness often prevents them from receiving the help they need. While tourists marvel at the Strip, they may not realise that just a few miles away, people are struggling to survive."

She gestured with her arms, emphasising her point. "There are even organisations trying to help, offering food, clothing, and support services. Yet, the scale of the problem can feel overwhelming. It's often easier for people to turn a blind eye than to confront the harsh realities."

Trevor, listening intently, chimed in, "It's a stark contrast to the luxury and excess that Vegas is known for. It's important to remember that behind the neon lights, there are real human stories."

Uncle Ken looked thoughtful. "You're right, Tanya. We often forget that every city has its struggles. It's easy to get caught up in the fun without acknowledging the deeper issues at play."

Aunty Tanya smiled, appreciating their openness. "Exactly! Awareness is the first step. When we visit, we can also think about ways to contribute or support local initiatives. Every little bit helps."

The group nodded in agreement, recognising the importance of balancing their excitement for Vegas with empathy for those facing hardship. As they enjoyed their beef jerky, the conversation deepened, encompassing both the vibrant life of the city and the challenges that lay beneath its dazzling surface.

On Wednesday evening, Trevor, Uncle Ken, and Manu set out to explore the vibrant streets of Las Vegas. As they drove downtown, they passed the iconic old Harrah's Casino and the historic Binion's, landmarks that spoke to the city's rich gambling history.

"The Binion's Casino never backs down," Uncle Ken spluttered, rolling his eyes with a mix of amusement and disbelief. "If you place even a single dollar bet, they'll take it, and I'm talking in the millions! It's a gambler's paradise, but you better know what you're doing."

As they continued their drive, the atmosphere shifted. Downtown Las Vegas had a gritty, old-school charm, markedly different from the pristine glitz of the Strip. The streets were bustling, but they bore the marks of time, with vintage neon signs and a more laid-back vibe.

They approached Fremont Street, where an expansive arched light board adorned the ceiling, illuminating the night with a dazzling light show. The vibrant colours danced above, captivating those passing by. "This is Fremont Street," Uncle Ken explained, pointing out the spectacle. "At night, it turns into a whole different world. It's fun to watch!"

As they navigated through the throngs of people, they spotted a zip line tour overhead. Adventurous souls soared above the crowds, suspended on cables, their laughter echoing as they zipped past the dazzling lights. "Now that's something I'd love to try!" Trevor exclaimed, his excitement palpable.

"Over there is the North Premium Outlet Mall," Uncle Ken continued, gesturing toward a modern shopping complex. "You'll find high-end brands like Gucci, Dolce & Gabbana, and Louis Vuitton."

Manu raised an eyebrow, confused. "Who are they? Why do people care so much about these names?"

Trevor smiled, eager to explain. "They're famous fashion designers known for their luxury bags, clothes, and perfumes. Their products are often seen as status symbols. People buy them not just for the quality, but for the prestige that comes with the brand."

"Oh, I see," Manu replied, pondering the concept. He wondered aloud, "But why spend so much on things that will wear out one day?"

Uncle Ken chuckled, appreciating Manu's perspective. "That's a good question! For many, it's about more than just the item itself. It's about the experience, the craftsmanship, and sometimes, the social status attached to owning something rare or exclusive. But you're right—things do wear out, and it's important to think about what truly matters."

As they continued their drive, the conversation flowed effortlessly, blending reflections on consumerism with the excitement of their surroundings. Las Vegas was alive with stories, each corner revealing a new layer of its multifaceted identity.

After their lively evening downtown, Manu was eager to explore more of what Nevada had to offer. The next morning, Trevor and Uncle Ken planned a day filled with adventure, starting with a visit to the breath-taking Red Rock Canyon.

As they drove out of the city, the towering red cliffs and unique rock formations came into view. "This is one of the most beautiful natural landscapes in Nevada," Uncle Ken explained, his voice filled with pride. "It's perfect for hiking and photography."

Once they arrived, Manu marvelled at the sheer beauty of the canyon. The vibrant colours of the rocks contrasted sharply with the clear blue sky. They embarked on a short hike along the Calico Hills Trail, where Manu felt invigorated by the fresh air and stunning scenery. He snapped photos, with Trevor's camera, trying to capture the magic of the moment.

After hiking, they headed back to the Strip for a quick lunch at a famous diner known for its hearty portions. "You have to try the burgers here," Trevor insisted. "They're legendary!"

With satisfied appetites, they made their way to the Neon Museum, an outdoor exhibition that showcased iconic Las Vegas signs from decades past. The collection included everything from vintage neon signs to artistic installations. "This place is like a time capsule of Vegas history," Uncle Ken said, pointing to a sign from the old Sahara Hotel. Manu was fascinated by the stories behind each sign, realising how much the city had evolved over the years.

Next on their itinerary was a trip to the Mob Museum, where they delved into the intriguing history of organised crime in America. The exhibits were interactive and engaging, with artefacts and stories that brought the past to life. "It's incredible to see how the mob influenced the growth of Las Vegas," Trevor remarked, as they explored the museum's many displays.

As the day turned to evening, they decided to visit the famous Las Vegas Strip once more, this time to catch a show. They managed to secure tickets to a spectacular Cirque du Soleil performance. The combination of acrobatics, music, and stunning visuals left Manu in awe. "I've never seen anything like this!" he exclaimed, his eyes wide with wonder.

The following day, they took a short drive to Lake Mead, where they rented a boat and spent the afternoon enjoying the sun on the water. Manu couldn't believe how crystal clear the lake was, surrounded by dramatic desert landscapes. They swam, laughed, and even attempted to fish, though their luck was limited. "Just being out here is enough for me," Manu said, soaking in the serene atmosphere.

To wrap up his trip, Manu insisted on visiting the Hoover Dam. As they approached, the sheer size of the structure left him speechless. "This is amazing!" he said, gazing at the massive concrete walls and the powerful waters of the Colorado River. As they took a guided tour, he learned about the dam's history and its significance in providing hydroelectric power to the region.

On their final night in Nevada, they returned to Fremont Street to experience the vibrant nightlife. The street was alive with music, street performers, and the glow of neon lights. They enjoyed dinner at a local eatery, where Manu sampled some classic Vegas fare, including shrimp cocktails and a slice of decadent chocolate cake.

As they headed back to their hotel, Manu reflected on his whirlwind trip. He had experienced the dazzling lights of the Strip, the natural beauty of Red Rock Canyon, and the rich history of Las Vegas. "Thank you for an unforgettable adventure," he said, gratitude shining in his eyes. "I've seen so much more than I ever imagined!"

Trevor and Uncle Ken smiled, pleased to have shared their love for the city with Manu. "There's always more to explore," Uncle Ken replied. "Next time, we'll find even more hidden gems."

That evening, after a day filled with exploration, the trio gathered for dinner at a cosy restaurant known for its hearty portions and classic American cuisine. As they indulged in their meals, Uncle Holf leaned back, a gleam in his eye that signalled he was ready to share one of his favourite stories.

"Speaking of hidden gems," he began, "have you ever heard about Area 51?"

Manu, intrigued, shook his head. "No, what's that?"

Uncle Holf chuckled, clearly excited to dive into the topic. "Area 51 is a highly classified U.S. Air Force facility located in the Nevada desert, just a couple of hours from here. It's been the centre of countless conspiracy theories and UFO sightings for decades. People think it's where the government conducts secret research on alien technology and experimental aircraft."

Trevor leaned in, equally captivated. "They say some of the most advanced planes in the world have been developed there. You wouldn't believe the kinds of aircraft they've tested!"

"Exactly!" Uncle Holf continued, his enthusiasm bolstering the conversation. "One of the most famous is the U-2 spy plane, which was used during the Cold War for high-altitude reconnaissance. It's designed to fly at altitudes where it's difficult for enemy radar to detect it, and it played a crucial role in gathering intelligence."

Manu's eyes widened. "So, what kind of workers go there every day?"

Uncle Holf took a sip of his drink before answering. "Well, accessing Area 51 is no easy feat. Employees typically work in highly specialised fields like engineering, aircraft design, and intelligence analysis. They undergo extensive background checks and are required to have security clearances. Most of them commute from nearby towns, and some even use private planes to get to work."

Trevor chimed in, "It's said that many workers arrive at a small airport nearby, where they board unmarked planes that take them directly to the facility. You wouldn't even know they were there unless you were part of the program."

"Wow, that sounds like something out of a movie!" Manu exclaimed, marvelling at the secrecy surrounding the place. "Do people really believe there are aliens there?"

Uncle Holf nodded, a grin spreading across his face. "Oh, absolutely! There are countless tales of UFO sightings and government cover-ups. Some believe that the government is reverse-engineering alien technology. Whether or not that's true, the mystery of Area 51 has certainly captured the public's imagination."

As their dinner plates were cleared, dessert arrived—a decadent chocolate lava cake that melted in their mouths. Manu savoured each bite while absorbing Uncle Holf's stories.

"Imagine if we could sneak a peek inside," Trevor joked. "I'd love to see what they're really working on!"

Uncle Holf laughed, "You'd probably be whisked away by men in black suits before you even got to the gate! But that's part of the allure, isn't it? The unknown, the mysteries that lie just beyond our reach."

As they finished their dessert, the conversation continued to flow, weaving tales of conspiracy, adventure, and the thrill of the unknown. Manu felt a sense of exhilaration; his trip to Nevada had turned into an unexpected journey filled with history, excitement, and a touch of intrigue.

After dinner, they stepped outside into the cool evening air, the lights of Las Vegas twinkling in the distance. "What an adventure this has been," Manu thought, already eager to see what else the next day would hold.

Sheri and Ron were busy with the research sponsor university and they were writing reports here and there while Manu was entertained by Trevor, Uncle Ken and Uncle Hoft.

Trevor's brothers, Martin and Tristan were in Germany visiting their grandmother and Manu did not get to meet them.

20

The Scholarship

After returning from Nevada, Manu immersed himself in the bustling activities of his butterfly farm, diligently collecting pupae and meticulously drying them. He eagerly awaited the commencement of the school year, anticipating his return to Omili Primary school for the eighth grade. Fond memories of the sophisticated lifestyle he encountered in Nevada lingered in his mind, where he absorbed valuable insights into the western way of life. He was enthralled by their lifestyle and made a firm resolution to enhance his own life and aspire to a prosperous future.

He was immensely grateful to Maoru for looking after his grandfather, while he was away in Nevada and invited her again to sleep in the extra room at their new house, but Maoru declined as usual.

"Manu, I like it in the old hut with the butterflies. They whisper songs into my mind at night and I sing new songs every day, as I work in the butterfly farm," she smiled, relating her secret to Manu.

Maybe Maoru was a bit mad, as the folks around the settlement area said, but she was perfectly fine as far as Manu was concerned.

He admired her resilience and the way she poured her heart into every task. Whether she was tending to her garden or crafting intricate trinkets, Maoru approached her work with a passion that inspired those around her.

Her oddities were just a part of her charm. Whilst others might have scoffed at her butterfly songs—those whimsical melodies that danced through her mind—Manu found them refreshing. She had a unique ability to find joy in the most mundane things, transforming everyday chores into a work of laughter and creativity.

Maoru's weirdness wasn't a flaw; it was an indication to her spirit. She painted the world with her colourful imagination, reminding everyone that happiness could be found in the simplest of pleasures. Whether she was lost in thought or humming a tune, her hardworking nature shone through, capturing the hearts of those who took the time to really see her.

In a world that often-demanded conformity, Maoru stood out like a wildflower in a field of grass. And for Manu, that was more than enough. He cherished her quirks and admired her dedication, knowing that her unique perspective added a richness to life that was truly extraordinary.

"Manu, she sings new songs at the farm, and the butterflies gather around her as if she's a nectar-bearing flower," Bubu Pellie reported to Manu in a serious tone.

Manu smiled at Bubu, handing him his cup of tea and passing him a slice of buttered bread. "Bubu Pellie, it's her hair. She always colours it brightly, and that attracts the butterflies. They think she's a flower."

"Absolutely, she loves colouring her hair in vibrant shades," Bubu Pellie said with a smile as he savoured his tea.

A week before the school year started, Manu was weeding the hedges around his butterfly farm, when a black Toyota Mitsubishi pulled up next to his house. He heard Maoru calling his name and came from behind the hedges and saw the same woman who handed him the bouquet, when he was given the Young Achiever's award.

"Hello Manu, how are you doing?" the woman greeted him with a lovely smile.

"Hello Wanda, welcome. I am quite good thank you," Manu smiled at Wanda, as he took her hand.

"This is Willie. He works in the foreign currency section at our bank," Wanda introduced, pointing to a young man on her right. Willie and Manu exchanged smiles and shook hands warmly.

"Please come," Manu realised that they were on an important errand, so he invited them to sit on the veranda of his house on the bamboo chairs around the bamboo coffee table. He signalled Maoru to bring some refreshment. After a minute, Maoru brought each of them a *kulau* to drink and a bunch of sweet yellow bananas.

"How can I help you," Manu asked the two visitors, as Bubu Pellie listened and nodded.

"Well Manu, we bring you good news. Please brace yourself," Wanda smiled and gestured at Willie to talk to Manu.

"It is my pleasure to announce to you, Manu, that Edward Clifford in Australia, has heard of your plight on how you rose from your struggles, as a young boy and fulfilled your dream. Edward is impressed and quite stunned with how you have handled the situations that should have put you down. To support you in your education, Edward has sent a cheque of K6,000.00 to the ANZ Young Achiever's Fund. This money is not to be withdrawn and given to you, but every year, ANZ will pay your school fees, uniforms, shoes and stationery up to grade 12."

"But who is Edward Clifford?" Manu asked, curiosity getting the better of him.

"Edward Clifford used to work in Papua New Guinea. He is about 80 years old now and he buys your butterflies. He is one of your fans, who has your butterflies framed and hung in his living room," Willie explained, smiling.

Manu smiled and said thank you to Willie. They rose and shook hands, while Wanda shook Bubu Pellie's hand.

Before Wanda and Willie left, they went for a walk in the butterfly farm, so Willie could take some pictures of Manu and his butterflies and send them to Edward Clifford in Australia.

It was a pleasant, fulfilling day for Manu. This time he was pleased indeed, that a kind man in Australia, wanted to support his education. Manu was truly thankful that there were some very good people out there, who are willing to help those who try their best to help themselves.

Manu explained to Bubu Pellie that the largest birdwing, found only in Morobe Province and sold at a high price, would be preserved and sent to Edward Clifford in Australia as a gift from him. Bubu Pellie nodded thoughtfully.

When the school year resumed at Omili Primary school and Manu was thrilled to get back into class. He worked with conviction at school and when he got home, he helped Maoru and Bubu Pellie in the butterfly farm. Some of the flowering plants were dying, so they had to plant new ones, after tilling the soil again.

Whilst they tilled the soil and were in the process of replanting the vines and other plants, the butterflies kept hovering everywhere over the garden. Manu was worried that they were going to leave and then come back later, but then he realised that the citrus and breadfruit trees were also the best hangout places for the butterflies.

Bubu Pellie and Maoru worked diligently while Manu was at school. When he returned home, they allowed him to explore the farm, giving him the opportunity to inspect the day's progress. Meanwhile, they prepared and cooked the evening meal.

After dinner, they washed the dishes and cleaned the house, while Manu settled at his study table to complete his schoolwork.

One Sunday afternoon, Manu was engrossed in the *Goosebumps* series by R.L. Stine, specifically the book titled *The Ghost Next Door*.

Sheri had gifted him the entire series, which included about twenty *Goosebumps* books in total.

As he smiled, he recalled that special day.

"Well, Manu, you never did catch the changing being in the Blue Mountains, so at least R.L. Stine can give you some goosebumps," Sheri laughed as she handed him the neatly wrapped books on Christmas Day in Nevada.

"Sheri, Manu is not easily scared," Ron chimed in with a playful wink at Manu.

"Thank you, Sheri! I already like them," Manu replied, his mouth full of Christmas pudding.

Just then, he heard Bubu Pellie calling his name. Manu stepped out onto the veranda and saw Kaia and Chay standing below the steps, waiting for him. "Hey, how are you two?" Manu yelled as he raced down to them, shaking their hands enthusiastically.

"Manu, my main boy! Wow, you look like a white boy!" Kaia exclaimed, causing Bubu Pellie and Maoru to laugh heartily.

The air was filled with joy as the boys clapped, slapped, and playfully punched each other in greeting.

Maoru stood by, smiling in delight, perhaps surprised that boys greet each other with playful jabs instead of hugs.

"I heard you went to America! Hey, do you remember Chay?" Kaia asked, as lively as ever, just like the days when they used to carry golf clubs together.

"Yes, Chay, my main boy! How are you doing?" Manu exclaimed, slapping Chay on the shoulders, and Chay responded with a playful punch to his back.

Before long, they were all chatting in their familiar 'caddies' language,' just like they used to at the golf course, sharing jokes and laughter as if no time had passed. The friendship flowed effortlessly, filling the air with a sense of nostalgia and joy.

Manu was thrilled to see his old friends again and invited them up onto the veranda. Kaia was already in full swing, excitedly sharing the latest gossip from the golf course.

"Yeah, and the woman turned out to be African, as we both discovered in the end," Kaia continued, while Manu and Chay chatted about other topics.

"What did you say, Kaia?" Manu asked, a bit confused.

"Oii, she wasn't African; she was a Black American woman who worked for the United Nations!" Chay shouted, bursting into laughter. The three of them erupted into a lively discussion, their voices blending together in a chorus of friendship.

"I was saying that Chay and I have been caddies for a dark-skinned woman for a week, thinking she was Papua New Guinean. But on the last day, we finally asked her, and she told us she was American. Yes, Chay, you are correct for once!" Kaia exclaimed, pointing at Chay with a triumphant grin.

"We should have known, especially since she paid us well—like K20.00 each per day! We really looked after her, too. Chay carried the umbrella and shielded her from the rain, while I took care of her hat. But she acted more like a white woman; she bought us lunch and treated us to cold water!" Kaia rambled on in his typical animated style.

As Kaia continued to speak, Manu and Chay couldn't help but laugh, reminiscing about the good old days. It felt just like back then, when they would chuckle over Kaia's jokes, completely forgetting their rumbling stomachs and simply enjoying each other's friendship.

Bubu Pellie bought each of them a plate of rice with corned beef and a kulau each. They ate and chatted away, truly content in the presence of each other's company.

"Hey, Manu, my main boy! Tell us about one unique adventure you had in America," Kaia blurted out suddenly, his eyes sparkling with excitement.

"What America? You nitwit, he went to Nevada!" Chay retorted, his voice rising in mock exasperation.

"Nevada is in America, you empty-headed golf course fly!" Kaia shot back, and just like that, the air was filled with their laughter, a chorus of joy and friendly banter echoing around them.

"One afternoon, Sheri, Ron, and their son Trevor took me to the hot springs near Hoover Dam. It was about a two-and-a-half-mile hike down a scenic canyon, and when we arrived, we found an Olympic-sized swimming pool filled with natural hot springs. It was incredible—like nothing I had ever seen before. I tell you; it was both relaxing and a lot of fun to swim in."

"You mean there was hot water mixed with normal water from the ground?" Chay asked, looking puzzled. Kaia seemed just as confused.

"Yes, Chay, there was natural hot water—much larger than the swimming pool at the golf course," Manu explained patiently.

"Don't interrupt him, golf-course fly! Let my main boy finish the story!" Kaia suddenly looked angrier than confused. Chay nodded in agreement, and they both waited eagerly for Manu to continue.

"Trevor and I soaked in the hot pools at night, surrounded by floating candles, and we even napped a bit. We spent the night in tents, and in the morning, we went hiking to the Valley of Fire, where the red rocks were absolutely breathtaking," Manu shared with his friends, reliving the adventure.

"Wow, white people really love to explore unusual natural sites, while we regard places like that as sacred," Chay sighed.

"Of course! Those places are sacred, nitwit! If you mess around too much, the water sprites and canyon shape shifters will whisk you away to their dimension!" Kaia exclaimed in his usual loud voice.

Manu and Chay exchanged glances and burst into hysterical laughter.

Kaia is a legend, always saying the most unexpected things. His friends find it hilarious, as he is a natural-born comedian.

"Seriously, if Chay were there, he would have already been consumed by the eyes in the Valley of Fire!" Kaia yelled, and the three of them collapsed onto the floor of the veranda, laughing uncontrollably.

In the afternoon, Manu guided them through his butterfly farm. Kaia and Chay were both impressed and delighted to see how Manu was engaged in something entirely different from what the boys were doing at Bumbu settlement. The vibrant colours and delicate creatures filled them with a sense of wonder, highlighting Manu's unique passion.

"Manu, I always knew you were a smart boy, and I've always believed in your capabilities. I'm so proud of you, my main boy," Kaia told him, giving a hearty slap on the shoulder. Chay chimed in, playfully punching Manu on his right arm in agreement.

Manu led the boys to the Kamkumung firewood market, where he spotted his old mates, those he used to sell firewood with not long ago.

"Hey Manu, we heard you went to America, boy!" Muino shouted, rushing over to greet him. Before long, a crowd of his former firewood-selling friends gathered around, shaking hands and catching up on old times.

By the time Manu returned home, darkness had fallen. Bubu Pellie had already lit the lanterns, hanging each one in its proper place, casting a warm glow throughout the home.

Manu's school year had been a whirlwind of hard work and determination. Balancing his studies with the demands of his butterfly farm was no small feat, but he remained focused and committed. With the support of Bubu Pellie and Maoru, he cultivated a thriving environment for the butterflies, ensuring that each stage of their life cycle was nurtured with care.

Every morning, before school, Manu would tend to the farm, checking on the caterpillars and ensuring they had enough food. Bubu Pellie often joined him, sharing his wisdom about the plants that attracted butterflies and helping him create a vibrant landscape. Maoru, always eager to lend a hand, crafted special habitats that mimicked the butterflies' natural environments, making the farm a haven for these delicate creatures.

Throughout the year, Manu watched his efforts pay off. The farm flourished, attracting more butterflies than he had ever imagined.

Each new arrival brought a sense of accomplishment, filling him with pride. His schoolwork reflected this dedication; he studied diligently, often staying up late to complete assignments, knowing that education was the key to his dreams.

As the year progressed, Manu's hard work culminated in the completion of his Grade 8 National Exams. He felt a mix of relief and hope, knowing that he had done his best. The success of his butterfly farm and his academic achievements were testaments to his perseverance, setting the stage for the exciting opportunities that lay ahead.

Doctor Sherf always visited at the end of the month to collect the dried butterflies and leave more supplies for Manu. At the end of October, just after Manu had completed his Grade 8 National Exams, Doctor Sherf arrived one afternoon in his Land Rover, parking outside Manu's house.

Manu was already at the door, having recognised the familiar sound of the engine. Maoru was there too, enthusiastically greeting Doctor Sherf and helping him unload the supplies.

"Welcome, Doctor. How are you?" Manu called out, hurrying over to shake his hand.

"I'm quite tired, my boy. If the spare room is available, I'd like to spend the night. I can't drive any longer in this state," he sighed, throwing his hands up in exasperation.

"Of course, Doctor! We're honoured to have you spend the night with us; the spare room is always available for you," Manu replied, feeling a surge of excitement at the thought of having the doctor stay.

Maoru, overhearing their conversation, quickly sprang into action. She dusted the spare room, made the bed with fresh linens, and asked Bubu Pellie to hang an extra lantern to brighten the space.

As the evening settled in, the warm glow of the lanterns filled the home, creating a cosy atmosphere. Manu, filled with anticipation, sat with the doctor in the living room, eager to hear stories of his travels and his many adventures. Doctor Sherf, despite his fatigue, shared tales of his experiences in remote villages, inspiring Manu with visions of a future where he could make a difference.

As they chatted, the sound of laughter and the clinking of dishes wafted from the kitchen, where Bubu Pellie was preparing a special dinner in honour of their guest. That night, the house was not just a home but a hub of warmth, laughter, and dreams waiting to take flight.

21

Our Very Own Entomologist

As Manu stepped through the gates of Lae Secondary School, his heart raced with a mixture of excitement and apprehension. The chatter of students filled the air, and he felt both exhilarated and nervous.

"Look at that scholarship kid!" whispered a group of students nearby. Manu caught their gaze and straightened his shoulders, determined to prove himself.

"If that was not enough, he's got a butterfly farm!" another stated as he walked by.

"Hey, don't worry! You've got this!" said his friend, Leo, whom he had known from Preparatory at Omili Primary School was walking with him on their first day.

"Oii, coinless humans!" Leo yelled at the group of grimacing chattering group.

"Jeles nogat marasin[11]," he continued in Tok Pisin.

The group dispersed and went into the hall.

---

11 There is no medication for jealousy

Manu nodded, his pulse quickening. "Yeah, I just want to make the most of this opportunity."

In Grade 9, he dove headfirst into his studies as the terms progressed, quickly making a name for himself as a diligent student. His favourite subject, biology, captivated him. Every day in class, he felt a spark ignite within him and he yearned to know more.

"Alright class, today we're exploring local ecosystems," announced Mrs. Tali, their biology teacher. "I want you to think about the role of insects in our environment."

Manu's eyes lit up. "Insects are crucial! They help with pollination and decomposition!" he blurted out, earning a smile from Mrs. Tali.

"Exactly, Manu! You're on the right track," she replied, encouragingly. "Let's see what you can create for our upcoming project."

Determined to excel, Manu poured his heart into his project on local ecosystems, meticulously researching and gathering data. He spent hours in the library and even ventured into nearby fields to observe insects in their natural habitats and sat for hours studying the butterflies in his farm. It was such a revitalising project and he loved it.

"Manu, you know a lot already, without any teacher's instructions, huh?" Leo pondered one afternoon as they worked together. "I didn't know insects could be so interesting!"

"They're amazing!" Manu replied, grinning. "Without them, our world would fall apart. Just think about it. And yes, Doctor Sherf, taught me a lot. I owe it all to him."

As the project deadline approached, Manu felt both anxious and excited. The day of the presentation arrived, and he stood in front of his classmates, his hands slightly trembling.

"Today, I'll be sharing how insects contribute to our ecosystems," he began, his voice steadying as he spoke. He animatedly explained the intricate relationships between insects and plants, his passion shining through.

When it was over, applause erupted in the classroom.

"Great job, Manu!" Mrs. Tali exclaimed. "You've really brought this topic to life."

Weeks later, during the school assembly, the principal announced, "And the 'Best Student Award' for the biology project goes to… Manu!"

His heart soared as he walked up to receive the award. The applause felt like a warm embrace, and he couldn't help but smile.

"See? I told you!" Leo shouted from the crowd, beaming with pride.

"I couldn't have done it without your support!" Manu called back, his voice brimming with gratitude.

As Manu entered Grade 10 at Lae Secondary School, the stakes felt higher than ever. The academic pressure intensified, and he found himself juggling a demanding study schedule plus working in his butterfly farm every weekend for an hour or so.

Bubu Pellie and Maoru continuously worked in the butterfly farm, grew vegetables selling them at the market and Manu started a canteen under their house, so everyone was busy every day.

Manu had also gone back up to the Tree House to keep the place, over the first term holidays as Sheri and Ron flew to the states to attend Martin's university graduation.

He noticed flora and fauna he had taken for granted before. Like the ants that crawl up the Mother Tree. There were so many different species and the Mother Tree was their home. It was like as soon as he started studying biology, the universe was revelling how beautiful the world was. It was hard to explain.

"Manu, you're burning the candle at both ends," Leo said one afternoon, spotting his friend pouring over textbooks in the library. "Are you sure you can handle this?"

"I have to, Leo," Manu replied, rubbing his tired eyes. "Every little bit helps before I get home. Plus, I need to keep my grades up."

"Just remember to take breaks! You don't want to end up like a zombie," Leo joked, nudging him playfully.

"Speaking of zombies, I watched this crazy short movie while keeping the Tree House for the doctors." Manu recalled, his eyes lighting up with excitement.

"Really? What was it about?" Leo whispered, glancing around to make sure the librarian wasn't eavesdropping.

"It was about a group of kids who stumble upon an abandoned lab in the woods," Manu began, his voice dropping to a conspiratorial tone. "They find this experimental serum that was supposed to enhance human abilities, but instead, it turns people into zombies."

"No way! That sounds wild!" Leo leaned in closer, intrigued. "Did they actually drink it?"

"Yeah! One of them thought it was a prank and took a sip. The next thing you know, he's turning green and acting all weird," Manu continued, his eyes wide as he animatedly described the scenes. "They had to run and escape while trying to figure out how to reverse the effects."

"Did they succeed?" Leo asked, completely absorbed in the story.

"Barely! They had to work together to find the antidote hidden in the lab, all while dodging their friend, who was now a zombie trying to eat their brains." Manu chuckled, shaking his head. "It was both hilarious and terrifying."

"Manu, you're making me want to watch it right now!" Leo exclaimed, stifling a laugh. "But seriously, how did they end it?"

"They figured out that the antidote was a mix of some weird fruit and their friend's favourite snack—chocolate bars!" Manu whispered, grinning. "In the end, they managed to save him just in time."

"Classic! Only in a zombie movie would chocolate save the day," Leo laughed. "But hey, what if you turned into a zombie one day? Would you still want to study insects?"

"Absolutely! I'd just be a zombie entomologist!" Manu replied, grinning. "Imagine me wandering around, mumbling about the importance of pollinators while trying to eat brains."

"Now that's a horror movie I'd watch!" Leo smiled, shaking his head in disbelief. "But seriously, you need to take breaks before you turn into a zombie for real."

"Yeah, you're right. Let's grab a snack and recharge," Manu agreed, feeling energised by their banter. "But only if there's chocolate involved!"

"Deal! And I promise not to let you drink any weird serums!" Leo laughed as they gathered their things and headed out of the library, the weight of their studies momentarily lifted by their lively conversation.

Throughout the second term, Manu immersed himself in his studies, knowing that the end of the internal marks was approaching. He was determined to prepare for the PNG Grade 10 National Exams in the third term. The weight of his responsibilities at home felt a little lighter when Uncle Kia, a relative of Bubu Pellie, arrived from Goroka.

Uncle Kia managed the canteen and worked closely with Bubu Pellie. A devoted Seventh Day Adventist, he would close the canteen at 6 PM every Friday to attend church services all day Saturday, only reopening at 6:30 PM that evening. Manu admired Uncle Kia's firm faithfulness in both the small tasks and the larger responsibilities he carried.

"Uncle Kia is just like Bubu Pellie," Manu thought, appreciating their shared kindness and commitment. However, there was one small hiccup: Maoru, had taken quite a liking to Uncle Kia. Every time she served him food, she would stare and giggle, her cheeks flushed with youthful admiration.

One evening, Uncle Kia chuckled, "I have a wife and three kids at home," his voice warm yet firm. Manu caught a glimpse of Maoru's face as it fell, frowning with disappointment. He felt a pang of sympathy for her.

On Saturday, while Uncle Kia was at church, Manu decided to lift Maoru's spirits. He called her over and handed her K150. "You're appreciated more than anyone in our home," Manu told her, smiling.

Her eyes lit up with gratitude, and she beamed at him, wrapping her arms around his waist since he had grown quite tall. "Aiiyaa, naispla pikinini. Mi save bai yu lukautim mi[12]," she sobbed, her voice trembling with emotion.

Manu felt a warmth spread through him at her words. "Of course, Maoru. We're in this together," he reassured her, pulling her into a gentle hug. In that moment, he knew that he would always be there for Maoru and that was exactly what Bubu Naris would want him to do.

Despite the challenges of studying for the National Exam, Manu refused to let them derail his ambitions. At the beginning of the year, he had joined the school science club, eager to immerse himself in new experiences and collaborate with like-minded peers.

"Welcome to the Science Club! We have a competition coming up, and I think you'd be a great addition to our team," Mrs. Tali encouraged during their first meeting in the second week of Term 1.

"Count me in!" Manu replied, excitement bubbling within him. He felt revitalised and ready to tackle new challenges alongside his classmates.

By the second week of Term 3, Manu and his team were deep in rehearsal sessions for the regional science fair. Their focus was on sustainable agriculture, exploring the crucial role of insects in enhancing crop yields.

"Why not showcase our small ecosystem model?" suggested Aisha, one of his teammates, her eyes sparkling with enthusiasm as she gestured toward their carefully assembled display. "We can demonstrate how beneficial insects like bees and ladybugs help farmers."

"Great idea! And let's make sure to highlight organic farming practices during our presentation," Manu added, feeling the excitement in the room. They gathered around the model, rehearsing their lines and preparing to share their findings.

---

12 Wow, what a wonderful son. I know you will look after me

"Okay, I'll start with the introduction," Aisha said, taking a deep breath. "Then you can dive into the specifics of how insects contribute to crop health, right?"

"Exactly! I'll explain the pollination process and how it benefits the entire ecosystem," Manu replied, his voice filled with determination. The energy in the room was infectious as they practiced, each teammate eager to contribute their part and support one another.

Late nights became their norm as they worked diligently on their project at Aisha's house. The buzz of ideas and laughter filled the room as they assembled their model, each team member contributing their unique strengths. Aisha's father, a lecturer at the University of Technology, would often peek in, offering encouraging words and insights that helped refine their ideas.

"Manu, do you think we can actually win?" Aisha asked one evening, her eyes wide with anticipation and a hint of nervousness in her voice.

"Why not? If we believe in our project and work hard, we can do anything!" Manu replied, his voice filled with determination. He could sense the excitement building among his teammates, and it fuelled his own resolve.

Finally, the day of the science fair arrived. Aisha's parents dropped them off at Malahang Technical College, their warmth and encouragement boosting their spirits. Manu's heart raced as he set up their display, meticulously arranging the components of their ecosystem model. The room buzzed with excited chatter, the air thick with anticipation and the energy of competition as Grade 10 students from Morobe Province prepared their presentations.

When it was their turn to present, Manu stepped forward, his nerves momentarily forgotten. "Today, we'll show you how insects can transform agriculture and help us build a sustainable future," he announced confidently, his voice ringing clear. He and his teammates passionately explained their project, illustrating the vital roles insects play in pollination and pest control. The judges listened intently, nodding as they absorbed their findings.

When the presentations concluded, the tension in the air was intense.

"And the winner of the regional science fair is... Manu and his team for their innovative project on sustainable agriculture!" the head judge declared.

Cheers erupted around them, and Manu felt his heart swell with pride, a rush of exhilaration washing over him.

"Did we really just win?" Aisha shouted, her face lighting up with joy.

"Yes! We did it!" Manu exclaimed, embracing his teammates, their laughter and cheers echoing in the room.

"Who knew studying insects could be so rewarding?" Leo quipped, grinning as he joined the celebration, his eyes sparkling with pride for his friend.

That victory deepened Manu's understanding of ecological systems and solidified his passion for the study of insects. As he stood there, surrounded by friends and celebrating their achievement, he knew that every challenge he had faced had only made him stronger and more determined to pursue his dreams. This was just the beginning, and he felt ready to take on whatever came next.

This was not something new.

He knew that hard work has positive feedback. Always.

Together they had worked hard and they had achieved something remarkable, and he knew that with this support, there were no limits to what they could accomplish in the future.

Manu approached the National Exams with a mix of excitement and determination, knowing that his hard work would soon pay off.

After weeks of studying late into the night, he tackled each subject with confidence, particularly shining in his science exams. When the results were announced, his heart raced as he scanned the list, and a wave of joy washed over him upon seeing his high marks, especially in biology and chemistry.

As he celebrated with friends and family, Bubu Pellie clapped him on the back, beaming with pride. "You see, Manu? All those late nights paid off! Hard work truly makes a difference my boy!"

"Absolutely!" Uncle Kia chimed in, his eyes twinkling with joy. "But let's not forget the power of faith. God has been guiding you through this journey. Remember to thank Him for your success!"

Manu smiled, feeling a profound sense of accomplishment. "Thank you, Uncle Kia. I've been praying for strength, but I know it was my commitment that got me here."

Bubu Pellie nodded enthusiastically. "And that dedication to understanding ecological systems and the role of insects was crucial! You really put in the effort!"

"Thanks, Bubu! I couldn't have done it without your support," Manu replied, his heart swelling with gratitude.

"And now, this is just the beginning," Uncle Kia said, his voice filled with conviction. "With hard work and faith, you can achieve anything. Just keep trusting in the path God has laid for you."

"Right! I'm excited to explore more in science," Manu said, determination shining in his eyes. "I want to make meaningful contributions to the world."

During the Christmas holiday, Manu found himself at the Blue Mountains once again, this time with Doctor Sherf, who was tasked with keeping the Tree House while Sheri and Ron embarked on a two-week ecological adventure to Guadalcanal in the Solomon Islands. After their adventure, they would head to the States for Trevor's wedding to Carmelia.

Before the couple left, Doctor Sherf and Manu set up a video recording to congratulate Trevor and Carmelia.

"Alright, let's make this memorable!" Doctor Sherf announced, adjusting the camera with a twinkle in his eye. "Trevor, my boy, you're getting hitched! You're an awesome young man. Honestly, you should have been a scientist!"

Manu chuckled, "Seriously! I remember how passionate Trevor was about the terrain and the rock formations when we went camping. He could have discovered a new species if he wanted to!"

Doctor Sherf leaned back, his laughter booming through the Tree House. "The boy was unbelievable! I still can't forget that time he climbed up the Mother Tree like Tarzan! I arrived for a visit, and there he was, swinging from branch to branch like it was child's play! That kid could charm the leaves off the trees. It's no wonder he found someone as amazing as Carmelia."

"Absolutely! They're perfect for each other," Manu agreed. "I can already see their adventures together—full of laughter and maybe a little bit of chaos!"

"Here's to them!" Doctor Sherf raised an imaginary glass. "May their love be as strong as the roots of the Mother Tree!"

As they wrapped up the recording, Manu felt a surge of excitement for Trevor and Carmelia's future, knowing their journey together would be just as adventurous as the ones they shared during his visit to Nevada.

By Grade 11, Manu's fascination with entomology had blossomed into a full-fledged passion. He spent countless hours in the library, poring over books about insects and their crucial roles in ecosystems.

"Hey, Manu! You're like a walking encyclopaedia on bugs now!" Leo teased one afternoon as they sat together during lunch.

Manu chuckled. "You know, insects are incredible! Did you know that without pollinators like bees, we wouldn't have most of our fruits and vegetables?"

"Alright, Mr. Entomologist, I get it! But don't forget to take breaks. You need to socialise too!" Leo nudged him playfully.

"Socialising is overrated when there are insects to research!" Manu replied, grinning.

His teachers noticed his growing enthusiasm and encouraged him to take advanced science courses. "Manu, you have a real talent for this," Mrs. Tali remarked during a meeting, her eyes sparkling with encouragement. "I think you should consider taking AP Biology next year."

"Really? That would be amazing!" Manu said, his heart racing at the thought of diving deeper into his passion.

Encouraged by his teachers, Manu also began volunteering at local environmental initiatives. He joined a community group focused on educating others about biodiversity and the importance of protecting natural habitats.

"Alright, everyone! Today, we're going to talk about why insects matter!" Manu announced enthusiastically to a group of curious children during a workshop.

"Why do they matter?" a little girl asked, tilting her head in confusion.

"Well, without insects, our world would be very different! They help plants grow, break down waste, and even provide food for other animals," Manu explained, smiling at the eager faces before him.

"Cool! Can I be an insect helper too?" she asked, her eyes wide with excitement.

"Absolutely! Every little action counts. If you plant flowers, you're helping bees!" Manu replied, feeling a swell of pride as he inspired the next generation.

As the months passed, Manu's commitment to environmental conservation didn't go unnoticed. At the school's annual awards ceremony, he was announced as the recipient of the "Outstanding Service Award" for his community work.

"Manu, please come forward," the principal announced, his voice brimming with pride. "Your dedication to educating others about biodiversity and your tireless efforts in our community are truly commendable!"

As Manu walked up to the stage, the applause erupted like a wave, filling the auditorium with warmth and encouragement. He glanced back at his friends, their faces beaming with joy and support.

"Thanks, everyone!" Manu laughed, his heart swelling with a mix of happiness and gratitude. "This award is for all of you who believe in the power of education and the importance of our environment!"

his voice rang out clear and steady, radiating conviction as he spoke to the crowd. The cheers intensified, and he felt a rush of inspiration coursing through him.

That afternoon, when he returned home, Manu showed the award to Bubu Pellie. "Look what I won!"

Bubu Pellie's eyes glistened with pride, hugging Manu in a warm embrace. "You're collecting awards year after year! Congratulations, my boy!" he exclaimed, his voice thick with emotion.

At that moment, Bubu Pellie knew he had made the right decision to let Manu explore the Blue Mountains. It was hard to explain how the universe aligns for those who work hard and keep their minds open to learning.

"This is just the beginning, Manu. Your journey is only getting started!" Bubu Pellie told his grandson

In Year 12, Manu poured his heart and soul into his studies, focusing intently on biology and chemistry as he prepared for the PNG National Exam.

"Manu, are you ready for the big biology test?" Leo asked one morning, sliding into the seat next to him.

"Ready as I'll ever be! I've been reviewing the life cycle of insects non-stop," Manu replied, a grin spreading across his face. "Did you know that some butterflies can taste with their feet?"

"Only you would know something like that!" Leo chuckled. "Just don't forget to breathe during the exam!"

As the weeks passed, Manu's hard work culminated in exceptional grades. His teachers praised his dedication, and he felt more confident than ever.

"Manu, your lab reports are outstanding! Have you considered applying to universities abroad?" Mrs. Tali encouraged him during a one-on-one meeting.

"I've been thinking about the University of Queensland in Australia," he admitted, excitement bubbling in his chest. "They have a fantastic entomology program and there's a scholarship for that course."

"Go for it! You have the talent and the passion. I believe in you," she warmly encouraged him.

With her words in mind, Manu submitted his application, pouring his heart into his personal statement. He wrote about his journey, his love for insects, and his dreams of making a difference in the field of entomology in his country, Papua New Guinea, where there were millions of exotic insects still to be discovered in the virgin forestlands.

A few weeks later, Manu returned home from school one afternoon, and spotted Kaia sipping a drink in front of the canteen under their house, as Uncle Kia talked with him.

"Hey, my main scientist boy! Good to see you, nais wan!" he yelled in his trademark style.

"Hey, bos tumas, nais wan!" Manu replied, shaking his hand.

Kaia was now engaged to the pastor's daughter, Lilau, and worked as a handyman at the church grounds. But he was still the same Kaia—loud and hilarious.

"Pastor told me to bring this to you," Kaia slapped Manu on the back as he handed him an envelope.

Manu recognised the stamp on the envelope right away. "I think I got something from Queensland!" he called out, his voice trembling with anticipation.

Uncle Kia looked over the counter, eyes wide with curiosity. "Hey Manu, my main boy! Aussie, Aussie, oi oi oi!" Kaia yelled, mimicking the Australian golfers at the club.

Manu paused, clutching his stomach as he doubled over with laughter. Kaia was absolutely hilarious, and the thought of him heading to Bible College next year was just too exciting to ignore.

"Should do me right. All I want is peace," Kaia had said to Manu and Chay the last time they met at Anderson's Foodland. Those two old friends from the Golf Course days had always stuck together. Chay was now a supervisor at the Papindo shopping centre.

"Never thought I'd see blue fly working in a shop," Kaia joked when he first heard about Chay's job. "He can't tell a K2 from a K100 note!"

Manu and Chay erupted into laughter, enjoying Kaia's endless rants about Chay's new role.

"You'll be a grandfather soon, golf course camel!" Chay shot back, never one to take the teasing lying down. They laughed helplessly until tears streamed down their faces.

"The insect doctor will spray you, blue fly!" Kaia snapped at Chay, and even the people at nearby tables couldn't help but chuckle at the banter. "He is my main boy!"

It was hard to believe that Kaia was actually ready to settle down with a nice Christian girl. Yet life has a way of surprising us, and the future is always full of unexpected turns.

With trembling hands, Manu tore open the envelope and read the letter aloud.

"We are pleased to inform you that you have been accepted to the University of Queensland for the Bachelor of Science (ENTOMA2461)."

"YES!" he shouted, jumping into the air. Kaia and Uncle Kia erupted in cheers, hugging him in a warm embrace.

"Hey, golf club carrier! I am so proud of you!" Kaia exclaimed, breaking into smiles and laughter. "Wait till the golf course fly hear this wonderful news!"

Manu and Kaia laughed hilariously, while Uncle Kia looked confused.

"This is a dream come true! I can't believe I'm going to study what I love!" Manu exclaimed, his heart racing with joy.

The excitement was so loud that Bubu Pellie and Maoru rushed to the house from the butterfly farm.

"What's going on?" Maoru breathlessly scampered to Manu and Kaia.

"What's all this commotion? What is going on?" Bubu Pellie yelled as he dropped his spade and knife on the steps.

Manu looked over at his grandfather and handed him the letter. Bubu Pellie's hands were lined with the marks of hard work, and his thinning grey hair showed the years he had devoted to family and community. As he read the letter, his eyes lit up with disbelief, then filled with tears of joy. He was overcome with emotion, as he pulled Manu into a tight embrace, sobbing tears of happiness that reflected his pride and love.

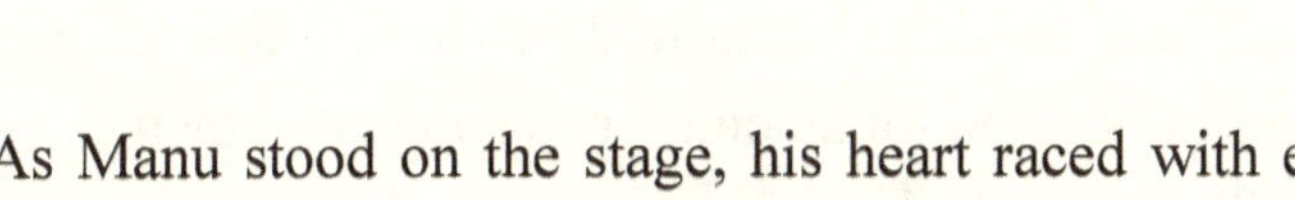

As Manu stood on the stage, his heart raced with excitement. The auditorium buzzed with celebration as he and his classmates received their Grade 12 Certificates, marking the end of a significant chapter in their lives. Friends and family cheered, their faces glowing with joy.

Manu's eyes sparkled as he spotted Bubu Pellie in the crowd, tears of happiness glistening in his eyes. Maoru was dressed nicely in her colourful meri blaus, with a new hairstyle, standing as far away as possible from where Uncle Kia was.

As he stepped off the stage, Maoru rushed over and placed a lei around his neck. Manu hugged her just as Bubu Pellie came over and embraced him, with Uncle Kia trailing behind.

"Hey, remember, I made a mumu for you early this morning. Bring Kaia and Chay!" Uncle Kia reminded him.

Then his friends rushed toward him, laughter and cheers filling the air.

"Look at you, Manu! We did it!" Leo exclaimed, clapping him on the back.

"Yeah, mate! You're officially a graduate now!" Chay added, grinning widely. "I always knew you had it in you!"

Kaia, ever the jokester, chimed in, "Next stop, University of Queensland! Just don't forget us little people when you're the insect doctor!"

Manu chuckled, shaking his head. "I could never forget you guys. You're the best part of this journey!"

"Let's celebrate!" Leo shouted. "Ice cream at Anderson's? My treat!"

"Count me in!" Kaia replied, already bouncing on his heels. "I can't wait to see you in your lab coat, Mr. Entomologist!"

As they made their way outside, Manu turned to his grandfather and called out, "Bubu, everyone come over, and Aisha's father will take some pictures."

After the long photo session, Manu told his family that he was going to Anderson's Foodland for an hour or so and would then bring Kaia and Chay with him to the house.

"Hey, Manu!" Chay called out, nudging him playfully. "You've got a bright future ahead, but remember, you owe us a round of drinks when you make it big!"

Manu laughed, feeling the warmth of their companionship. "Deal! And I'll make sure you guys are the first to visit!"

With smiles all around, they headed off, ready to celebrate not just graduation, but the journey ahead.

After the ice cream session, Manu took Kaia and Chay home, still buzzing from the day's events. As they walked in, the rich aroma of Bubu Pellie's cooking greeted them. The table was laden with mumu chicken, taro, kaukau, breadfruit, highlands kumu, lamb flaps, goat meat, and cow meat and variety of fruits and vegetables with can drinks at the end of the table.

"Whoa! It's a feast fit for a king!" Kaia exclaimed, his eyes widening. "I didn't know graduation came with a buffet!"

"Only the best for our superstar!" Chay said, elbowing Manu playfully.

Maoru beamed at them as she set the table. "I made all your favourites! Come, eat and celebrate!"

Kaia's jaw dropped playfully as he spotted a familiar face among the church members who had come. "Wait a second! Is that my fiancé?" he whispered to Manu, chuckling discreetly.

"Yeah, that's Aisha," Manu replied, suppressing a grin.

"Manu, my boy!" Kaia called out, raising his voice dramatically. "You've graduated, and now you're going to have to impress all these beautiful ladies! Good luck, my friend!"

The room erupted in laughter, and even Bubu Pellie chuckled, shaking his head at Kaia's antics.

Before everyone settled down to eat, Bubu Pellie stood up for a brief speech, his eyes sparkling with pride. "Congratulations, Manu! You are destined for greater success," he proclaimed, his voice warm yet firm. His words were short and to the point—Bubu Pellie never liked to drag things on.

"Now, let's eat!" he declared, a smile breaking across his face as he gestured to the table.

As everyone ate, the room filled with lively conversation and laughter. Kaia was animatedly recounting a funny story from school, and the others chimed in with their own tales. Amidst the joy, Manu couldn't help but notice Maoru, who kept shooting daggers at Uncle Kia from across the table.

Manu chuckled silently, finding the whole scene amusing. "What's with the glare, Maoru?" he teased under his breath, trying to stifle his laughter.

"Just keeping him in check," she replied with a smirk, her eyes narrowing playfully at Manu's uncle.

"Good luck with that!" Manu laughed, knowing Uncle Kia's religious rules and family obligations.

After the gathering, Manu bid farewell to his friends and church members, their laughter and warm wishes echoing in his ears. He then headed to Bumbu River with Uncle Kia for a refreshing swim, the cool water washing away the excitement of the day. Meanwhile, Maoru and some church ladies stayed behind to clean up, chatting and laughing as they washed the utensils.

That night, as Manu entered his room, he felt an inexplicable pull toward a small box tucked away on a shelf. Inside lay the tightly wrapped red cloth that Bubu Naris had given him years ago, on her deathbed at Angau Hospital.

He could vividly recall that moment. She had sat on the edge of her bed, her frail voice steady yet filled with warmth. "For you. Open it later when we go home," she had said, her eyes shining with love. Manu's heart had swelled with gratitude as he promised to cherish it. Sadly, she never came home with him and Bubu Pellie; she had passed on that gloomy day, leaving a void in his heart.

Now, with a mix of anticipation and nostalgia, he carefully unwrapped the cloth. As he unfolded it, a small note slipped out. His hands trembled slightly as he picked it up and read the words: "Your full name is Emmanuel, which means God is with us."

A wave of warmth washed over him, and tears brimmed in his eyes. This wasn't just a poignant reminder of his grandmother's love; it reflected the journey that had brought him here and the path still ahead.

With the red cloth in hand, Manu felt a profound sense of connection. He understood that he carried her spirit with him, a guiding light for the adventures he had experienced and those waiting for him at Queensland University. He smiled, feeling fortified by her presence, ready to embrace whatever came next as Emmanuel Aneva.

The End

Epilogue
The Author

I grew up in the most beautiful forestlands, a realm where time seemed to stand still. That life, that time, is now in the past, but the wonderful thing is that I hold on to the memories, vibrant and alive in my mind.

Oh, how I loved and envied the trees—so tall, so proud, so powerful, their leafy crowns reaching for the sky. The era I grew up in was nothing short of magical. As a feral child of the 70s and 80s, I roamed freely through the lush underbrush, swimming in pristine, crystal-clear rivers that sparkled like jewels in the sunlight.

Even then, I sensed that the trees held ancient secrets—roots that delved deep into the earth, whispering stories we cannot hear. I believed they shared their wisdom through their roots, connecting generations across time.

My great-great-grandfather, my grandfather, my father, and I all stood beneath the same towering giants that still stand today. We are here today and gone tomorrow, but the trees remain, steadfast and eternal, secret keepers of our history. Did you know that?

My stories speak of forestlands because I am of the forest, the rivers, and the mountains. In this book, I draw from my reservoir of memories to illuminate the forests. It is a world that only a fortunate few get to experience, and I count myself among the lucky ones.

The Indigenous peoples of the islands may be separated by the sea, but their ancestral beliefs lie side by side. The land and the sea are sisters, providing for their children—humans, flora, and fauna alike.